TEXAS LADY

SANDY SULLIVAN

TEXAS LADY

DEDICATION

I'm dedicating this one to some friends who encouraged me from the beginning to get my story published:

Cathy Gehret: Thanks for all your feedback and help. I know how much you love this story so this one is for you.

Shaylynn: You have been inspiration in helping me get to this point in my ever expanding career in writing. Thank you so much.
Becky Hollada: My youngest daughter. Thanks for your editing and help with the original version of this. You've been instrumental in helping me develop my writing skills.

And last but not least - Clay Walker - The love you have for your fams is an inspiration to me. You give so much to each and every one of us and I can't thank you enough for being my inspiration for the hero in this book.

For those who don't know Clay, he's a country artist who's been singing and playing for his fans since for a long time. His first album came out in 1993 and I've been hooked ever since.

Romance

Texas Lady
Copyright © 2022 Sandy Sullivan
E-book ISBN: 9781944122751

First E-book Publication: September 2022

Cover design by Dawne Dominique
Edited by Rebecca Hollada
All cover art and logo copyright © 2022 by Sandy Sullivan

CHAPTER 1

Texas Lady

Sandy Sullivan

Morning dawned bright and cold in the Texas sky. Sun reflected against the glass of the windows on the sprawling ranch house of the Double J. The flowers in the yard had not yet begun to bloom, and frost glistened on the leaves of the budding trees.

Elizabeth Johnston rolled out of the huge bed with its warm, downy mattress, only to have the cold morning air send shivers down her arms when it hit her bare skin. Dressed in long johns and wools socks, her developing form stayed hidden beneath the over large clothing handed down from her much larger brothers.

Even at sixteen, the promise of the stunning beauty already glowed bright. Her long, curly chestnut hair framed her round face and her sky blue eyes sparkled with enthusiasm.

Studying her reflection in the mirror, she turned her head left and right before she stuck her tongue out. With a soft giggle, she poured cold water from the pitcher into the washbowl resting on the mahogany dresser.

When the cold water hit her skin, she gasped.

"Darn it, that's cold!"

She grabbed the washcloth lying next to her, and scrubbed her face until the pink of her skin almost masked the sprinkle of freckles across her nose. Rinsing the soft off with more cold water, she picked up a towel warmed by the fire.

"There. Finished."

The trunk at the base of her bed housed every stitch of clothing she owned and all were the clothing of a boy since that's what she found comfortable. With a quick flip of the lid, she pulled out a pair of boy's trousers, a blue flannel shirt, camisole, and clean socks. The long johns and dirty socks hit the floor before she shimmed into the camisole until it rested near her slim waist. The flannel shirt came next, then the jeans over her buttocks and hips. Tucking the shirt into her waistband, she tightened the trousers around her waist with a piece of hemp rope, and knotted it tight.

Sitting in a small chair in the corner she slipped on the clean socks before she pulled on mud-caked boots, and stomped her feet to wedge them in.

"Thank goodness for big brothers."

Crossing in front of the mirror, she checked her reflection.

"It'll do, I guess."

A quick swipe of her hair brush through the tangled curls brought tears to her eyes for a moment. Once the tangles disappeared, she tied it back away from her face with another piece of rope.

The door opened with a twist of her wrist and she almost ran into one of her brothers hurrying down the hall.

"Good grief, little sister. Watch out! I almost ran you down." Ray quickly sidestepped her. "Are you all right?"

"I'm fine, Ray. You are like a bull in a china shop, but I love you anyway." A huge smile graced her face as she followed him into the living room, bustling with activity.

Elizabeth shook her head.

Ray stood over six feet tall already and turned many a woman's head with his broad shoulders, his wavy brown hair and bright green eyes. At nineteen, he already had his share of women vying for his attention.

"I love you too, Liz," he said, kissing her on the forehead.

A bright smile lit his face when he took his seat at the table and started shoveling food onto his plate, while Carmen tsk'd at him near the edge of the table.

Elizabeth's gaze moved over the woman who'd been like a second mother to all the children since they were small.

Her parents had employed her long ago when they first arrived in Texas, and she had been a solid inspiration in their lives. Carmen had never married, nor had any children.

"Men!" Carmen rolled her eyes at the men at the table already filling their plates high with food. "They never get their bellies full, hey *chica*?"

Elizabeth laughed when she sat next to Ray and started to fill her plate. "Not in this house, Carmen."

Her gaze found her other brothers, John Jr. and Matt along with her parents, John and Margaret. The large loving family spent many a meal at this table, sharing dreams, thoughts and troubles.

She'd been born in Texas and raised there all her life, but she knew her parents had moved from a small town in Tennessee after the War Between the States when John Jr. and Matt were small. Her father was a Confederate soldier and had anticipated the end of the war being hard. He'd managed to save some money and change it into Union gold to start over. When the carpetbaggers flooded the southern states, John immigrated to Texas with his family. Cattle was easy and profitable, thus the Double J was born.

The conversation at the table turned to work for the day. The boys and their father discuss the plans for moving some of the cattle nearer the house in preparation for shipment to Houston while Elizabeth listened.

"Dad, how many do you think we need to move?" John Jr. asked, his green eyes dancing with enthusiasm.

"Oh, probably five hundred head or so. We'll need to hire some more hands from town to get them moved and branded." Her father's gaze moved over her brothers sitting across the table from him. "Maybe Jeff can come over and help." Her father's twinkling blue eyes, the same bright color as her own, stopped on her face. "Lizzie, you need to stay here and help your mother. The range is no place for a young lady,"

"What? Why now? I've never missed a round up before. I don't understand."

"Do as your father says, Elizabeth," her mother interjected with a frown, before she stood and gathered the dishes.

"But, Mother! That's not fair! I can ride and rope as good as Ray and you both know I can." Indignation zipped down her back. Her parents had never denied her riding roundup before. Why were they starting now?

"Elizabeth!" John growled, giving her a stern look. "You'll do as you're told young lady, and I'll hear no more about it."

Elizabeth flopped back down on the bench near the table and folded her arms across her chest. Tears well up in her eyes and one lone droplet slid down her cheek. Knowing how hard it would be for him to resist her, she gave him her most forlorn expression. Those looks had always gotten her what she wanted before, so she hoped it would work this time.

"Don't look at me like that, Elizabeth. You are becoming a young woman now, and you must start acting like one." His eyes softened just a little. With a grumble, he said, "Mother, do something with her." He got up from the table, grabbed his hat hanging by the door, and walked outside with her three brothers following close on his heels.

"Mother, this is not fair. I don't want to be a young lady! I want to ride and work the cattle with Father. I can become a young lady later. I'm only sixteen!" Tears rolled down her cheeks.

Taking the seat next to her on the bench, her mother wrapped her arms around her shoulders.

"It's not fair. Why do I have to learn to be a young lady? I want to be able to run a ranch, work the cattle, and have my own property like Father. I have no use for frills, fluffy dresses with yards of petticoats under them, or for sipping tea and batting my eye lashes at the young men while we dance. I hate dances! I hate dresses, and I hate tea!"

"Elizabeth. You are a young girl, not a young man like your brothers. Although times are changing, you cannot own property unless it was willed to you by your husband," her mother reminded her softly. "Someday, you will wish for a handsome young man to whisk you away to his home after you are married, cook and clean for him and raise his children. That's what young women do, not ride horses, rope and brand cattle, and track mud into the house."

"I don't want a husband and babies, mother." She sniffed slightly, rubbing her nose.

"I realize now that I have failed in attempting to teach you the ways of woman. I've let you run wild with your brothers when I should have been showing you how to cook, clean, and be a good wife for your husband. Today, we will start where I have failed so miserably up to this point." Her mother gently guided her from the bench and steered her in the direction of her bedroom.

"I don't think I like the sound of this," Elizabeth said, drying her eyes with the sleeve of her flannel shirt as she preceded her mother into her room.

"First, we find you something decent to wear young lady." The door closed behind them with a resounding click.

* * * *

In the north field of the ranch, John Sr. squinted against the sun, watching his three sons gathering the young bulls and herding them toward the temporary pen. The young son of his best friend and neighbor rode with them. Jeff had grown up with his own boys and they couldn't be closer if they were siblings.

John watched as Jeff worked with Ray. The two boys always rode in perfect harmony, seeming to know the move the other would make before he made it.

The two were about the same height at six feet even though his son was a year younger. Many a young woman would be besieged by the two, each trying to woo her before the other. It was a game with them as to who could steal a few kisses before the other.

Their features were almost opposite. Jeff had eyes the color of cinnamon and black hair with Ray sporting bright green eyes and light brown hair. The two were such a contrast; it was almost funny when they decided to both focus their attention on one particular woman. Both boys had the ladies young and old, wrapped around their little fingers.

John Sr. and Jeffery's father, Ernest, had become friends in the early years in Hempstead. Ernest had moved to Hempstead shortly after John and Margaret had with his wife Donna and Jeff, who was only a small child. They had bought the land adjacent to the Double J. The Rocking W was about half the size of the Double J at only five hundred acres. Over the years, the old friends had shared hands across the borders of the two ranches and driven their cattle to market together, and the boys had all become friends.

* * * *

"Hey, Ray," Jeff said behind the handkerchief across his mouth and nose, when he rode near Ray. "Did you see Amy Cross yesterday at the general store?"

"Nope. Didn't go into town yesterday at all. Why?" Ray got between the next heifer and her calf, attempting to separate them.

"She was lookin' mighty pretty. Had her hair all up in curls on her head, pretty bonnet on and everything. She was askin' about you." Jeff rode between the next heifer and her calf expertly driving the calf into the pen.

"Really?" Ray asked behind his own handkerchief. "About what?"

"She asked where you were. Her and Aubrey Dillon had been over at the dress shop lookin' at the new cloth brought in last week. You think they might be going to the dance weekend after next?"

"I dunno."

They rode near the stream to take a break in the shade trees. Ray pulled off his handkerchief, dipped it in the stream, and wiped his sweaty face and neck as Jeff dropped on his knees beside him.

"I might just ask that pretty little Aubrey to go with me. I think she likes me." Jeff sat next to Ray on the knoll for a few minutes. The shade of the tree felt good while the soft breeze blew across their skin. "She's been flirting with me an awful lot when I'm in town."

"Could be. So what did Amy say?"

"She came up with Aubrey and asked me if I'd seen you in town. Course, I said no since I hadn't seen you. She looked a little disappointed, I'd say."

Ray's gaze focused off into the afternoon sun. "Maybe I'll ask her."

"Where's Elizabeth today? Not like her to miss a roundup." Jeff glanced around trying to discern if she was there and he just hadn't seen her.

He'd known Elizabeth since she was born and thought of her like a little sister, too. Her nature got her into trouble more times than not, so he felt it was his duty, along with her brothers, to keep her safe.

"Dad wouldn't allow her to come along this year. He says she needs to learn to be a young lady now that she's growing up. She's sixteen already."

"Sixteen, really?" It startled him to realize his little Elizabeth was that old, but then again, he thought of himself as a man at twenty. "She'll be a real lady pretty soon then. I can't imagine her anything other than little Elizabeth who tagged along with her big brothers fishing, hunting, riding, and shooting. Heck, she shoots better than you!" Jeff punched Ray in the arm teasingly.

Ray toppled to the ground, but jumped up quickly and chased Jeff back to their horses where his friend's father waited impatiently.

"I believe you two have work to do." John gave them a stern look.

"Sorry, Dad," Ray said, climbing onto the back of his horse.

"Sorry, Mr. Johnston," Jeff replied, pulling up and straddling the saddle. "We were just trying to cool off a bit."

"Let's see that we get the rest of these calves separated this afternoon. Then we can see what mischief you two can get into." John turned his horse back toward the awaiting cattle.

The two young men eyed each other for a moment before Jeff yelled and kicked his horse into a fast gallop. "I'll race you back!"

* * * *

Over the last two weeks, her mother managed to get Elizabeth to wear a dress, at least in the house. She still managed occasionally to get outside in the late afternoons to ride the ranch with her brothers and work the cattle. Conceding that much, her mother willingly gave her a little freedom since she at least tried to learn some of the feminine attributes. Table manners, proper layering of clothing and even how to dance encompassed the agenda, driving her crazy. Every evening, Elizabeth complained to her father about the endless dribble her mother tried to teach her. Unfortunately for her, her father would not falter in his and Margaret's decision to teach her how to be a lady.

Now, while the wagon rolled into Hempstead, Elizabeth frowned at the thought of being compared to those stuffy girls she had gone to school with. They had never liked her anyway but to be trussed up like a turkey on Thanksgiving made her cringe even more. Everyone would be comparing her to girls like Aubrey Dillon and Amy Cross, and she feared she would come up lacking. She had always been more comfortable around the boys than the girls.

Her mother had threatened to leave her at home to get her into the pretty dress her parents had the local seamstress make for her. The dress was white with small lavender flowers and a large lavender sash around her petite waist with yards of petticoats underneath. Soft kid boots on her feet completed her ensemble. Her mother had arranged her long chestnut hair atop her head in soft curls that framed her face.

"You look absolute enchanting, sweetheart," her father complemented when she'd come out of her room, but she only grumbled about worthless petticoats, annoying boots and how in the world was she supposed to do anything with all of it.

When the wagon came to a stop near the livery, she could see lanterns placed around the area set aside for dancing, illuminating the night. Long tables covered with red-checkered tablecloths sat on the side of the makeshift dance floor. Each one held an overabundance of food brought by each family in celebration of the coming summer. Her gaze moved over the crowd noting all the people she'd known her entire life. This was the biggest festival in the area before the summer work began. The liquor flowed freely among the men while the women kept a sharp eye on the children running wildly through the milling crowd.

The spring flowers had begun to bloom, and the scent of lavender permeated the air. Elizabeth took a deep breath to inhale the intoxicating scent and it lifted her spirits slightly. She absolutely loved the smell of lavender.

"Dad, Mom—we are going to head on over to see who is here," Matt said when the boys dismounted from their horses and tied them to the hitching post near the wagon.

"All right, but you boys be careful," her mother said, when her father came around the wagon to help her down, then put his big hands on Elizabeth's waist and lifted her down, too.

"You look beautiful, Lizzie. I knew you would look lovely in that dress when your mother picked out the fabric."

"I hate it." Her anger and stubbornness was apparent when she spun around and stomped toward the crowds while trying not to trip over the length of the dress and the small boots that encased her feet.

Her parents followed slowly behind her and Elizabeth heard her mother say, "I've tried, John. I don't know what else to do. She's so defiant."

"Like her brothers, I fear, Mother. We may have to follow through with our original plan, I'm afraid."

Elizabeth approached the dance floor and noticed her brothers and Jeff standing off to the side, so she walked slowly around the outside. She didn't want her presence to be known to her brother's friend, fearing he would make fun of her if he saw her. If he compared her to Aubrey Dillon, whom she knew he liked and she couldn't stand, and found her lacking, she'd have to hurt him. Ray told her Jeff was going to ask Aubrey to the dance. At this point, Aubrey was nowhere to be found when Elizabeth attempted to scoot by her brothers.

Ray saw her first and exclaimed, "There she is. Hey, Liz, come over here." He motioned with his hand and all eyes turned to her.

Elizabeth could see no way out of this predicament, so she slowly walked to where they stood.

"What's the matter, sis?" Matt asked.

"You know I can't stand this kind of dressing up."

"You look so pretty though." He gave her a hug and pulled her to his side. "You almost look like a girl!"

Elizabeth elbowed him in the side for the last remark, but when the others chimed in their agreement, she started to relax a little. A small smile flittered across her mouth and her eyes lit up when Jeff smiled at her, and their eyes locked for a moment before she turned away.

All eyes turned to the dance floor when the local fiddle player started to tune his instrument and the other members of the makeshift band worked their way to the front of the stage. The crowd moved in closer so it could hear.

The portly, somewhat balding mayor, stood in front of the band. His obvious brand new black suit with a bowtie tied tight around his large neck, almost crinkled when he moved.

Holding up one large hand, he said, "Attention everyone, attention. We've all gathered here tonight to celebrate the spring planting season and subsequent cattle drives. We're all here to have a good time, so no fighting. All guns must be checked with the deputies at that table over there by the refreshments and all you young bucks behave yourselves. With all of the beautiful young ladies here tonight, I'm sure you can all stay busy dancing without getting into trouble."

He stepped away from the band, and the music started to play with a loud twang and screech. Everyone cringed but laughed, when the fiddle player turned shades of red. He quickly recovered and started a nice, slow waltz. The rest of the band joined in while young men grabbed partners and moved onto the makeshift dance floor.

Elizabeth was left on the side next to Jeff when her brothers wandered off to find a partner.

"You sure look pretty, Elizabeth," he said with a grin. "I wouldn't have recognized you in that dress if Matt hadn't said anything. I don't think I've ever see you in a dress before."

"Thanks. You look mighty handsome yourself, for a boy, that is. I don't believe I've ever seen you in anything but muddy jeans before."

"Boy? I'm a man now if you didn't notice. I'm almost twenty years old!" He tilted his chin proudly.

"Well, being twenty years old doesn't necessarily make you a man, you know." Her gaze raked over his broad chest and noted the way he filled out his pressed shirt. A small amount of dark chest hair peaked above where he had left the first couple of buttons undone.

"Where is little Miss Prissy Aubrey? I thought you were asking her to the dance?" She blushed before she lowered her gaze.

He certainly doesn't need to know my feelings for him run deeper than those for a big brother.

Jeff had always teased her mercilessly when they were growing up, just like any brother would. He had always treated her nice and tried to protect her from the ribbing her brothers gave her constantly. Being the only girl in the house except her mother, her brothers wanted to protect her but also made her feel like a baby most of the time. Jeff didn't treat her that way.

"Jealous?" A crooked little smile flashed at the corner of his mouth.

"No! Of course not!" Her quick response sounded hollow even to her when her eyes met his. She focused on the dirt beneath her boots, kicking at a small clump. "I was just wonderin' since Ray said you asked her."

"I did bring Aubrey to the dance. She's over at the refreshment table with her mother, but I saved one dance for you. Will you dance with me, little Elizabeth?"

He flashed his sexy crooked half smile in her direction.

Elizabeth's heart melted when she looked into his eyes. He always could get her to do just about anything with that smile.

Holding out her hand to him, she said, "I'd like that."

He took her hand, pulled it into the crook of his arm, and led her onto the dancing area. When he slipped his strong arm around her tiny waist, she sighed as a soft, melody played in the background. They twirled around the dance floor and Elizabeth knew she died and gone to heaven. Her dream was coming true! Jeff was holding her in his arms and smiling down at her. Her sixteen-year-old heart thought for sure he cared for her more than just a sister. He couldn't hold her like this and not feel something akin to love for her, could he?

The stars, twinkling in the night air, shone brightly over their heads, making her feel as if this night couldn't be more perfect than it was right now.

* * * *

She sure is going to be a beauty someday. Jeff looked into her sky blue eyes and smiled. *Some man would be lucky enough to call her his own.*

When he glanced over her shoulder, Aubrey caught his attention while she pouted off to the side. She obviously didn't like the fact of him dancing with Elizabeth.

Ah! Jealousy could be advantageous. A huge smile spread across his face, and he looked back at Elizabeth.

As the beautiful melody drifted off, Jeff escorted her back to the side of the dance floor to where her brothers stood.

"Thank you for the dance, Elizabeth. It was a pleasure." He unceremoniously deposited Elizabeth with her brothers. "I'll see you all later."

Approaching the young blonde, he slipped an arm around her waist and kissed her cheek.

"What were you doing dancing with her?"

"Jealous, Aubrey?"

"You're here with me, Jeffery Walker. Remember that."

"It was only one dance. I've grown up with Elizabeth. She's nothing more than a little sister to me. Besides, you're the one

I want to share my kiss with behind the barn." He skimmed his lips over the heated skin of her neck. "I know you want that too."

Her eyes closed and she tipped her head. "Maybe. Don't be so sure of yourself."

One eyebrow cocked and he smiled. "I know what you want, Aubrey."

* * * *

Elizabeth stood open mouthed. Hadn't he just held her in his arms and smiled at her? Anger rolled down her back when she watched him work his magic on Aubrey, holding her hand in his and flashing that same smile at her. Fuming, Elizabeth turned her back on the pair and said, "I'm going to go find Mother and Father."

Her brothers looked at her puzzled when she stomped off, kicking up dust.

The rest of the dance passed slowly for Elizabeth while she watched the others dancing and having a good time. In her heart, she was sure Jeff cared for her, but she couldn't understand why he continued to escort Aubrey around. He retrieved the blonde's dinner plate for her, and danced, completely ignoring Elizabeth like she wasn't even there.

The evening wound to a close. Elizabeth helped her mother and some of the other matrons of the town clean up.

Still fuming from Jeff's dismissal, she stood at the back of the wagon packing some of the dishes they had brought with them, when she heard giggling coming from near the back of the barn. At first, she tried to ignore it, thinking it was probably one of her brothers with one of the local girls, but she then heard Jeff's unmistakable laugh. Unable to fight her curiosity, she followed the sounds.

Rounding the corner near the back of the livery where the lights of the dance failed to illuminate, she stumbled on Jeff and Aubrey obviously locked in a warm embrace. Jeff's mouth seemed to be fastened to Aubrey's neck and she giggled in response.

Elizabeth stared at them in complete shock. Aubrey noticed her over Jeff's shoulder and began pushing him away.

"What's wrong Aubrey? I thought you liked what I was doing?"

"Jeffrey Walker!" Elizabeth stomped toward him with angry indignation, her dress swishing behind her.

Jeff whirled around to face her, surprise in his brown eyes.

"Elizabeth? What are you doing back here?"

"I was following the sounds." Anger made her voice crack. With hand firmly planted on her hips, she said, "How could you?"

"Elizabeth, I'm sorry, but I don't understand," he said with a completely dumbfounded look.

"You are a rotten, uncaring, pathetic excuse of a man! I hate you, Jeffery Walker!" With palms flat on his chest, she shoved.

Caught off guard, he landed with a large splash in the horse trough, soaking both his clothes and Aubrey in the process. Aubrey stood sputtering and then began to wail. A moment later, she took off running toward her mother.

With a satisfied smile, Elizabeth turned on her heel and ran back to their wagon while Jeff attempted to drag himself out of the trough. Her father and mother were already there and had been searching for her.

"Elizabeth? What was that noise?" her mother asked.

"Nothing, Mother. Are we ready to go? I'm sure tired." Elizabeth fought the giggle bubbling in her throat when she heard the cussing and splashing coming from behind the barn.

Her father lifted her onto the seat of the wagon and then lifted her mother beside her. Walking around the back of the wagon, he hopped up next to them, grabbed the reins, and flicked them over the rump of horse.

The moment he pulled away and turned the wagon toward home, Jeff rounded the corner of the barn. Elizabeth looked over her shoulder and, with a large grin, waved triumphantly, then turned back around and starting talking with her mother about the dance.

* * * *

Jeff fumed while he stood in the middle of the road, water dripping from his nose, making a large puddle around his feet.

The Johnston brothers walked up, and Ray asked, "What happened to you?"

"Your little minx of a sister happened to me. Little witch pushed me into the horse trough while I was out back with Aubrey."

They all laughed and slapped him on the back.

"Interrupted something, did she?" Matt asked as they began to walk toward their horses.

"You could say that. I guess I'll just have to find another time and another place to continue our little conversation." A smile lifted the corners of his lips when he thought about what Elizabeth had interrupted.

"Conversation was it? I doubt that!" Ray said, and they all laugh again.

CHAPTER 2

Elizabeth squinted at the dreary morning as the rain pelted the window to the dorm room where she had spent the last four years of her life. She hated the weather in Pennsylvania. It was always either raining or snowing. Never mind the heat during the summer! This little room she shared with her friend did nothing to lighten her mood. It was smaller than her room at home and painted stark white. The curtains on the window were a slate gray and did little to brighten the room. One small bed for each girl, a small dresser with a larger mirror they must share, and a smaller table to put their personal things in, were the only furnishings. Her mind wandered back to home and the day her parents told her she would be leaving, while she absently ran the silver hairbrush through the tangles.

The day after the spring dance had dawned bright and sunny when she had awoken. With a large smile at the memory of Jeff standing in the street, soaking wet slipping across her mind, she had begun her day.

After she dressed, she walked into the front room for breakfast, as the entire family fell silent. Her brothers had quickly made an escape from the house when her parents said, "Lizzie, we need to talk to you, sweetheart."

The conversation started with, "It's what's best for you," and "You'll love it there."

"Away? What do you mean you're spending me away?"

"Mother and I have decided you need more of a disciplined routine to learn what is required of a girl your age. You need to learn to be a lady, Elizabeth, and the only way that will happen is for you to go to a school that teaches these things. Your mother has tried to teach you, but you always seem to be able to weasel your way into doing what you wish rather than what needs to be done. I will be taking you to the rail station in two days so that you may travel to Arrington Hall in Pennsylvania. It is a very respectable school for girls, and they will teach you how to behave." When he'd finished his speech, he frowned.

"That's not fair, Father! How can you send me away? Do you hate me that much?" Hot tears began rolling down her cheeks, but she quickly brushed them away.

"We don't hate you, Elizabeth. You know that." Tears welled up in her mother's eyes, and she hugged Elizabeth to her chest. "We love you sweetheart."

"Then how can you send me away?"

She knew her mother almost gave in when she looked at her father, but he shook his head stubbornly at her questioning glance. "It's what's best for you."

"Carmen will accompany you, as well as John. I would send Ray, but I know you would be able to talk him into bringing you home since he favors you."

"Mother?" She turned tear filled eyes to her mother one last time in a desperate plea.

Her mother just bowed her head.

"I hate you! I hate both of you!" Elizabeth shouted, jumping to her feet. With one last looked, she ran into her room and slammed the door.

Two days later, she found herself riding in the wagon with her trunks in the back, full of the new dresses her mother had commissioned for her before they even had planned her departure. Carmen was sitting next to her with her father driving the wagon and her brother John riding his horse behind.

Sadly, she kept her eyes forward, not daring to look at her father for fear she would start crying again.

I refuse to cry another tear. I'll take this for what it is and fight with every breath once I get to this school. I'll make them kick me out. See if I don't.

When the train station came into view, Elizabeth straightened her back in resolve. She hated the thought of leaving her home, but her parents weren't to be dissuaded in their plans. The wagon came to a stop, but she refused to allow either her father or her brother to help her down. She stood solemnly while they unloaded her trunk, but almost lost her composure when her father took her in his arms, gave her a big bear hug, and kissed her on the cheek. "We love you, sweetheart, and you'll be fine."

She'd climbed aboard the train with her brother and Carmen, but refused to wave when the train pulled out of the station. Anger still sparked her defiance and she wanted him to know that she was not about to forgive him, for sending her away, not yet anyway.

The ride to Pennsylvania had been a long one. The scenery from the train window had been very pretty, but she hadn't been interested in the view. John had tried talking to her as well as Carmen, but she kept to herself not talking more than what was required to order her meals. After switching trains several times on the way, she finally had arrived at the school. She hated it from the moment she'd arrived. The school was very stately since it had been built many years ago with grand columns adorning its front with marble steps leading into the main hall. The décor was elegant in its simplicity with gold brocade curtains hanging from the tall windows and pictures of past board members hanging in the front hall. A tall elderly man who'd introduced himself as the headmaster met them, and in turn, he informed them where she would be staying and when her classes would begin. She was sure it had seen many a young woman grace its halls of learning, but she hadn't been impressed. Its grand appearance didn't appeal to her since all she wanted was to return to the sprawling acres of her birthplace.

"Liz, you'll be all right. You'll fit in here, just wait and see, and when you come home, you'll be the perfect lady, all beautiful and smart." John had given her a small smile and a big hug

"Come, *chica*. I'll help you to your room before we leave for home." Carmen put her arm around Elizabeth and escorted her from the great hall to her assigned room.

That was four years ago. She hadn't seen her family since except for when Ray had visited one Christmas. Tears had soaked his shirt when she'd seen him and begged him to take her home, but he refused.

"Liz?"

"Yes, it's me, silly. Gosh, it's good to see you. I missed you so much. You have no idea!" She hugged him tightly.

They had spent the next few days talking about home, their parents, and how much everyone had changed including her. When he had to leave for home, she had been sad, but she knew that he was pleased with her transformation. She really didn't like the school at first, but she had grown to tolerate it at least. Everything had rubbed her wrong at first. They refused to let her wear her jeans, made her use her manners, and even had taught her how to be coy with the young men. One of the things that surprised her in her lessons was the fact they discussed literature, history, and even business to some degree in order for the girls to be able to hold their own in a conversation with a suitable young man.

Now, Elizabeth snuggled back under the coverlet and tried to forget what today meant. Tonight was the year-end ball at school, and she really didn't feel like going except it meant tomorrow she was going home.

"Home!" She smiled, and flipped the coverlet off, shivering in the cold of the morning. Goose bumps flittered across her skin. Today would be the longest day of her life, she knew. She absolutely would not be able to focus on her studies at all knowing what this evening brought. Quickly washing her face, she pulled her clean underclothing from her dresser and slipped them on. The armoire held the dull gray dresses she'd worn every day since she'd been at school. Grabbing it, she slid it over her head, and buttoned up the front. Lord, how she hated the drab dress they made them wear.

Sitting on the side of the bed, she pulled her stockings on her petite feet, slipped on her black button-up boots, and fastened them with the buttonhook. Noting her reflection in the mirror, she ran the brush through her thick hair and pulled it back in a pretty white ribbon.

Grabbing her shawl, she headed down the long corridor to the dining hall, the same place where she had taken her meals for the last four years and she wouldn't miss it at all. The food was terrible, and the company even worse except for Michelle. When she found her best friend, she slid onto the bench beside her, and she smiled.

"There you are. I thought you were sleeping in this morning since you hadn't come down for breakfast yet."

"Today? Not on your life! I can't wait for this day to be over except that I'll miss you terribly. You are the only sane thing in this whole place." Elizabeth hugged her friend.

"Well, maybe I'll move to Texas with you," Michelle said with a smile as she hugged her friend in return.

They had become quick friends when they both arrived at the school. Michelle had tried to help Elizabeth adjust since she could see Elizabeth was not the least bit comfortable with all the ladylike things they were trying to teach them. Michelle had tutored Elizabeth after their classes were over each day, instilling the need for her to learn the curriculum. "Someday you'll need all of these things, Elizabeth. Someday you'll meet a nice gentleman and want to get married. You'll need to be able to hold your own in polite society," Michelle told her.

Elizabeth would always answer, "I just want to go home. There is not much call for being able to hold a conversation in polite company in Texas."

Her thoughts came back to the present, and she wasn't going to allow anything to dampen her spirits today. Not even the fact that she would miss Michelle terribly, or the meanest teacher on all the earth, Miss Williams. She had even whacked Elizabeth across the knuckles a few times over the years, but today even she couldn't stop the smile playing across Elizabeth's lips.

It will all be over soon, and I can't wait to get home.

As the afternoon wore on, the sky began to clear from the morning drizzle that had plagued them. The sun even had decided to smile down on the girls for tonight's festivities. All of them were atwitter over the coming dance, but the girls that had been there for four years were the most anxious. This year it was their turn to be the belles of the ball.

The students from the boy's school from across town were invited tonight, and all the girls at school were flittering around like butterflies. Their giggles could be heard throughout the hall while they prepared for the dance.

The two girls were cloistered in Michelle's room trying on every pretty dress they owned, for tonight was the only night they were allowed to wear the beautiful silk dresses their parents had purchased over the years. Many of the dresses had to be altered over the last few weeks since the girls had completely blossomed into young women.

Elizabeth had chosen a gorgeous blue silk dress that was the exact color of her eyes, with a high waist and a modest bust line. It had white ruffles around the neckline, the sleeves, and the hem and a white sash to be worn around her tiny waist. Michelle had helped pile Elizabeth's long curly hair up high on her head with small wispy curls hanging down on her neck that teased along the ruffles of her dress.

Michelle's dress was lavender with deeper purple accents along the neckline and hem. It complemented her skin tone perfectly. Elizabeth helped Michelle with her blonde curls as well while the time for the dance grew closer.

"Are you going to dance with Gregory tonight?" Michelle asked curiously while they finished checking their appearance in the mirror.

"I don't know. He's a nice and all, but I just don't want him to think I like him that way."

Gregory Webster was a handsome man with blond hair and blue eyes, broad shoulders, and a well-built physique. Born into wealth, he was used to getting whatever he wanted, from women to money, and he expected it from everyone he came into contact with. He had yet to be turned down by any woman, and he didn't accept that Elizabeth wasn't impressed with everything he had. His parents owned a large plantation in Virginia, and being the eldest of the family, he was set to inherit his family home and fortune. When he had come to Pennsylvania, it was in order to secure a bride of good breeding, not just to attend a school for young men, and he had his mind set on her. He had used every chance he had gotten over the last two years to attempt to impress her. Handsome, yes, but when she told him about her home in Texas and how badly she wanted to return there, he laughed.

"Texas? You can't be serious, Elizabeth." His indignation was apparent one afternoon when they walked outside the school about a year ago.

"Don't call me that!" Her brothers and father called her Lizzie, but she had been so hurt by what had happened at the spring dance before she left, she hadn't allowed anyone of the male persuasion to call her Elizabeth. Her heart still stung from Jeff's dismissal, even after three years.

"I'm sorry. What did I say?"

Surprise was evident in his voice, at her reaction to her name when he turned concerned eyes toward her. "Never mind. It's nothing. Just call me Liz, all right? I just prefer Liz," she said. "Besides, what's wrong with Texas?"

"It's dirty, smelly, full of cows, gunslingers, and just plain nasty! People get killed there from what I've heard.

"No it's not. It's beautiful! In the spring when the bluebonnets are in bloom and the trees start to grow new leaves down in the hollow with the sun shining, you've never seen anything so pretty. There is a beautiful pond near my parents' house that is so clear you can see the fish swimming under the water. There is a beautiful waterfall that cascades over the rocks and splashes into the pond. I don't know how you can say it's dirty and nasty."

"I'm sorry, Liz. To me, it's a dirty place that I care not for. I just don't understand how you could love such a place. The comforts that are plentiful here in Pennsylvania, or Virginia, for that matter, are abundant. We have parties, fox hunts, summer cotillions, and courting, just to name a few."

"I love it because it's home. Have you ever been there?"

"Well, no, but I've heard about it, and I'd rather not see it personally. I'm much too civilized to be comfortable in a place like that. Now if you wish to talk about my home, then I can oblige you. It's very grand! There are large columns that stand at the front entrance with porches that wrap all the way around the front. We bred horses there and raise tobacco."

"Horses? I love horses! What kind do you have? Many of the horses we have on our place are mustangs that have been roaming the ranges for years. They are so majestic when you watch them run across the plains in a large group or when a stallion keeps moving his mares so the younger stallions won't try to challenge him for them. It's magnificent."

"The horses we raise are thoroughbreds. We raise them to race."

"Race? What do you mean race? I don't understand."

"The horses are bred to be fast, I mean really fast, and we have races several times a year and people come from miles around to bet on them. If there is one horse that wins several times at different races, he can be sold as a stud for someone else's mares at a very profitable rate. It carries on the bloodline and breeds more horses to race."

"I see." She wasn't quite sure if she liked the thought of this type of horse breeding. The wild mustangs breed many times over the years but this type of controlled environment didn't appeal to her.

"It's really very profitable, Liz. It's one of the best money-makers my family has invested in."

"Is everything about money here?" She was confused by the feelings that she didn't really care for his way of life.

After that day, she had tried her hardest to avoid Gregory, but he had persisted. She figured he thought he could persuade her to stay in Virginia with him when he went home. After all, he was a Webster of Virginia. Who wouldn't want to be his wife?

Not me.

The clock struck seven, and the girls made their way into the great hall for the evening's festivities. Elizabeth was disappointed that her family wouldn't be there tonight to see her, but her father had written and said it would be impossible with the spring cattle drive. They had over a thousand head to move in a few weeks' time, and they just couldn't get away.

When Elizabeth and Michelle made their way into the main area for the dance, Elizabeth saw Gregory standing to the right side. Their eyes met and he began to make his way toward her. She grabbed Michelle's arm and started across the room in the opposite direction.

"What are you doing?" Michelle was startled when Elizabeth dragged her along.

"I'm avoiding Gregory. Come on."

"Oh, all right."

They rounded the outside corner of the building and ran smack into her brother John. He grabbed her shoulders in an attempt to steady her.

"Pardon me." He looked down into the blue eyes of his sister. "Lizzie?"

"John!" She threw her arms around his broad shoulders and squeezed tight. "What are you doing here?"

"I came with Mother, Father, Matt, and Ray of course." He motioned behind him indicating the rest of her family. "We came for your final night here at school."

Elizabeth squealed in delight, wiggling out of her oldest brother's arms and in turn hugged each member of her family.

"I thought you weren't coming."

"We wanted you to be surprised, little sister." Ray hugged her tight.

"My goodness! Look at you!" her father said as she hugged him. "You look absolutely beautiful."

"I can't believe you are all here! This is the best day ever."

"Oh my! I've completely forgotten." She stepped aside to introduce her friend to her family. "Mother, Father, this is Michelle. She has been my best friend here."

"Michelle, this is my mother, Margaret; my father, John; my brothers Ray, Matt, and John Jr."

"I'm pleased to meet you. I've heard so much about each of you, I feel I already know all of you."

"Well, let's go inside, shall we? The dance is about to start, and I'm sure I've saved at least one dance for each of you, except you, Mother, of course. I'm sure we can convince Father to dance with you though." Elizabeth giggled and took Ray's arm.

Elizabeth and Ray made their way back toward the great hall, chattering away with Matt following closely behind them, and her mother and father close behind. She glanced over her shoulder to see John Jr. extend his arm to Michelle.

"Shall we?"

"Thank you," Michelle said, blushing slightly when she took his arm for him to escort her inside.

Elizabeth smiled at the picture of her brother and her friend before Ray swept her up in a dance. Attempting to avoid Gregory, she kept her dance card full. During the dance with her father, she noticed Gregory watching her from the side of the crowded room.

"Is there a special young man you've got your eye on, my little girl?" her father asked, seeing her gaze transfixed on the young blond gentlemen.

"I'm sorry, what, Father?" She pulled her eyes from Gregory and hoped he would just leave her alone.

"I had noticed you watching that good-looking gentlemen in the corner just now. Someone special I hope?"

"No, Father. Actually he's just a friend."

"Really? That doesn't look like the glance of a friend, Elizabeth."

"I believe he wants more than friends, Father, but I'm not interested in him that way." The dance ended and her father escorted her back to the side of the dance floor, and Gregory started making his way toward her.

"I think I'm going to get some air." Elizabeth excused herself and slipped out the side door.

While she stood by the railing of the balcony, Gregory approached from her left and she groaned almost out loud.

"Liz, are you avoiding me?"

"Don't be silly, Gregory." Elizabeth tried to be cordial even though she didn't want anything to do with the man next to her.

"I've been trying to dance with you all night but you seem to have been very occupied."

"My family is here. I haven't seen them in four years, so I've been spending time with them. I'm sorry if you have felt slighted."

"I forgive you," he said, slipping his arm around her waist and drawing her closer while he tried to nuzzle her neck.

"Gregory, stop it!" She pushed against him, attempting to dislodge his arms from around her. "Keep your hands off me!"

"But, Liz, I thought you understood that I want you for my wife."

"I don't believe your audacity! I'm your friend, Gregory. That's all. I'm sorry if you felt there is a future between us."

With his eyes blazing with anger, he puffed out his chest. "You would turn down a marriage proposal from a Webster? Do you know how many women would be honored to be getting a marriage proposal from me?"

"I'm sorry, but I don't love you."

"Love? What's love got to do with this?" His face flushed a deep shade of purple from his rage. A moment later, he turned his back to her trying to regain his composure, grasping the railing of the balcony so hard his knuckles turned white.

She stood completely still, not sure what he would do next. He was so angry with her; he could have easily struck her in his rage.

After a few minutes he had regained his composure and turned to face her again.

"Lizzie, I'm sorry. This was not the way this was supposed to happen." He got down on one knee, pulled out a gorgeous diamond solitaire from his pocket, and grasped her hand. "Will you marry me, Liz?"

Pulling her hand from his, she said again, "Gregory, please. You have to understand. I can't marry you. I don't love you."

He sprang to his feet, and with a cry of outrage, he raise his hand to strike her. Ray stepped from behind the pillar next to Elizabeth, grabbing Gregory's fist in his hand just as it was about to strike her.

"You will *not* hit my sister." Ray flung Gregory's fist back.

Elizabeth slid behind Ray while Gregory sputtered in his rage. He quickly backed down, turned his back on them, and walked away.

"You still seem to know how to get yourself into trouble, little sis."

"Thank you," she whispered and hugged him. "I don't know what he would have done if you hadn't come out here. How did you know I might need you?"

"Brother's intuition. Let's go back inside. It's a bit cool out here."

They watched Gregory work his way back around the building. Once Gregory had disappeared, Ray turned to her, put his arm around her shoulder and escorted her back inside.

The rest of the evening passed without incident. The family avoided Gregory while he scowled from the corner of the room until they left.

The family returned home to Texas the next day as a jubilant Elizabeth chattered and practically bounced on the train seat all the way home. She just couldn't wait to get home.

CHAPTER 3

Elizabeth sat on a rock near the naturally fed spring about a half a mile from her parents' ranch house. She had always loved coming here as a young girl to swim in the summer when it was so warm. Now, after returning home from school, she could relax and dangle her feet in the cool water and dream about where her life would go from here. Yes, she had learned the ways of a lady with proper manners, the etiquette of how to dress and how to behave around gentlemen, but she was still that free-spirited little girl who loved to ride her horse across the plains with the wind blowing her curls on the inside.

She smiled remembering how the wind felt in her hair when she rode, while the breeze lifted her long curls and then settled them back down on her neck.

With a wicked grin, she glanced around, contemplating if she should or not.

There isn't anyone around. What would it hurt?

Quickly standing, she began shedding her shirt, trousers and her chemise, as well as her under drawers. She stripped down to bare skin before jumping headlong into the deep water of the pond.

God this feels wonderful!

Her mother would kill her if she could see her now after spending four years at finishing school only to find her daughter, naked as the day she was born, swimming in the pond.

Surfacing in the center with a loud giggle, she rolled over on her back, easily skimming across the water. Her brothers had taught her to swim many years ago in this very pond. Of course, it had been a long time since she had swum here, but it felt so refreshing, she just couldn't stand not getting into the water.

It felt so good to be home again, back where she belonged. She would have never left if her parents hadn't shipped her off to that girl's school, but she really hadn't any choice in the matter. They had made up their minds long before she had been sent away. She hadn't been able to even come home for holidays and birthdays. Every holiday had been spent at school, usually her and Michelle, except for a few of the teachers who had no family to speak of. Michelle's family had spent much of their money putting her through the school, so they couldn't afford to bring her home for holidays. Elizabeth's parents had said it was best that way since she had fought them so hard about going in the first place. They probably would have relented if she had been able to come home. Perhaps it's why they never let her. They knew her all too well. She had been home only a few days, and she already missed Michelle, but she was glad to be home.

She realized it was getting late, so she swam to the side of the pond where her clothing sat in a nice neat pile on the rock. Feeling as though eyes were on her, she looked around, peering into the brush near the rock. After a moment, she shrugged, climbed from the water, and reached for her clothing.

"What is this? A mermaid perhaps?" a deep voice said from behind the rock.

She squealed, grabbed for her chemise to cover herself, and whirled around to see who had interrupted her. Her heart pounded, and she narrowed her eyes when the man stepped from his hiding place. Brown eyes bore through her scant clothing, raking her body from head to toe and she flushed with embarrassment.

"Jeffery Walker! What are you doing here?" Her indignation was clear in her voice while she stood there dripping wet with nothing on.

When he realized who stood in front of him, his eyes opened wide in shock. "Elizabeth? Is that you?"

* * * *

Jeff was completely surprised at the vision standing in front of him. He hadn't seen Elizabeth since the spring dance four years ago when she had unceremoniously shoved him into the horse trough after she had caught him kissing Aubrey Dillon. She had been so proud of herself that night, but he had spent an uncomfortable ride home in wet clothing.

"Of course, it's me, you ninny. Who else would be swimming in this pond? After all, it is on Double J property. Now, please turn around like a gentleman so that I can get dressed."

"Well, you never know. Besides, it's half on Rocking W property too, you know." His eyes met hers. Desire raced along his nerves. He'd caught a peek of some luscious curves before she'd grabbed her clothes. After another quick glance, he turned around. "I didn't know you were home. I'm surprised Ray hadn't mentioned it since I had just seen him in town last night," he said over his shoulder.

"I just got home a few days ago," she replied, her words muffled slightly as she pulled her shirt over her head. "You may turn around now."

He turned to see she'd mostly returned her clothing to its proper place, but her hair was beginning to dry and wildly tangled about her head. Her blue eyes shot daggers at him when he raked his eyes appreciatively over her, and he began to smile.

Elizabeth had changed dramatically from the last time he had seen her. At the time, she'd been only sixteen and hadn't completely filled out her womanly form. The woman standing before him was magnificent! Soft rounded bosom and a tiny waist showed off the curves to perfection. Although she didn't know it, he had seen even more of her beautiful body when she had emerged from the pond. Of course, at the time, he hadn't known it was Elizabeth. He really hadn't come here with the intention of spying on whomever was swimming in the pond, but he'd heard a horse nicker softly to his when he rode near the nearby. He hadn't recognized the horse so he had gotten down to investigate. With so many rustlers in the area, he had to be careful.

"Would you please stop looking at me like that?"

"Like what?" His gaze slid over her again.

"Oh, never mind." She slipped her boots back on and stomped off to where her horse stood tied.

He followed behind her, watching her backside sway with appreciation. Why hadn't he noticed how nicely her backside fit in her brother's trousers before now?

When she approached her horse and attempted to slide her foot into the stirrup, he came up behind her, grasped her small waist, and easily lifted her into the saddle.

Elizabeth landed with an unladylike *thump,* and she grabbed for the reins quickly.

* * * *

Staring down at him from atop her horse, she realized he was still the most handsome boy she had ever seen. *Man,* she corrected herself in her mind. After all, he is twenty-four years old now and had easily grown another three inches since she had been gone. Her head barely reached his shoulder, and she was tall for a girl at five feet eight inches herself.

"Are you headed back to the ranch house now that you are well refreshed?"

"Yes," she said with a sheepish smile. "Mother is going to kill me, I'm sure. She never did understand how I could swim in the pond anyway, much less now."

"I'm sure all will be forgiven, even if you do look a little disheveled."

"Do I?"

"It's not all that bad, Elizabeth. You just look, um, how shall I say this without sounding crude?"

"What?"

"You look like you've just had a wild romp with someone in the field."

She could see the laughter in his eyes. "I do not! Do I? I can't go home like this!"

"It will be fine. Just run your fingers through your hair. Do you have anything to tie it back with?"

"No. I didn't bring anything with me. I really hadn't planned on going for a swim this afternoon when I headed out here."

Taking the bandana from around his neck, he said, "Here. You can borrow this to tie back your hair until we get back to your parents' place."

"Thanks." She took it from him, ran her fingers through her long hair as she attempted to make it somewhat presentable, and then tied his bandana around it at her nape to secure it in place the best she could.

"Shall we go?"

"Yes, I supposed we should. Why were you out here today anyway?"

"I was riding out to check on some of the cattle in the pasture back to the east, and your horse nickered at mine so I thought I'd check it out."

"You really don't have to ride back to the house with me. I know the way."

"I'm sure you do, but there have been some problems out here lately, so I just think I'll ride along, if you don't mind."

"I don't mind, I guess." She really didn't want him riding home with her. Her parents and her brothers didn't need to know they had run into each other near the pond. She would have enough explaining to do about her appearance without ex-plaining Jeff's presence, too.

Glancing at him, she wondered what he was thinking. Several times he looked at her when he thought she didn't notice. The changes in him weren't glaring, but apparent to her, none-the-less.

His eyes had gotten a slightly deeper brown, if that was possible. His hair was a bit longer near the collar and had a little bit of a curl at the ends that she could see under his black cowboy hat. His chest was broader, and she could see small springy curls of brown hair from around the opening of his shirt near his neck.

I wonder what it would feel like to run my fingers through those curls. She quickly looked back at the road in front of them. *My goodness! Where did that come from? You would think I'm some sort of brazen hussy with all that's flittering through my mind at the moment.*

A talk with her mother might be in order this evening. Then again, maybe not. Mother wouldn't understand.

* * * *

Jeff shifted his gaze toward Elizabeth from time to time during their ride.

She sure has grown up.

The little girl he remembered from four years ago no longer existed, and the woman who now rode next to him took his breath away.

The jealousy of his relationship with Aubrey she'd displayed before, made him laugh, but now, Aubrey couldn't hold a candle to the beauty before him. Her hair had gotten so much longer and curled at the ends. Her eyes were still the same deep blue he remembered. Her eyes had always been so bright and full of feeling while they were growing up. He could usually tell what her thoughts were by looking into her eyes. As a child, she never could keep secrets from him. He usually knew when she had been up to something and when they had played tricks on her brothers together, her laughter had been contagious. They had always been friends, but now, it felt rather awkward. She was a young woman now and not the little girl he used to play with who had been all legs and uncoordinated. Now, she could turn any head in the room.

When they rode up to the house and directed their horses toward the hitching post in front, her brothers Matt and Ray were sitting in the cool shade of the porch. They both stood and approached the pair when they dismounted and tied their horses to the railing.

"Elizabeth? Jeff?" Ray asked with a questioning raise of his eyebrow.

"Uh, hi Ray. I found this little nymph near the pond, and with all the troubles we've had lately, I thought I would escort her home."

He kept to himself just how close to the pond he had found her.

Blue eyes focused on him and she said, "Jeff kindly escorted me home. Thank you."

"You are certainly welcome. I'm glad I could be of help."

"You look like you found the pond refreshing, Liz," Ray's teasing words brought a smile to Jeff's lips. "Care to stay for dinner, Jeff? I'm sure Mother wouldn't mind. You know you are always welcome."

"Thanks, Ray. I think I'd like that," he said, glancing at Elizabeth again. "That is, if Elizabeth doesn't mind."

"Why would she?"

"Well, I know she just got home and all. I don't want to intrude."

"Intrude? How do you figure that? You are like family and you know it," Matt said with a questioning look.

"All right, all right," Jeff said with a wide grin and holding up his hands in surrender. "I never could turn down a meal that your mother puts out. She's one of the best in the county. Of course I know Carmen does most of the cooking."

"Then it's settled," Ray said, slapping Jeff on the back once he had stepped onto the porch, and motioned for Juan to put the horses in the barn.

* * * *

Elizabeth looked at Jeff through her lashes then turned on her heel and headed into the house.

How will I ever to make it through dinner with him sitting at the table and my thoughts running in the direction they are?

She sailed into the dining room and met her mother's glare.

"Elizabeth! My gracious! What happened to you? Don't tell me. You went swimming again," her mother said when she took in Elizabeth's appearance with her tangled curls and damp clothing.

Elizabeth bowed her head and walked to her room to change her clothes before she attempted to brush out her hair.

While she sat in her room brushing out her tangles, she took in her reflection. Her form had certainly filled out, from what she could tell. The same blue eyes stared back at her in the mirror. Her hair was longer, reaching her petite waist.

I need to have Mother trim it. One tangle resisted the brush. *If I hadn't got into the pond, my hair wouldn't be such a mess.*

Her mind wandered back to the scene at the pond, and her cheeks began to flush when she thought about the way Jeff looked at her when she was standing there with little to no clothing on. No man had ever looked at her like that before. Gregory didn't even look at her with the same kind of heat in his eyes.

It was almost like he'd touched me. Goose bumps rose on her arms. *This is silly. It is only Jeff for heaven's sake! He's like one of my brothers.*

Once she had all the tangles brushed out, she pulled her hair back and up on top of her head, showing off her slim neck, accenting the square neckline. The burgundy red of the dress highlighted her coloring to perfection. It accentuated the red highlights in her hair and the tan coloring of her skin that she had never been able to get rid of. During her time in school, they had tried everything from rubbing lemon juice on her skin to refusing to let her outside when the sun shown, but it never went away completely. It was a part of her, just like the color of her eyes or the wave of curl on her head.

A soft knock sounded on the door.

"Come in."

Her mother came inside and approached to help her secure her hair on top of her head. "You have such beautiful hair, Elizabeth. It's so soft and shiny," she said, pushing the pin into her hair to secure the last curl. "Now, shall we go out to dinner?"

"Thank you, Mother." Elizabeth hesitated when she stood up and walked to the door with her mother following on her heels.

"Everything all right, sweetheart?"

"Yes. I'm just glad to be home, but I miss Michelle," she said, trying to hide her feelings from her mother. She really didn't want to face Jeff again after this afternoon. She blushed to her hair roots just thinking about how he had seen her with pretty much nothing on. The blush deepened when she thought about the heat in his eyes when they raked over her skin.

"Are you sure there isn't anything else bothering you?

"Yes, I'm sure," Elizabeth said, pulled the door open, and heading into the dining room, shuffling her feet like she was headed to her own hanging.

CHAPTER 4

All the men stood when the two women made their way into the dining room.

When Elizabeth stopped near the table, a sexy little crooked smile quirked at the side of Jeff's mouth as their eyes met. Her heart skipped a beat, and she almost stumbled.

"Oh! I'm sorry."

"Are you all right?" Ray asked, catching her arm.

"Yes, thank you. I don't know what's gotten into me." Her heart sank into the pit of her stomach. The stop they'd left for her was right next to the man who sent all of her nerve endings on high alert.

Oh Lord, how am I going to sit next to him all evening?

With a deep breath, she worked her way around the table and sat down.

I'll make it through this night if it kills me.

Biting her lip, she scooted sideways and asked, "May I have the potatoes, please?"

"Certainly."

Grabbing the bowl, he handed it to her, but when their fingers touched, electricity shot up her arm, to settle low in her belly. Tension crackled between them when her eyes locked with his. Quickly, pulling her hand back, she almost dropped the bowl.

"Elizabeth," her mother exclaimed. "You must be more careful, dear. You almost dropped that into Jeffery's lap."

"I'm sorry, Mother, Jeff. The bowl was just hotter than I thought."

A little smirk crossed his lips. "You're forgiven of course."

Lord, it's going to be a long night.

The conversation around the table changed to the rustlers who had been plaguing the ranchers in the area for the last few months.

"Has your father lost many head, Jeff?" her father asked.

"Probably a hundred or so, I think. He'd mentioned getting a town meeting together with all of the ranchers to decide what we are going to do about it."

"That would be a good idea, I think, Father," Matt said.

The other boys chimed in with their agreement, and John raised his hand to halt the conversation again.

"Possibly, but I would like to talk to your father first, Jeff, before we get everyone riled up in town."

"When I head home later, I'll mention to him you would like to talk to him."

"Thanks. Let him know that I should be near the house tomorrow. I have some repairs to do around here."

"Certainly, sir," Jeff replied.

Once they'd finished their meal, Margaret rose from her place at the table and asked Elizabeth to help her clear the dishes while the men moved outside.

* * * *

Ray wandered off away from the others and motioned to Jeff to follow. They walked about several feet away from the others, and Ray asked, "Are you still seeing Aubrey?"

"Why? Interested in her yourself?"

"Nah, just curious." Ray kicked at the dirt beneath his feet. "Is there something going on between you and Liz?"

"I'm not sure I know what you mean, Ray. There's nothing between Elizabeth and me. Hell, today was the first time I've seen her in four years."

He shuffled his feet, kicking up a little dust in the process and avoiding looking at his friend.

It wouldn't do any good to tell Ray, I think his sister has turned into a very beautiful woman.

"Well, I know my little sister, and she was acting awfully strange at dinner tonight. I saw the looks you two were shooting at each other even if the others at the table didn't. I've never seen her act so skittish."

"What looks? Elizabeth is like a little sister to me, you know that."

"The hot look you gave her when she approached the table would say otherwise. I thought you two were going to set the house on fire."

"It's just the look of appreciation for a beautiful woman, nothing more. She certainly turned into a pretty thing while she was gone though."

"Just make sure you keep your hands off her, all right? She's off-limits to you. Otherwise, I may have to kick your butt for you." The narrowing of Ray's eyes assured Jeff he meant every word.

"Sure, Ray, sure."

After a moment of uncomfortable silence, the two of them headed back to where the other men still stood talking on the porch. The conversation concerning the rustlers picked up again, relieving Jeff of his wandering thoughts about the woman he'd thought of for so long as a child, but no more.

* * * *

In the house, Elizabeth cleared the table with her mother, taking the dishes into the kitchen where Carmen stood waiting to clean up.

"Elizabeth? Did you hear what I said?" her mother asked.

"I'm sorry, Mother. No, I didn't."

I need to focus instead of dwelling on that disturbing man.

"I asked you if you would like to write to Michelle and invite her to come out here and visit you. John sure seemed taken with her when we attended your graduation."

Elizabeth smiled, remembering how John and Michelle had become almost inseparable while her family was in Pennsylvania. She hadn't gotten a chance to ask Michelle about it before they left.

"I'd love that, Mother! I shall sit and write to her tonight so it can go out in the post tomorrow."

This could be just the thing she needed to get her mind off a certain brown-eyed cowboy who had taken up residence in her mind from the moment she'd returned.

Shoot. He's always been on my mind. Ever since my fourteenth birthday.

Michelle could keep her out of trouble at least while she was here. She was good at that! Besides, she might be able to play matchmaker while Michelle visited. Wouldn't it be lovely if Michelle and John got married! She clapped her hands in glee at the thought.

"What are you up to, young lady?"

"Oh nothing."

"Nothing? I know that look. You are planning something."

"Just a little matchmaking. It's nothing, really."

"You had better be careful. That could backfire and cause lots of problems, you know. I don't think I've ever seen a match-making scheme work out for the best."

"I'll be careful, Mother, and it's not like they don't already like each other."

Her mother just shook her head and headed back into the front room to work on her needlepoint.

Elizabeth followed her quickly, and when her mother settled into her rocker near the window, Elizabeth headed off to her room to write the letter to Michelle.

Besides, this will give me a reason to avoid Jeff for the rest of the night.

* * * *

After Jeff left, the rest of the men disbursed and John Sr. sat down next to his wife with a heavy sigh.

"What's wrong, John?"

"Nothing you need to worry your pretty head about, my dear."

Setting the needlepoint in her lap, she gave him a worried look. "Don't try to protect me, John. I know this situation with the rustlers is bad. We've lost quite a few head of cattle I'm sure, but don't want you to keep me in the dark. I'm here to stand beside you. You are my husband."

"I know, my dear. I just don't want you to worry. The boys and I will handle things."

"Do not patronize me, John Johnston! I'm not some willy-nilly female who will be pushed aside when things get rough. This is my home too, and I'll not stand beside and let anyone take away what we have worked so hard to build," Margaret said, her eyes blazing.

"All right Mother. I'll tell you what's going on. You're right. We've lost too many cattle and our financial situation can't handle much more. I didn't want to worry you with all of the details. It's a man's business.

"What can I do to help?"

He tangled their fingers together and stroked her palm.

"Nothing at the moment, dear. You and Elizabeth need to stay close to the house. I wouldn't put it past these outlaws to harm either of you and I couldn't handle it if something happened to my two beautiful women. For the time being, there isn't much else to be done. We need to stay on top of the cattle and move them closer to the house. I hope it's enough to dissuade the rustlers and hopefully they'll move on to the other areas soon."

"Should we keep a rifle close by?"

"Probably. At least you and Elizabeth would have some type of protection should me and the boys be out in the pasture."

* * * *

Ray came striding into the room, buttoning up his shirt and tucking it into his pants.

"Morning, sis."

He kissed her on the cheek, and she gave him a sidelong look.

"Good morning to you, too. It's about time you were ready to go. Good gracious! We're wasting daylight."

"What's your hurry this morning, or are you just trying to avoid being here when Jeff comes over later."

The penetrating look he gave her, didn't sit well when he sat down and pulled his boots.

"I'm doing no such thing. I want to get to town to make sure this letter to Michelle goes out today." She grabbed her shawl and slipping on her gloves. "I've already had Juan bring the wagon around."

"My, you are in a hurry this morning."

Thirty minutes later, the wagon rolled along through the sunlight filtering through the trees while Elizabeth shifted on the seat.

"Sis, are you sure you're all right? I mean, I saw the way you and Jeff were looking at each other last night at dinner. I love Jeff like a brother, but I don't think you should have anything to do with him. You know what I mean?"

"I don't understand what you are talking about, Ray. I'm sure I didn't look at Jeff any differently than I have all of my life." Heat curled up her neck to splash across her cheeks.

"Well, I thought you should know he's been seeing Aubrey Dillon again and has been for some time now."

"He is?"

"Yes, he is. I think he is even going to ask her to marry him."

"Oh." She bowed her head, hoping he wouldn't see the hurt on her face. "I'm sure they'll be very happy together. After all, they've sort of been together for a number of years now."

"Yes, yes they have."

They were silent for the rest of the trip to town.

I don't care if Jeff seeing Aubrey. I don't.

Ray pulled the wagon in front of the general store, coming to a rough stop before he set the brake.

"I'm going to give the order Mother gave me to the clerk and then head over to the livery."

"I think I'll walk over to the dress shop and see what new fabrics Mrs. Bradley has," she answered after he had hoped down and came around the side to help her down.

* * * *

Ray watched his sisters retreating figure with a frown. He hoped neither Jeff nor Aubrey were in town today.

I'm protecting Elizabeth, but if she finds out I lied about Jeff asking Aubrey to marry him, she'll kill me.

"Don't tell me that was Elizabeth?" Ray heard behind him.

Allen Simpson leaned against the railing of the store, his eyes glued to Elizabeth.

"Hi, Allen. What have you been up to lately? I haven't seen you in town in a while."

"You didn't answer my question. Was that your sister?"

"Yes, that's Liz. What's it to you?"

"Nothin'…I was just appreciating the view. That's all," he said, raising his hands in defense. "No need to get your drawers in a bunch. She's sure changed. Turned into a real beauty, she has."

"She sure has," another deep drawl said.

Ray and Allen turned to see Jeff walking toward them.

"Hey, Ray. I didn't know you and Elizabeth were coming into town this morning," Jeff said, stopping next to Ray.

"I wasn't really a planned trip, but Elizabeth needed to send a letter this morning so we thought we do some other shopping for Mother."

"Oh? Who she sending a letter to?" Jeff asked and Ray noticed how his gaze never left Elizabeth until she went inside the dress shop.

"A beau she had at school. They had grown very close while she was there, and she's inviting him to come out and visit her here at home."

"She had a beau at school?" the two men said in unison and then looked at each other with a scowl.

"A guy named Webster. Gregory Webster." He stretched the truth even further. Liz hated the guy, but he wanted to protect her from Jeff and in turn, it seemed, from Allen, too. Allen had the reputation of a womanizer who had broken many hearts in town in his three years in Hempstead.

Allen had moved to Hempstead with his family when his father opened the local bank in town. He was a pompous ass, and Ray didn't like him anyway.

"Well, anyway, I've got to get this order to Mr. Giles if we are going to get it filled sometime today. See you two later."

* * * *

"Well, I've got things to do," Jeff said, before he headed in the direction of the dress shop.

"Me, too." Allen headed toward the bank, trying to be inconspicuous, and then cut down the alley behind the general store where he'd planned to meet his contact.

"Is everything set?" the man asked when he approached.

"Our east coast buyer will be in town in a few weeks. We'll set up the drop outside of town." His gaze shifted from side-to-side to make sure no one saw him talking with the stranger.

I don't need anyone getting suspicious.

"Good. Make sure no one sees me leave." The stranger moved toward the front of the store keeping to the shadows and then blending with the foot traffic on the boardwalk.

Allen followed close behind, watching so that no one saw them talking, then headed toward the bank.

Getting in on this will make me very rich. I'm tired of relying on my father for my station in life.

Once he reached the imposing brick structure, he strolled in and headed for his father's office.

"What are you doing here, Allen?" his father asked when he reached his desk.

"I need a little cash."

"What for now? You're forever needing money." The scowl on his father's face pissed him off.

Damn old man! He ground his teeth together until his jaw hurt.

"Investing. I'm looking at buying some land outside of town."

"Where?"

"Near the Double J."

Hmpf. "Let me investigate it first before you go buying anything."

Son of a bitch!

"I need some spending money, too."

His father's eyes narrowed a moment. Slipping open the drawer to his left, his father pulled out his wallet, threw several bills across the desk and then grumbled under his breath about irresponsible children.

Allen picked up the money, gave his father a frowning look and then left the bank, heading for the nearest saloon.

* * * *

The bell tinkled over the door, and Elizabeth turned to see Aubrey coming inside the dress shop.

"Aubrey, my dear, I'll be with you in just a moment," Mrs. Bradley said. "Will you excuse me, Elizabeth? I'll be right back."

"Of course." Elizabeth debated whether to talk to Aubrey. After the conversation with Ray on the way in, she was dying to know if the other woman and Jeff were indeed planning to get married.

"I'll be right back, Aubrey. I have your dress in the back room." Mrs. Bradley disappeared into the room behind them.

"Elizabeth? Elizabeth Johnston, is that you?"

"Hello, Aubrey. How nice to see you," she replied, plastering a smile on her face.

"My, my! Haven't you changed."

"Thank you, Aubrey. You have changed quite a bit yourself."

Aubrey's large bust almost spilled over the top of her gown. *My mother would kill me if I wore a dress like that.*

"Aubrey, I need to ask you a question and please tell me if it's none of my business, but are you and Jeff seeing each other?"

"Why yes, yes we are. Actually we have been seeing each other for quite some time now and I'm sure he'll be asking me to marry him shortly. In fact, we are having a special dinner tonight here in town. After all, it's our anniversary of sorts. We've been together for four years now."

"I see," Elizabeth said, dropping her eyes to the floor at her feet.

"I even ran into him a little bit ago and he said he was buying me something special to celebrate tonight. I'm sure it will be an engagement ring."

A moment later, Mrs. Bradley came out from the back with Aubrey's dress. Elizabeth excused herself and left without another word.

The tears brimming in her eyes began to run down her cheeks blinding her for a moment. Seconds later, she slammed into a solid wall of muscle.

"Elizabeth, what's wrong?" Jeff asked, grasping her shoulders in his hands.

"Nothing," she said wiping the tears with her gloved fingers. "I'm fine. Just leave me alone."

"No. Something has happened. Tell me."

"Just leave me alone, please! Haven't you done enough already?" She pulled from his grasp and all but ran back toward the wagon.

* * * *

Jeff continued to stand in the same spot watching Elizabeth head back to the wagon with a puzzled expression. The bell on the dress shop tinkled and he looked back to see Aubrey.

"There you are," she said, coming up beside him and grasping his hand. "Would you like to have dinner with me later?"

"Uh...sure," Jeff said absently, returning his attention to Elizabeth.

"Something wrong?"

"No, I guess not. Where would you like to have dinner?"

"That restaurant over on First Street is nice. How about there? It's very romantic."

"That's fine. How about I meet you there about five? I have some things to do at home before then, and I have to run an errand out to the Double J."

"Of course. I wouldn't want to take you away from your duties at home. Will you be following Ray and Elizabeth out there?"

"No. I believe they will be in town for a while getting supplies before they head home. I'm headed out there now, so I probably will be back in town before they even head for their place." He glanced back at the Johnstons' wagon.

"Good," she grumbled.

"Pardon?"

"Nothing. I just had to cough a little from the dust." She looked at him through her lashes and gave him a coy look. "Well, I will see you later then."

"I'll see you in a little while."

Not paying much attention when Aubrey left his side, he headed toward the livery to retrieve his horse. The path put him next to Elizabeth's wagon.

Neither of them said a word when he stopped next to the wagon and his eyes met hers. Tears still lingered on her lashes, and he swallowed hard. A woman's tears had never affected him this much before, but hers made him feel like he had broken her heart.

"Damn," he murmured, and then turned toward the livery

Astride the animal, he jabbed him in the ribs and tore out of town like the devil was on his heels, toward the Double J.

CHAPTER 5

Three weeks later, Elizabeth stood on the railway platform waiting for the train to arrive. Excitement zinged through her to see her friend again and she fought the urge to bounce while she waited. Michelle had written two weeks ago, saying she would love to visit Elizabeth in Hempstead and she would immediately make plans to arrive on the fifth of June for a long visit. Now, Elizabeth stood there looking in the distance for the telltale sign, the steam from the locomotive as it came around the bend near town.

Standing next to her was John Jr. When he'd heard Michelle would be coming for a visit, immediately volunteered to go into town with her to meet Michelle's train.

"What time is it?" she asked her brother again for the tenth time in a ten-minute span.

"Two minutes later than you asked me last time, Liz. The train usually runs a little late, you know that so keep you petticoats on." He smiled and shook his head at her impatience.

"I'm just eager for her to be here already."

"Really? I hadn't noticed at all."

"Oh, bother with you." She turned and peered at the horizon, watching for the train.

"It should be here shortly. See," he said, pointing to the cloud in the distance.

Elizabeth turned to him with a huge smile on her face. "There it is."

They both stood very still when the train pulled into the station. Steam billowed from under the engine in a rush and Elizabeth stood on her tiptoes trying to see. When Michelle stepped down from the train, Elizabeth squealed, ran over to her, and threw her arms around her.

"I'm so glad you are here," she said, hugging her friend.

"Me too." Michelle hugged her back and then stepped away. "You brought company, I see." Michelle smiled and Elizabeth saw her blush when she looked at John. "Well, hello again."

"Hello. It's nice to see you again." John blushed and Elizabeth had to fight a giggle.

This is going to be easy, Elizabeth thought, noticing the color on her brother's face. *My goodness! I've never seen him blush before.*

"Liz!"

Elizabeth heard her name called from a familiar voice near the train. With a tilt of her head, she gave Michelle a questioning look.

"I couldn't help it, Elizabeth. He said he had business in Texas so he insisted he accompany me." Michelle leaned toward her and whispered in her ear, "I'm sorry."

"Liz, it's so good to see you." Gregory caught her up in a hug and swung her around in a circle. Once he set her back on her feet, he planted a wet kiss on her cheek.

"Gregory? What are you doing here?"

"I came to see you, of course. I've missed you. Besides, I had business in the area, and when I heard Michelle was coming to visit you, I had to come along." He draped his arm across her shoulder with a bit too much familiarity.

She wiggled out from under his arm, and said, "John, you know Gregory Webster. He was at the dance at school right before we came home."

"Ah, yes. Nice to see you again," John said but Elizabeth could tell it wasn't sincere when John's eyes narrowed.

"Well, we should be getting back to the ranch. Gregory, there is a hotel over on Second Street that has some nice rooms. I'm sure you'll be comfortable there."

Elizabeth motioned for John to get Michelle's trunks so they could be on their way back to the house and away from Gregory.

John and Michelle walked over to pick up her trunks, leaving Elizabeth with Gregory for a moment.

"Liz, I'm so happy to see you." He attempted to wrap his arms around her shoulders again, but she pushed at his chest trying to avoid him.

"Gregory, I don't know why you came here. I realize you were probably hurt by how things ended between us after the dance, but really, you shouldn't have come."

"Come now. Believe it or not, I didn't just come to Texas to see you, although it was my first intention." He leaned forward attempting to plant a kiss on her cheek.

"Gregory, really. We are in public." Glancing around her at the crowd, heat crawled up her neck when she noticed several people staring.

"All right. Have dinner with me then. I won't take no for an answer, Liz."

"But...it's Michelle's first day here, and I want to spend time with her."

"I realize that, my dear, but she'll be here all summer, correct?"

"Well, yes but..."

"Then you must have dinner with me. I'll only be here a short time. Please?"

"All right but not tonight. Tomorrow?"

Maybe if I can sit down and really talk to him, I can get him to leave me alone.

"Wonderful! Shall I pick you up at your parents' home?"

"No, I'll have one of my brothers bring me into town and meet you at the hotel. There is a nice restaurant in there," she answered as John and Michelle returned to her side. "Shall we go?"

"I'll see you tomorrow then. About six?"

She turned around to see him following a few feet behind them. "Yes, six is fine."

John lifted her onto the seat of the wagon next to Michelle, who was sitting in the middle.

"Fabulous! I shall see you then."

John snapped the reins over the back of the horse and the wagon pulled away. Elizabeth fought a shiver of revulsion at the beading look in Gregory's eyes while he watched them leave.

The two of them twittered with conversation all the way back to the ranch house.

When they crested the small hill before reaching the house, Michelle gasped, "Oh my!"

The sun, had started to set behind the hill that stood proudly behind the house, causing the entire building and yard filled with flowers, to be bathed in gold.

"It's absolutely beautiful here. I can certainly understand now why you wanted to come home so badly."

"I'm glad you like it. Dusk is probably my favorite time of the day when the sun is setting behind the hill. Look! Mother is waiting for us."

"Probably wanting to make sure we made it home with our precious cargo here," John said, smiling down at Michelle, and Elizabeth smile when her friend blushed to her the roots of her blonde curls.

They pulled up to the porch and their mother said, "It's about time, you two. Dinner was ready thirty minutes ago."

"Sorry, Mother." John hopped down and walked around the wagon to help the two ladies down.

"Well, hello again, Michelle. How was your trip?"

"Very long, Mrs. Johnston, but worth it."

John grabbed the horse's reins and set about putting them away for the night, while the women walked into the house.

"Well I'm glad you are here finally." Elizabeth hugged her friend before she steered her into the house. "You can wash up in my room before we eat. I'll show you where it is."

After the two girls had washed up, they returned to the dining room where Margaret had laid out a fabulous meal in celebration of Michelle's arrival.

All her brothers were fighting for a place next to Michelle and she giggled before she took her seat.

"Oh Lord," Elizabeth grumbled, watching her brothers making fools out of themselves. "I supposed no one wants to sit next to me." She exaggerated her look of hurt look before she took an empty place at the table.

"It's not that we don't want to sit by you, sis. It's just you're our sister. Michelle's a guest and a very beautiful one at that." Matt sat next to her and hugged her to his side. The rest of the men at the table mumbled their agreement.

"Well, I must forgive all of you then," she replied with a smile. "Pass me something to eat, will you?"

The men gave a hearty laugh when Ray said from her other side, "Of course. We wouldn't leave you to waste away before you got anything to eat."

"That certainly won't happen any time soon." A chuckle left her lips when she agreed with their observation.

"Liz, what's this about dinner with Gregory tomorrow night?"

She glared at John Jr. across the table and wished he hadn't said anything.

I really don't want to explain Gregory's appearance to Mother and Father, nor do I want to explain why I'm having dinner with him tomorrow.

"The young man is here? In Hempstead? He's trouble, Liz. I think you need to stay away from him."

"Well, Father, since it was brought up, I didn't realize he was coming here until he got off the train with Michelle."

"I'm really sorry, Elizabeth. I wish I had never come now."

Michelle looked like she fought tears across the table and Elizabeth felt terrible.

"No, Michelle. I really glad you are here. I wish Gregory hadn't followed you, but I know he would have come either way. He knew where I was from. It was just a matter of time, I'm afraid." She wasn't angry at Michelle, she was angry at Gregory. "As for dinner tomorrow night, yes, I'm having dinner with him at the hotel. I'm hoping a heartfelt discussion with him will set him straight." Elizabeth looked down at her dinner plate and tried to hide the apprehension she felt.

Somehow I don't think it will work, but I have to try.

"Well, you won't be going alone, young lady. One of your brothers will accompany you. I'm sure Ray would love to," her father said, glancing at Ray.

"Of course. I would love to show the gentleman the backside of the livery."

"No you won't, Ray." Their mother gave Ray a fierce look across the table.

"Yes, Mother. I'll behave myself as long as he does. I'm sure I could find a lovely young lady in town who would love to have dinner with me tomorrow night while I keep an eye on Liz."

"It's settled then. Ray will accompany you, Lizzie, and keep an eye on you," her father said, then changed the subject. "What's for dessert, Mother?"

Everyone laughed at his remark, and the mood suddenly lightened tremendously. The evening passed without any more talk of Gregory Webster, though he was very much on the mind of one young lady.

* * * *

The next morning dawned with bright blue skies and the hint of the warmth that would be prominent later in the day.

It would be a scorcher today. Elizabeth squinted against the sunlight while she waited for Michelle to awaken. She'd always been an early riser and today was no exception.

Since her return to the ranch, she had taken up most of her before-school behaviors, much to her mother's chagrin. Her clothing continued to be mostly boy's pants, although she needed some slightly bigger now that her hips had filled out. The smaller trousers didn't fit any more, but she could still fit in the shirts she'd saved. She still dressed like a lady for dinner and when she went to town so not to disappoint her mother.

Today, she had on her trousers, a button-up shirt, and work boots, ready to ride out with Ray to check fences. Michelle planned to spend the day with John, so Elizabeth thought she might as well get some work done.

"Ready, sis?" Ray said, coming through the front door with his hat in his hand and heading to the barn with her close on his heels.

Ray had gotten very handsome over the last few years. His shoulders had gotten broader and a mat of chest hair peeked through the collar of his shirt. His waist had stayed trim, and he had gotten rather tall. He now stood over six feet and five inches.

I sure wish he'd find a nice girl to settle down with. She loved him with all her heart and she wanted to see him happy.

"Ray?"

"Yes?"

"Have you found anyone special that you like to spend time with? I mean, you said you were going to ask someone to go to dinner with you tonight so you could keep an eye on me."

"If you mean is there someone special in my life, no, there isn't. I really am not into settling down yet, sis. Good grief! I'm only twenty-three! Are you trying to marry me off already?" A warm, impish grin flashed across his lips.

"No, not at all. I wondered. That's all. I'd rather not share you with anyone yet."

"What about you?"

Curiosity sparkled in his eyes but she couldn't look at his face for long, afraid he would be able to tell she lied. "No. Not really I guess."

"What about this guy you are having dinner with tonight? Are you sure you aren't just playing hard to get or something?"

"Gregory? He was very nice at first at school, but he got very possessive, and I really didn't like him in that sort of way. He just wouldn't take no for an answer. Now, I hope I can get him to understand that."

"Well, let's just hope he knows how to keep his hands to himself because I won't hesitate to make him wish he had, if you know what I mean."

"I love you, Ray," she said once they'd mounted their horses and headed out toward the north pasture, which bordered with the Rocking W. She loved having protective older brother's sometimes.

After riding for about an hour, checking the fence, they found a spot needing repair. They dismounted and Ray pulled supplies from his saddlebags and was preparing to mend the fence when he realized he would have to go back for fencing.

"I'm pretty sure there is wire in that line shack about a quarter mile back. I'll be right back. You stay right here and make sure none of those cows over there try to get through."

After he remounted, he kicked his horse and headed back in the direction they had come while Elizabeth stayed to guard the fence break.

She hadn't sat there more than about five minutes when someone crested the hill to her left and headed toward her. Her shoulders stiffened, thinking it could be rustlers. When she realized it was Jeff, she relaxed slightly.

The two of them hadn't run into each other since their encounter in town three weeks ago. Avoiding him had become second nature these days and right now, she sure wished she could ride away.

"Elizabeth?"

An appreciative glance from the top of her head to the tips of her boots, sent shivers down her arms to settle low in her belly.

"It sure didn't take you long to get back into those trousers again."

"What do you want, Jeff?" Eyeing him from under her hat, she shifted uncomfortably in the saddle.

"Still upset with me, I guess," he said, moving with his horse when the animal side stepped. "I wish you would tell me what's wrong. I thought we were friends?"

Before she could answer, Ray rode back up from the line shack with the fencing. "Hey, Jeff, I didn't know you were out this way today."

"Well, with all the trouble going on, I thought I'd better check things out and I just happened on Elizabeth. Need some help with that?" He dismounted and walked over to Ray.

"Listen, Ray, I'm going to head back to the house since Jeff is here to help you. I'm not feeling well anyway. I think the heat might be a bit much for me, just yet. It's been quite a while since I've been out in this kind of heat."

"Sure, sis. I got this. Make sure you feel well enough for your dinner date tonight," Ray said and she glared at him before she kicked her horse into a gallop and headed back toward the house.

* * * *

"Dinner date?" Jeff asked after she'd left.

"She has a date with that gentleman friend she knew from school I told you about since he's here in town now. He's meeting her at the hotel tonight for dinner. He came all the way from the East to see her. Kind of romantic, I think."

Ray made sure Jeff had all the details and then some. He wanted Jeff to think Elizabeth wanted to have this date with Gregory. Maybe Jeff would leave her alone that way and continue to pursue Aubrey. Not that he felt Jeff wasn't good enough for his sister, he knew the way Jeff treated women, and Ray thought that if he got too close to Elizabeth, she'd end up getting hurt.

"Here. Let me get that." Jeff bent down to help secure the barbed wire Ray was holding. The two men didn't talk about Elizabeth any more while they worked together to repair sections of fence that had been damaged. When the sun began to set, the two men parted ways, each with their own thoughts concerning Elizabeth and her dinner date.

CHAPTER 6

Elizabeth sat in her room in front of the mirror while Michelle tried to get her hair just right.

"Are you sure you want to do this?"

"I really don't have much choice. I need to make him understand I don't care for him in the way he wants me to."

"Well, I'm just glad Ray is going with you. I don't trust Gregory."

"I don't really either. I just hope I can get him to understand my feelings don't run that way."

"I have a feeling you care for someone else though."

"It doesn't matter," Elizabeth said, lowering her eyes. "He doesn't think of me in any way besides like a sister."

"Who is he?" Michelle asked, taking Elizabeth's hands between her own. "You can tell me, Elizabeth. We've always shared everything. If someone has your heart, tell me. Maybe I can help."

With a rush of air from between her lips in a heavy sigh, she said, "His name is Jeffery Walker. I've known him my entire life. He is best friends with Ray, and I've had a crush on him forever it seems like, but he's going to marry someone else. A girl in town named Aubrey is to become his wife although I don't know when."

"Are you sure?"

"Yes, she told me so herself a few weeks ago at the dress shop. I haven't seen her since, but she had told me they were to have dinner together that night and she was sure he was going to ask her. He even went to the jeweler that day. I saw him go there with own eyes." Tears sparkled on her lashes, but she brushed them away as quickly as they appeared. "Well, I must go. I don't want to keep Gregory waiting." She stood and hugged Michelle. "Thank you for helping me with my hair. You always could do such wonderful things with it."

"You are welcome. I wish there were something I could do. I only want to see you happy."

"I know. Thank you. I wish it didn't have to be this way, but I guess the Lord has other plans for me," she said, grabbing her and opening the door to find Ray waiting for her with the buggy. "Shall we go?" Her steps dragged as she approached the buggy. *I feel like I'm going to my own funeral.*

Ray came around and gave him her hand to help her into the buggy then walked back around to the other side to drive. Elizabeth waved when they pulled away from the house and headed to town.

"Are you all right, sis?"

Concern shone bright in his eyes when he caught her gaze with his. "Yes, I'll be fine. I just wish this night were over with. I really don't want to face Gregory again, but I see no other choice."

"Just don't let him do anything to harm you."

"He's not like that, Ray. I'm sure things will be fine. I just have to convince him that I don't care for him the way he obviously cares for me," she replied with more conviction than she felt.

They rode the rest of the way into town in silence.

As they pulled up to the hotel, Elizabeth said, "Who are you meeting for dinner tonight?"

"I asked Julia Adams. You know, Deputy Adams's daughter? I'm going to head over to their place and pick her up as soon as I drop you off."

Raising a questioning eyebrow is his direction, she grinned. "Ah, I see."

"No you don't. She's just a friend, nothing more."

"Friends can develop into other things too, Ray." Her thoughts drifted to Jeff and she sighed.

"I'll be right back. Wait out here until I return. I don't want you alone with Webster." Ray flicked the reins over the horses' rumps and pulled away.

Elizabeth stood outside of the restaurant for a few minutes until the bell over the door tinkled and Gregory stepped outside.

"There you are. I thought maybe you weren't coming." He took her hand in his and slipped it through his arm, ready to escort her into the restaurant.

"I, uh...I was just about to come inside," she murmured, trying not to appear nervous when he took her hand in his.

"Wonderful. I have been waiting for this all day."

* * * *

In the shadows of the building next door, Jeff stared at the pair as they went inside. His eyes narrowed at the sight of Elizabeth walking arm and arm into the hotel with the stranger.

The soft breeze brought the scent of her perfume to his nose. He couldn't hear their words, but it had appeared to him that she was looking longingly into the stranger's eyes when they spoke.

I'll move a little closer so I can keep an eye on the pair inside. I'm only doing it to keep her safe. I'm not jealous or anything.

Ray and Julia approached in the buggy, so Jeff stepped back so they wouldn't see him. He didn't need Ray knowing he was there watching Elizabeth.

When they walked into the restaurant, Jeff took his former position near the window so he could see what was going on.

Elizabeth and the blond man sat near the back of the restaurant and Jeff ground his teeth together when the guy took her man in his, stroking her palm with his fingers.

Get your damned hands off her. Don't let him touch you, Elizabeth. No man should touch you like that, but me.

"Where the hell did that thought come from?"

* * * *

At the table, Elizabeth sat quietly trying to decide how best to bring up the subject at hand.

"Liz, I'm so glad you agreed to have dinner with me tonight."

"You didn't leave me much choice, Gregory."

"Yes, well, I'm still glad you are here. I've missed you so." He took her hand in his and raised it to his lips.

"We really need talk." She pulled her hand from his but was interrupted by the waitress arriving with their meal.

"After we eat, my dear. I hate discussing things while I eat. It irritates my palate, you know."

While they ate, Elizabeth picked at her food, not really hungry because of the conversation she still needed to have with him, but he ate with gusto. She hadn't realized before how atrocious his manners were for someone who had grown up having all the finer things in life.

She wrinkled her nose when he pushed away from the table with a satisfied sigh after completely devouring his meal.

"That was delicious! I'm surprised at the quality of the food in such a backwards town such as this."

"Are you finished, Miss Johnston?"

"Yes, I'm finished, thank you," Elizabeth replied, pushing her plate away.

"Would you like some dessert, sir?"

"Yes, yes I would. What do you have this evening?"

"We have blueberry pie, apple pie, and chocolate cake with chocolate icing."

"I will have a piece of the apple pie, I believe. Anything for you, Liz?"

"No thank you. I'm fine." Elizabeth scowled. She really wanted to get this over with. "Gregory, can we talk now? I really need to say a few things while I have your attention."

"Well, all right then, talk away."

"I know when I left Pennsylvania after the dance, you were not happy with me. I realize you were upset because I had spurned your advances and your proposal of marriage." She folded her hands in her lap to still her shaking hands.

"Yes, I was a bit upset, you might say, but I've forgiven you and I want you to know the proposal of marriage is still open."

"And I appreciate that, really I do, but you must understand my feelings for you have not changed from before. I don't love you, Gregory, and I don't want to be married to someone that I do not love. Call me a romantic if you must, but those are my feelings. If it means I remain a spinster, then so be it."

"I just don't understand you, Liz. I would lay the world at your feet, and yet you spurn me at every turn."

The hurt expression on his face didn't fit his persona at all.

"I'm sorry. I never meant to hurt you, really. It's just I've cared about someone else for a long time."

"Ah...I see. Some local boy." He eyes narrowed to slits.

"You could say that, yes. Now, I really must go. I need to get home before it gets too late."

"Of course, my dear let me walk you out. Did you say your brother came into town with you?"

"Yes, he did. He's having dinner with a lady friend in the corner. I'll just stop by their table and let them know I'm ready to go." She steered Gregory in the direction of Ray and Julia after they got up from the table and Gregory paid the waitress for their meal.

"Ray, you remember Gregory." She reintroduced them when they got close. "Well, hello, Julia. It's nice to see you again. This is Gregory Webster from Virginia. He's just in town for a few days."

"Yes, of course. Webster." Ray stood and Elizabeth almost laughed because she knew her brother did it so Gregory would remember exactly how much taller he was.

"Nice to meet you," Julia said with a smile.

The tension between the two men was palpable in the air and Elizabeth fought the urge to step between them.

"Likewise, I'm sure." Gregory kissed her gloved hand with all of his eastern charm.

"Ray, Gregory and I have had our talk, so I'm ready to leave." She hoped her brother could read the plea in her eyes.

"We will be finished shortly, I'm sure, and then we'll be ready to go."

"That's quite all right. I'll just take Elizabeth outside for a bit of air before you start for home."

Gregory took her arm and headed for the door. Elizabeth looked pleadingly over her shoulder at her brother, but she knew he couldn't leave his dinner date without an explanation.

* * * *

Jeff still stood in the shadows of the building next door, but when he saw Elizabeth and her beau head for the front of the restaurant, he stepped back so she wouldn't see him. He had been watching her while she dined with the easterner, keeping a close eye on his every move. Jeff knew he was the slimy type just by the way he dressed with his slicked-back hair and small, thin mustache. He didn't like him. Nope, not one bit. The pair came out the door, and Jeff flattened himself against the building.

"Liz, walk with me a little, please? It's the least you can do."

Jeff saw her glance nervously to where her brother continued to eat. "All right, but just for a moment. Ray will be here shortly."

"Wonderful!" Gregory took her hand, pulled it into the crook of his arm.

Jeff slipped out of his hiding place, but kept himself a good distance behind them when they began to walk down the boardwalk.

"You know, Liz, this local boy of yours obviously doesn't care for you the way you care for him. Otherwise, he would never have let me have dinner with you, then walk with you out on the boardwalk. Are you sure there is someone else, or are you just telling me a story."

"I don't know what you mean, Gregory."

"I think you are just trying to play with my feelings, Elizabeth." His snarl was clear to their shadow as Gregory turned toward her and pushed her into a darkened corner of the church.

"No! Stop it!"

Jeff grabbed the man by his shoulder, pulled back his fist and hit Gregory, sending him flying at least ten feet away. "Keep your filthy hands off her." He hoped the man would get up. It would give him reason to hit him again, but the man only shifted slightly, staying where he was on the ground. "Elizabeth, are you all right?" He gathered her in his arms and held her to his chest.

"Yes." Her muffled voice met his ears as she buried her head in his chest and he kissed her hair. "Come on, I'll take you home." Not daring a look back at the man still sitting on the ground, he led her back toward the livery where his horse was stabled.

"But Ray..." she said when he led her away from Gregory and back toward the restaurant. "He's still inside."

Ray and Julia came out of the restaurant and Ray looked around with a puzzled look until he saw Elizabeth walking with him.

"What happened?"

"I'll tell you later," Jeff grumbled, passing the pair. "After I take Elizabeth home."

"Uh... sure, Jeff."

At the livery, Jeff cinched the saddle on his horse, put his foot in the stirrup, and swung onto the big gelding. He then held out his hand to Elizabeth and removed his foot from the stirrup to allow her to mount behind him. She hiked up her dress to her knees, stuck her foot in the stirrup, easily swung herself behind him, and held onto his waist when the horse began to move.

They rode along in silence for several minutes while Elizabeth held tight to his waist, He didn't like how her touch sent heat straight to his groin.

"Thank you for helping me," she murmured against his back.

"You know I wouldn't let anything happen to you, Elizabeth."

He squeezed her hand where it rested against his belly. She rested her cheek against his back as they rode the rest of the way to her parents' home.

When they reached the ranch house, her parents came rushing out.

"Oh my! Elizabeth, what happened?"

Elizabeth slid off the side of the horse and she could see her mother's gaze shift to her ripped dress and mussed hair.

"Jeffery Walker! What have you done?" Margaret exclaimed with a furious look at Jeff.

"It wasn't me," Jeff said innocently when he slid off his horse. "It was that easterner."

At the same time, Elizabeth said, "Mother, it wasn't Jeff. It was Gregory. Jeff helped me."

"Well, let's get you inside, young lady."

Her mother ushered Elizabeth through the door and shut it tightly behind them. Jeff could only stare after Elizabeth. "I sure hope you know I would never do anything to hurt her, Mr. Johnston."

"I know, Jeff, I know," he replied. "It just looked a bit suspicious when you rode up with her on the back of your horse and with her dress torn and all."

"Thanks for believing me." He looked at Elizabeth's father before resting his gaze on the door.

"Let me see if she is decent so she can thank you herself." Her father reached for the doorknob, went inside, and closed the door behind him leaving Jeff by himself.

Jeff stood on the porch with his hands in his pockets feeling like a schoolboy. "Hell!"

* * * *

A few minutes later, Elizabeth came outside and found him pacing the front porch like a new father.

She smiled when he didn't immediately turn around. With a quick clearing of her throat, she attempted to get his attention.

He swung around at the sound. "I'm sorry. I didn't hear the door open."

"It's quite all right. You looked like you were lost in thought. I just wanted to say thank you again for helping me. I don't want to think about where things would have gone if you hadn't been there." She shuddered at the thought.

"You really need to be more careful with the company you keep, Elizabeth. You could have really been hurt."

Anger flared when she heard his words but to her. They sounded condescending. "And just exactly what does that mean?"

"All I'm saying is you need to be more careful. He clearly wanted more from you than you were willing to give."

He obviously had no idea the anger rippling through her at his words. "So, are you saying I must have been teasing him to give him the impression I was willing to give up something I hold dear?"

"Teasing, hell no. I don't know what he thought, Elizabeth, but it sure seemed like he felt you were willing if he was."

"Well, I'm sure you would know all about that, Jeff, since your sweet, little, innocent Aubrey was so willing to give up her kisses to you four years ago. I'm sure you've probably gotten much closer than that since then."

"Aubrey? What does she have to do with this? Are you still mad at me because of what happened four years ago? It didn't mean anything, not then and not now."

"Well, I don't particularly care what happens between you and Aubrey since you mean nothing to me. Thank you for helping me tonight. Good night." Anger still vibrated through her when she whirled around, and walked back into the house with a slam of the door.

CHAPTER 7

Elizabeth flew through the front door and headed to her room with Michelle on her heels muttering under her breath, "Men!"

"Elizabeth?"

Fury zinged through her at Jeff's audacity while she paced from one end of her bedroom to the other.

"I just don't understand men at all, Michelle. First, he rescues me from Gregory. All the while, he must have been thinking that I was teasing Gregory so that he would think I wanted his advances. Then he saying that I should be careful with the company I keep at the same time! I know for a fact that he has been *very* friendly with a certain Aubrey Dillon in town! I mean if they are going to get married and all, why don't they just do it?"

Michelle sat on Elizabeth's bed with her eyes wide with wonderment.

Elizabeth realized her friend no clue what she ranted about, but she continued anyway, needing to release the pent up frustration she felt. "I mean it's not that I'm jealous of Aubrey, you understand. Really, he means nothing to me except that he's Ray's friend and all, but where does he have the right to dictate to me whom I should keep company with!"

With her eyes wide with understanding, Michelle said, "Um...who are we talking about exactly, Elizabeth?"

"Jeff, of course." Her anger began to cool and she finally flopped on the chair in front of the mirror and began brushing her hair. "Is it just me, or does he seem to think he can tell me what to do? After all, I'm not *his* sister or anything."

"I really don't know, Elizabeth. Is that the young man that brought you home?"

"I'm really being silly, aren't I?" Her anger deflated. "After all, I've known him since I was born. He's always been almost a part of this family and he was only helping me."

"You know I love you like my own sister, so I'm going to tell you frankly what I think is actually going on between you and that very nice-looking young man who brought you home." Michelle sent a sympathetic smile toward her like she knew without a doubt what was troubling Elizabeth. "You care for him more than you are willing to admit. In fact, I think you are in love with him."

Peering at her reflection in the mirror for a long time before she spoke, she answered, "I guess if I really want to admit it to myself, you're probably right in a sense. I certainly don't think of him as a brother, but I know he doesn't think of me like anything other than an annoying little sister so what does it matter anyway? Besides, his supposed to marry Aubrey."

"I never thought you'd be one to give up so easily. If you want something, you usually go after it."

"I know, but this is different. I'm not good with things pertaining to the heart. Look how badly things have turned out with Gregory. No, I just need to leave it alone even if I can admit I'm terribly jealous of Aubrey at this moment."

"We shall see. Besides, Gregory was not right for you. He's a pompous ass and he assumes because he's a Webster from Virginia, he can have whomever he wants and they will fall at his feet begging to be his wife."

She giggled at the thought. "Well, I don't know about you, but I'm ready for bed. It's been a long, trying day and I'm tired."

* * * *

The family sat in the dining room eating breakfast and discussing the work for the day.

"Matt? Why don't you and John head out to the south pasture and check the fences."

"Sure, Dad."

"Ray, maybe you should stay close to the house today. That way you can do some repairs on the barn and keep an eye on the women. I'm going into town today to talk to some of the other ranchers."

"Anything special need to be done?"

"No, just general cleanup, and maybe you can help your mother weed some of the garden today if you get done with the barn."

"Father, Michelle and I can help Mother with the weeding, too. It will be good to get out in the sun today."

Michelle entered the room and sat next to her at the table, but her eyes wandered to John across from them. "Of course. It's been a long time since I've had the pleasure of gardening."

"Ray could go with Matt, Father, and I'll stay here and do the repairs."

It was obvious to all those at the table, John wanted to stay close to the house as knowing smiles passed among the other siblings.

"No, I think Ray needs to stay here. One of the horses kicked him last night when he was putting them away after his ride into town so he needs to rest it a bit and not ride today."

"Of course." Disappointment was clear in his voice while the family rose to start their day.

Sometime later, a rider approached the ranch house from the direction of the Rocking W while Elizabeth and Michelle worked the soil in the morning sun.

Elizabeth had resorted to her trousers and boots. Comfort was the rule of the day. She didn't want to fight with skirts this morning, even if she tolerated them for the most part.

At the sound of a horse riding into the yard, they all looked up from what they were doing to see Jeff.

Michelle said, "Ah...I believe your young man from last night has returned."

Elizabeth glared at her friend in silence before she turned around to watch Jeff swing down from his horse with all the grace of a man who'd been on horseback his entire life.

After a quick glance in her direction, he headed for the barn, not far from where she and Michelle worked and she could clearly hear the conversation between the two men.

"Can I help?"

"Sure. I can always use another hand with a hammer."

Jeff grabbed the hammer on the ground, some nails, and a board to help Ray fix part of the corral fence needing repair.

As their eyes met across the yard, the sparks that flew between the pair were obvious and it had nothing to do with anger. The heat passing between them was like a tangible thing in the air.

Michelle stopped next to her and said, "My, my. If it wasn't already getting a bit warm out here, I would swear the temperature just rose twenty degrees."

With her eyes never leaving the disturbing man next to the barn, she answered, "I don't know what you mean."

"Lordy, Elizabeth! You two just about set that bale of hay on fire!"

Quickly changing the subject, she said, "I think I'll go inside and get some lemonade. Care to join me?"

With a knowing quirk to her lips, Michelle replied, "Certainly."

Several moments later, her mother said, "Here, girls. Why don't you take some lemonade to Jeff and Ray? I'm sure they could use some refreshment as well." Her mother handed them two more glasses before the headed for the door to return to their gardening.

"Of course, Mother. I'm sure they are getting warm out there in the sun too."

Elizabeth walked across the yard in the direction of the barn with the two glasses in hand. She passed one to Michelle to give to Ray, when Jeff raised his eyes to meet hers.

"For me?"

"We thought you both might need something to drink out here in the sun." She handed him the glass. Their hands brushed, and electricity shot up her arm at the contact. Pulling her hand back abruptly at the contact, she almost dropped the glass. He looked confused.

"Something wrong?"

"No. Nothing." She lowered her eyes and took a shaky breath. "Listen, I'm sorry about last night. I think I overreacted a bit, and I wanted to apologize. I know you didn't mean what you said the way I took it, and I'm sorry."

"You know I care about you, Elizabeth, and I don't want to see you hurt."

He set the empty glass on the ground, before he took her hand in his.

"I know," she whispered, resting her eyes on where he held her palm in his and caressed it with his fingers. The heat coiled up her arm from his touch and settled somewhere in her chest. She brought her eyes to his. He could twist her heart around his finger with nothing more than a soft touch and his eyes held a promise she didn't know whether she wanted to explore. She knew he cared about her, he had even said as much, but she understood it wasn't the same way she cared for him.

When one of the horses in the corral came up behind Jeff and nudged him in the shoulder, the spell was broken, and she stepped back, turned on her heel, and headed back to the garden without another word.

When it was time for lunch, Elizabeth let Michelle bring the sandwiches she had made and the nice, cold water out to Jeff while she took her bounty to Ray, who still continued to work. She really didn't want another scene like earlier.

"Sis, I really think you shouldn't get too close to Jeff." Ray took the sandwich from his sister's hand.

"I care about him Ray, you know that, but I don't plan on letting him break my heart. I know he's to marry Aubrey. She told me so herself."

* * * *

When Michelle approached Jeff with the lunch she had brought, she said, "Well, hello. I don't believe we have met officially. My name is Michelle Collins. I'm a friend of Elizabeth's."

Jeff looked up and introduced himself extending his hand, "I'm Jeffery Walker, but my friends call me Jeff. My parents own the Rocking W, which butts up against this ranch. We all kind of grew up together."

"Ah, yes. Elizabeth had mentioned you a few times over the years." That wasn't necessarily the truth. Elizabeth hadn't mentioned him by name, but Michelle knew this was the young man Elizabeth had lost her heart to.

"She did?"

His surprise was evident as Michelle looked at the handsome man near her. "Of course! She is very fond of you, you know."

"She is?"

"Why, yes, of course. She told me so herself." Michelle smiled knowingly. Elizabeth would kill her if she heard the conversation Michelle was having with this handsome man.

Jeff's heated gaze slid to where Elizabeth still stood with Ray, and their eyes met across the yard. The longing passing between them could be felt even when they stood over two hundred feet apart.

I wish these two would just admit their feelings for each other.

"Well, I had better get back to the weeding." Michelle touched his arm, drawing his eyes back to her. "It was very nice meeting you."

"Likewise."

Michelle smiled again. He couldn't keep his eyes off Elizabeth. *Um...a very good thing.* She wandered back to the garden with plans swirling in her mind.

* * * *

Evening fast approached, and everyone returned to the house, gathering on the front porch to await the call for dinner.

Michelle and John sat off to one side talking in low whispers with an occasional giggle erupting from Michelle and a hearty laugh coming from John.

Elizabeth sat on the other side of the porch watching the two talk, and she knew there wouldn't be much work in getting those two together. *They are doing most of the work themselves.*

Her eyes moved to the tall, handsome man who stood not ten feet from her chair.

A moment later, she stood and brushed past Jeff, heading for her mother's flower garden. It was always peaceful there, and she really needed to think right now. The feelings were running crazily in her heart were confusing, and she needed some time alone. When she reached the fountain in the garden, she ran her fingers through the water and stared at her reflection. A sob shook her. She looked up at the moonlit sky and tears streamed down her cheeks.

Love hurts, and I don't think I like it very much.

She brought her hand to her chest in an attempt to hold her breaking heart together.

He is to marry Aubrey, and there is nothing I can do to stop it.

Not realizing he'd followed until he slipped his arms around her, she fought his grip for a moment and then relaxed against him, allowing him to hold her. He turned her in his arms and their eyes locked until his slid down and focused on her lips. Unable to resist the pull of the man who held her heart, her lips parted on a sigh. He bent his head and took them in the softest kiss she could ever imagine. Heat spiraled from her core to encompass her entire body, infusing her with feelings she didn't quite understand.

I love this man. The kiss deepened, and she felt his hands in her hair pulling at the pins.

"Oh Lord, Elizabeth."

His fevered whisper reached her ears when he had pulled his mouth from hers. He framed her face with his hands and stared into her eyes. When his lips met hers again, his hands began to travel down her back, sending goose bumps across her flesh. A moment later, his mouth left hers and started playing along her neck, bring back some semblance of sanity.

"Wait. We can't do this. You need to stop." She pulled back and looked into his eyes again. "What about Aubrey?

The cloud of passion lifted from his eyes as confusion rippled across his face. "Aubrey? What does she have to do with you and me?"

"You are supposed to be marrying her," she said, trying to wriggle out of his arms.

"Marry her? Aubrey?"

He released her, and she stepped back. "Yes, she told me you asked her to marry you."

"Elizabeth, I never asked Aubrey to marry me," he said, pulling her back into his arms and trying to kiss her again.

"You didn't?" She allowed the contact, but tried to decide whether or not he was lying. *He's never lied to me before.*

"No, I didn't ask her. I don't love her." He nibbled at the corners of her mouth until she opened her lips again for his kiss.

"Elizabeth? Jeff?"

They jumped apart guiltily when she heard Ray's voice.

"It's Ray!" Horror zipped down her back when she realized how close things had gotten to being out of control between them there in the moonlit garden. "He can't find us like this."

"I'll stall him while you put your hair back in place," he told her before he moved away. "Over here, Ray. I came out behind Elizabeth because she seemed upset about something, but she's fine now."

"Upset? Where is she?"

Her shaky hands attempted to put her hair right before she greeted her brother. If he saw her hair mussed like it was, he would kill her or kill Jeff. She wasn't sure which, but she really didn't want to find out right now.

"She's over there, but she's all right now. She wants a minute alone."

Elizabeth heard their conversation clearly from where she stood but didn't move to join them until the call for dinner rang out across the yard.

"Come on, let's go in the house. I'm starving."

Jeff steered her brother in the direction of the house while she brought up the rear, putting the last tendrils of her hair back in place.

Michelle stood on the porch with a knowing smile. Elizabeth's temper flared for a moment, then was gone. She couldn't be angry with Michelle. *It's not her fault she's right about my feelings.*

"Everything all right?" Michelle asked, tucking a small curl back into place in Elizabeth's hair.

"Fine."

Moments later when they'd all taken their seats, heat crawled up her neck and splashed over her cheeks when her eyes met Jeff's over the dinner table.

How am I going to make it through dinner?

A sexy smile quirked at the corner of his mouth and she felt like kicking him in the chins at the same time her heart flipped over.

The conversation among the men flowed rapidly when the talked turned to the happenings of the day. Matt and John talked about the pasture they had worked all on afternoon and asked why it seemed that there were more repairs required on the fence than usual.

Her father asked Ray and Jeff how things went at the house while he was in town, and Ray replied, "Things were fine, Dad. No problems around here of any kind."

"That's right, sir, other than Elizabeth and her friend adding a few more freckles across their noses since they were out in the sun all day."

"Really? I guess I hadn't noticed," her father said innocently. "You ought to be wearing a hat, Elizabeth. Otherwise, you'll burn in this heat."

"It was sure was warm out there today," Jeff said.

One eyebrow cocked mockingly and she ground her teeth together.

Oh Lord! He needs to stop looking at me like that. Her face got warmer by the minute and she lowered her eyes. The scene earlier raced through her mind and she started to fan herself with her napkin. "Is it a little warm in here?"

"No, I don't believe so, sweetheart. Maybe you should get some air," her mother replied.

"Yes, I think I will. If you all will excuse me a moment." Elizabeth rose from the table and went out onto the porch, the heat of Jeff's gaze following her until she shut the door between them.

She stayed on the porch for only a few moments before returning to the dining room and, feigning she didn't feel well, and heading to her room.

* * * *

"I hope she's all right. She probably just got too much sun today," Margaret said, watching Elizabeth disappear down the hall.

"You're probably right."

Jeff excused himself shortly afterwards saying, "It's getting kind of late so I should head on home. Thank you for dinner ma'am."

"You are welcome anytime, Jeff, you know that."

He grabbed his hat and departed shortly afterwards.

"Ray? I need to speak with you a moment on the porch, please," John Sr. said, standing and walking toward the door.

"Yes, sir," Ray replied.

Stepping out onto the porch together, John asked Ray, "Did something happen today between Elizabeth and Jeff?"

"Not that I'm aware of," Ray replied but not meeting his eyes.

"There seems to be something going on between those two, and I'm not sure I like it. I like Jeff, but he's not the type to settle down with one girl yet. He's still sowing his wild oats, I'm afraid. I don't want my little girl to get hurt."

"I know he's been seeing Aubrey Dillon."

"I'll just have to have a little talk with his father, I believe, before something happens between them." John looked out over his ranch and his eyes narrowed. Elizabeth was his pride and joy even if she was a little headstrong. He would protect her with his life.

CHAPTER 8

A few days later, Gregory stood in the office of the president of the local bank. "Thank you for your help, Mr. Simpson. I'm sure my father will be pleased with the advice you've given me on the investments that would be profitable in the area. Cotton processing appears to be the most profitable acquisition with the development of the railroad and its connections to Houston."

"Very true, young man. When the Houston and Texas Central extended the railway to our town, it has opened a whole new area of development for us. Your family would be wise to invest. Can I look forward to you opening an account with us soon, Mr. Webster?

"I will be wiring my father for funds in the next few days, Mr. Simpson, so you may look for me then." Gregory extended his hand to the banker.

"Wonderful! I'll look forward to it." Mr. Simpson escorted Gregory to the door of the bank. "Enjoy the rest of your day."

"I'm sure I shall." Gregory exited the bank with thoughts of making a surprise visit out to Elizabeth's parents' ranch. He really needed to apologize to her about his behavior. He needed to get back into her good graces if he was to make any headway with her.

Tipping his hat to the ladies in town, Gregory sauntered back toward the hotel, when his eye caught a beautiful blonde exiting the dress shop.

"Good morning."

"Good morning," she replied, batting her eyelashes. "You must be new in town."

"Well yes, you could say that. I'm actually here on business, you could say," he said, noticing the low cut of her neckline and her voluptuous bosom almost escaping the top of the gown. "I'm Gregory Webster."

"My name is Aubrey. Aubrey Dillon." She extended her hand, and he took it, lifting it to his lips.

"Well, Ms. Dillon, it's very nice to meet you. Are all the women in this town as beautiful as you are?"

"I really wouldn't know, Mr. Webster."

"I was just heading over to the hotel for lunch, would you care to join me?"

"I believe I would at that Mr. Webster. Thank you." She slipped her hand into the crook of his arm and they began walking toward the hotel restaurant.

Later that afternoon, Gregory rolled out of the bed in his hotel room and glanced back at the blonde lying on top of it propped up on her elbow, completely comfortable with her nakedness.

"That was a very nice way of spending the afternoon." He walked to the armoire and pulled out clean clothing.

"Um...yes, it was," Aubrey replied, her eyes sliding over him.

"But now, my dear, I really must go. I have someone I need to see, so if you don't mind, get dressed."

"Really. Someone I know?" she asked, watching him slip the trousers over his hips.

"Maybe."

"Oh do tell! I so love gossip." She sat up and pulled the sheet around her.

"You might know her at that. Her parents own a ranch on the north side of town called the Double J, I believe."

"Her? You don't mean Elizabeth Johnston, do you?" she said with a sneer.

"Why yes, actually."

"You can't be serious!" She got off the bed and grabbed her chemise.

"I'm assuming you know her then."

"Of course I know her. That harlot! My Jeffery needs to stay away from her. She's not good enough." Her face crinkled in a scowl.

"I'm sorry?" he said with a questioning look.

"Oh never mind. It doesn't matter." She adjusted her petticoats and reached for her dress.

He came back across the bedroom in a flash and grabbed her hair. "What were you going to say?"

"You're hurting me!" she said, reaching for his hand as tears sprang to her eyes at the pressure he inflicted on her scalp.

"I'm sure I can make it hurt a lot worse. I want to know what is between Elizabeth and this Jeffery, and you will tell me now! If you don't..."

With fear in her eyes at his veiled threat, she told him everything she knew about Elizabeth and Jeffery's relationship.

* * * *

Elizabeth stood outside of her parents' bedroom later that evening. Her father had looked worried at the dinner table, and she hadn't had a chance to ask him about it. When she mentioned it to her brothers, they just brushed off her worries, saying, "I'm sure it's nothing, sis. The rustlers have us all worried."

But she wasn't so sure. Her father had never looked that worried before, and her mother seemed to be a bit distracted, too.

"I'll figure out something, Mother. Don't worry about it," she heard her father say through the door.

"But, John, we could lose the ranch. We've worked so hard to make sure the future of our children was secured, and now we might lose it," her mother answered.

"I'll go into town tomorrow and talk to Mr. Simpson to see if I can get an extension. He's a reasonable man. He knows how the rustlers have hit every ranch in the area and how hard it's been trying to recover from that. We may just have to sell more of the herd that's left before fall."

"We won't have enough to replenish the herd next year then. We should never have sent Elizabeth to that school."

"She had to go, Mother. It was the best thing for her, and we both know it even if she didn't want to go.

"Yes I know, but it was so expensive!"

"Well, there is nothing we can do about that now. We will just have to get by."

Elizabeth left her parents' door and headed to her room. She felt terrible! It was all her fault.

I'll just have to think of some way to help. I will not allow my parents to lose our home.

Gregory arrived unannounced at the door of the Double J the next day. Due to heat of the day, Elizabeth, Michelle, and her mother had stayed in while the men did some work on the south pasture and her father made his trip in town to speak with Mr. Simpson.

When Elizabeth opened the door, she said, "Gregory. To what do we owe the pleasure?"

"My dear, Liz, I haven't had a chance to apologize for my behavior after our dinner. I acted total deplorably, and I wanted to see if you would give me a chance to make it up to you." He stepped inside the cool house and looked around.

Elizabeth noticed the look when he glanced around the room, and she didn't like it. She loved her home, even if it probably didn't compare to his. *He probably has more money in his pockets right now than half this town had in the bank!*

"Will you allow me to make it up to you?" he asked with a pleading look.

"What do you have in mind, Gregory?" she said, while a thought began to form in her mind.

Maybe there's a way to save the ranch after all.

"Just dinner, sweets, and maybe a walk. I wouldn't want to assume anything else at this point in time. Just between old friends, you understand."

"I supposed that would be all right." She tried not to shudder at the thought of being alone with him.

"How about tomorrow evening then? Meet me at the restaurant about six again?"

"Yes, that would be fine," she replied, trying to usher him back to the door.

"I look forward to it." He took her hand and kissed her fingertips. "Until tomorrow."

She watched him leave from the safety of the doorway.

"What are you thinking? Why would you have dinner with him again after what he did?"

"He's really not all *that* bad, Michelle." Elizabeth watched him ride over the hill before shutting the door.

"Yes he is, Elizabeth! If Jeff hadn't stopped him, who knows what would have happened!"

"I can handle him, Michelle."

"Well, you had better take one of your brothers with you again. I don't trust him," Michelle said with a shudder.

The next evening, her father argued with her while she readied herself for her encounter with Gregory.

"You are not going alone, Elizabeth Caroline. I forbid it!" Her father almost shouted in his anger.

"Father, I'll be fine. Gregory knows better than to do anything so foolish again, especially in the public area such like the restaurant." She finished putting her bonnet on and checked her reflection in the mirror near the door. "Besides, I'm twenty years old now, Father. I can take care of myself. I need to start making my own decisions."

She breezed out the door and approached the buggy her brother had hitched for her, climbing aboard and grabbing the reins. With a quick flick of her wrist, the buggy lurched forward and she headed for town.

* * * *

From his table in the corner, Gregory watched the other patrons of the restaurant while he awaited Elizabeth to arrive. Tonight, he wanted her alone, but he needed to be patient. Patience would be the only way to win her in the end. He knew now if he pushed her, she would retreat again and he had no intention of allowing that to happen. Besides, he could slate his lust with the pretty blonde for now.

"Ah, there she is," he said to himself as she breezed into the restaurant like a breath of fresh air. *She really is stunning.*

"Gregory," she said when he stood to help her with her chair.

"You look lovely as always. What would you like to drink?"

"Just water for me, please," she replied when he returned to his chair and the waitress arrived at their table to take their order.

"I truly want to apologize for my behavior previously. I acted boorishly and completely uncharacteristic of the gentleman I was raised to be. Your beauty just makes my heart race, and I lost complete control of myself that night. Will you accept my apology?"

Chewing her lips for a moment with a frown on her pretty face, she finally replied, "All right, Gregory. I accept your apology. We were friends at school, and I truly believe you are a gentleman and were raised as such, so I forgive you."

"That's wonderful!" He took her hand in his and raised it to his lips.

Pulling her hand from his grasp when their meal arrived, she said, "I'm a little surprised you are still in town. I know you don't care for Texas at all."

"I'm here because of you, my dear," he said, shoveling food into his mouth.

"Really."

"Of course. Well, I do have some business here in town, too. My father is looking to diversify our holdings, so he sent me here because of the growth that Texas has been experiencing."

"Ah, business. Of course. That explains why you are still here then."

"I wish you would give me a chance to win your heart. You know I care for you, and I always have. I know you don't love me, at least not yet. I can make you happy, I know I can,"

"Well, we shall see. I can't promise anything, but I would be willing to see you again as long as you can act like a gentleman."

"Of course, of course. The complete gentleman."

Things might just work out after all. Thoughts began racing through his mind and plans started to form.

After they had dinner, they went out onto the boardwalk and walked in the moonlight. He forced himself to act like the perfect gentleman the whole evening even though it was killing him! He wanted so much to swing her up in his arms and carry her up to his hotel room, but Elizabeth would never allow it.

"It's getting a bit late. I should be returning home. Thank you for dinner."

"You are certainly welcome, my dear," he said as they approached where her buggy was tethered. "This may be a bit forward, Liz, but when can I see you again?"

"Let me think for a minute." He didn't quite like the look on her face. Her eyes told him she certainly didn't seem to want to spend time with him. "If you'd like to come out to my parents' place, maybe we can go ride together and have a picnic."

"That sounds wonderful. How about tomorrow?"

"No, tomorrow isn't a good day. I have a lot of chores to do around the house tomorrow. Give me a couple of days."

"All right. How about day after tomorrow?" he said, pushing her into agreeing to see him.

"That should be fine."

She started to climb in the buggy, but he grabbed her waist and swung her up into it. "I'll see you then." He looked into her surprised eyes and almost laughed at her expression.

"Yes, yes, I'll see you then." She sat down and grabbed the reins. A gave him a curious look and then turned the buggy to head out of town.

After Gregory returned to his room, there was a soft knock. A smile spread across his lips when he came up off the bed and approached the door. Opening it, the smile on his face grew wider when he raked his eyes over the beautiful blonde standing in front of him.

"I've been expecting you, Aubrey." He grabbed her around the waist, pulled her inside his room, and shut the door behind them.

CHAPTER 9

"John! It's good to see you," the man on the porch said when John rode into the Rocking W. "It's been a while since you've been over."

"Good to see you too, Ernest. I'm sorry I haven't been by in a few weeks, but things have been pretty hectic around the ranch."

"Well, what brings you by?"

"How about if we take a seat here?" John suggested indicating the rockers sitting on the wide porch of the house. "Ernest, I need to talk to you about something that's come up."

"Sure, John. What's bothering you?" Ernest took the seat next to John in the cool shade of the porch.

"It's Jeff."

"What's that boy done now?" Ernest glanced out into the yard with a frown marring his face.

"Well, I'm not sure he's done anything really. It just seems there has been an attraction between Elizabeth and Jeff developing over the last couple of months. An attraction beyond just neighborly, if you know what I mean."

"Ah, I see. He's been hot after your little girl, has he?"

"Well, there just seems to be something going on between them. Not that I don't like Jeff and don't admire him or, for that matter, wouldn't mind him and my Elizabeth together but not now. He's still young, and I'm afraid he's not ready to settle down yet."

"I can understand your apprehension. What should we do about it?"

"Maybe we should just encourage him to stay on your ranch more than he has been."

"He's been over at your place quite a bit, hasn't he? I thought he was over there just yesterday in fact."

"No. He wasn't at our place," John said remembering the entire family had been in town yesterday, until the early afternoon when Matt and Ray had ridden out to check the cattle in the pasture near the house.

"Really. I could have sworn he said he was headed over there, and he was gone all day. I wonder where he went off to, then."

"I really don't know," John said, remembering last night talking with the boys and Matt saying they had been missing another thirty head of cattle.

* * * *

The next afternoon, Gregory arrived at the Double J with a brand new horse and buggy in order to take Elizabeth out for their picnic.

Michelle met him on the porch, greeting him with a quick nod.

"Michelle. It's nice to see you again. How has your visit with Liz been?" He alighted from the buggy and approached the porch.

"Very nice, thank you. Elizabeth will be out in a minute. She's packing your picnic."

"Wonderful. It sure is pretty day for a picnic."

He eyed the cloudless sky.

"Yes, it is. I'll go check on her progress. I'll be right back."

A few minutes later, Elizabeth opened the door and with a full basket in her arms. "I'm ready. Shall we go?"

"Here. Let me take that." He took the heavy basket from her and placed it in the buggy.

"Thank you."

"You are very welcome, my dear. No need for you to be lifting something as heavy as that," Gregory said, taking her hand to help her into the buggy.

"I'm not a frail female, Gregory. It really wasn't that heavy," she replied with a scowl as she settled into the seat.

"Well, there's no need for you to be doing those sorts of things with me around. I'm here to take care of you, Liz."

With a quick smile, he walked around the back of the buggy and slid into the driver's seat.

They rode away from the house in silence until she directed him to a spot near the stream separating the Rocking W from the Double J. A large oak tree at the top of the knoll with a large patch of soft green grass became their picnic area.

Off in the distance, she could hear the waterfall that fed the pool at the base.

My swimming hole.

The sound of splashing water tinkled in her ears. Her gaze wandered off for a moment while she remembered her encounter with Jeff there a few short days after her arrival home. She also remembered how he had caught her with nothing on and a flush of red crept up her cheeks.

"Liz?" Gregory asked, bringing her thoughts back to the present.

"Sorry. I was just thinking."

"About what my dear?"

"I, um...it was nothing really. I can just hear the waterfall from here. That's all." She couldn't possibly tell him that she was thinking of another man!

"You'll have to show it to me sometime then." He bit into the chicken her mother had prepared for their meal. "This is wonderful!" He took another bite.

"I'm sure Mother would be pleased you think so."

Their conversation turned to the people they knew from school and his business ventures in Hempstead.

Moments later, Elizabeth noticed a rider coming over the hill headed to where she knew the pond was.

The rider spotted the pair under the tree and changed directions, heading straight for where she and Gregory sat.

Oh Lord. This is all I need.

Although he was dressed all in black today and rode his big black gelding, she'd know that form anywhere.

Jeff frowned when he pulled the gelding to a stop. "Elizabeth? What are you doing out here? Especially with him?" Jeff demanded, dismounting.

"Having a picnic. What does it look like?"

"Excuse me? Do we know each other, sir?" Gregory asked a bit confused. "You obviously know, Liz."

"Elizabeth..." he corrected with a scowl. "Yes, in fact we know each other quite well, don't we Elizabeth?"

Her faced flushed at his innuendo. "Jeff, please don't start trouble."

"In fact, my fist knows your face rather well too, sir." Jeff said, facing Gregory.

"You!" Gregory said with a shocked expression when he realized who Jeff was. "You're the one who hit me in town!"

"Yes, I am. And I will do so again if you even think of doing anything improper with Elizabeth."

"Jeff!" Elizabeth exclaimed, springing to her feet. "That's quite enough! Gregory has been the perfect gentleman, and I expect he will continue to do so without any help from you."

"Well, just see that he continues to do so. Otherwise, I'll be making a late-night visit to his hotel room," Jeff growled over his shoulder, and headed back to his horse.

"You are not my brother, Jeffery Walker, and you cannot tell me who I may see and who I may not! What goes on between Gregory and me is none of your business!" she shouted at him, stomping in his direction.

"I'm making it my business, Elizabeth." He swung up on his horse and rode away with a scowling glance at Gregory.

"Exactly who was that again?"

"He's been a friend of the family since I was born. I guess he just think he's protecting me, but he just infuriates me!"

"There is a little more to it than that I'm afraid, Liz. He's almost...possessive."

"It doesn't matter anyway. I'm here with you and enjoying your company immensely, so let's not talk about him anymore, shall we?" Elizabeth gave him a brilliant smile, almost as if she was flirting with him.

After they had finished their lunch, the pair headed back toward the ranch house as she twittered nervously. She really didn't know what had gotten into her after she had seen Jeff. The fury she felt toward him for insinuating Gregory would be the least bit inappropriate with her, made her mad.

Even if he did before. She shook her head. *I don't need to think about it. I'll make sure he knows that kind of behavior won't be tolerated.*

"Thank you for the picnic. I enjoyed your company very much," she said when they arrived at the house.

"Thank you for accompanying me. It was a delightful afternoon." When he came around the side of the buggy to help her out, he asked, "Can I see you again?"

"We'll see. We need to take things slowly."

"Would it be all right if I kissed you good-bye?"

With a shifting glance to the door of the house, she replied, "I supposed that would be all right."

One arm snaked around her waist and he pulled her against his chest. Before he could fasten his lips on hers, she turned her cheek so his lips only grazed her face.

"Not good enough." He grabbed her chin in his hand and turned her head so that his lips locked on hers.

His wet, almost slimy kiss on her mouth disgusted her and she fought the urge to vomit until he lifted his head.

"I will see you again soon, my love." A wide grin lifted his mouth when he tipped his hat and sauntered over to the buggy.

She waited until he was out of sight, before she wiped the back of her hand across her mouth. "Oh yuck! That was absolutely disgusting."

Nothing like Jeff's kiss.

"Oh Lord. Where did that come from?" she murmured. "I can't let thoughts of him cloud my judgment right now. I need to stay focused on the problems at hand."

* * * *

That night at dinner, her father seemed deeply troubled when the talk of rustlers again dominated the conversation at the table.

"Father, what's wrong?" Elizabeth asked.

"It's nothing dear." He shifted his gaze to her mother.

"Father, didn't you say we lost more cattle from the east pasture today? I'm pretty sure I saw some men who didn't belong over there, this morning," Matt said.

"East pasture?" Elizabeth responded. "That is where Gregory and I had lunch this afternoon. Are you sure?"

"I saw them myself," Matt replied.

Everyone chimed in, "You did?"

"Yes. I saw the leader at least or I think it was the leader. He held back and took a shot at me, but I got a look at him."

"You weren't hit, were you?" their mother asked with a concerned look at her son, scanning as much of his body as she could see for any tell tale mark.

"No, Mother. I'm fine. Missed me by a mile," Matt said, reassuring her.

"Well, what did he look like?" Elizabeth asked with a curious expression.

"I couldn't see his face since he had a bandana over his mouth and nose, but he was dressed all in black and was riding a black gelding. He was probably six foot or more and had a broad chest. He was a good distance from me, but Lord, he was sure cocky! He even raised a hand in greeting before he disappeared." Matt clenched his fist at his side. "I should have gone after him!" He pounded his fist on the table in anger.

"Absolutely not, young man!" their mother exclaimed. "If you had done that, you could have been killed."

"But, Mother, they got away with more of our cows, cows we can't afford to lose."

"Cows can be replaced. You can't." A tear slipped down her cheek when she raised her hand to his cheek.

"That's right, son. It's not worth your life over a few cattle."

As Elizabeth remembered her encounter with Jeff this afternoon while she had been picnicking with Gregory, her brow furrowed in concern. Hadn't he been wearing black? But no, he had been alone, or at least until he had ridden over the hilltop, he had been alone.

She shook her head in denial, and her thoughts turned back to the matter at hand. When everyone had finished their meal, they adjourned to the porch to get a breath of air before retiring.

Elizabeth stepped off the porch and headed to her mother's flower garden after dinner. It was a bit of a sanctuary to her. She loved the flowers her mother grew and the lovely water fountain they had placed in the center. When she approached the fountain, her mind wandered back to her encounter with Jeff in this very spot not two weeks before. Her face grew warm when she remembered the feel of his lips on hers and how his hands had felt on her skin.

If Ray hadn't called for them, who knows what might have happened. She hadn't been with a man before after all, but she still had the yearnings of a woman in her heart for the love of a man.

I wonder what it would have been like to feel his hands on my bare skin, every inch of it. Her face flushed with color and her skin tingled at the thought while her mind raced on. What about his kisses on her skin?

"Enough of this." She dipped her hand in the fountain and splashed water on her face to try to cool the overheated skin before returning to her family.

When she came back to the porch, she overheard her father say, "We've got to do something quickly. The loss of the cattle is going to be the death of this ranch if we don't stop these infernal rustlers."

"We'll stop them, Father, if it means patrolling the fences around the clock, we'll stop them," John Jr. replied.

"Elizabeth. I didn't see you come back, sweetheart."

"Father, I need to know how bad things are. Please? I can't help if I don't know."

"It's man's business, sweetheart. You don't need to worry your pretty head over it," he said, brushing off her concerns.

With a stomp of her foot, she whirled around, retreated into the house, and slammed the door behind her.

When the house had turned dark and everyone had retired to their rooms, Elizabeth slipped out of her bed, tiptoed to the door, and quietly opened it so as not to disturb the other girl sleeping. Her eyes adjusted to the darkness of the front room quickly, and she headed in the direction of her father's study.

I need to find how bad things really are.

Approaching the study, she stopped for a moment when she thought she heard a bedroom door open down the hall. She froze, waiting for the noise to come again. None came. Slipping inside the office, she shut the door silently behind her.

A small candle on the desk flared to life when she stuck a match to the wick, generating enough light to see but not enough to give her away should someone walk by. Dozens of papers lay scattered across her father's desk. The journal he kept tally of the cattle in, sat open on the corner. Quickly scanning the pages, she noted the decreasing size of the herd over the last three months. Knowing without numbers next to them, indicated they weren't sold meant they had been stolen. "It's worse than I thought," she whispered to herself.

The financial journal was next. She flipped to the page showing the most recent month's finances and realized the numbers were in the negative. "Oh my!" she whispered and then noticed stuffed in the pages farther back in the journal was a tax notice for this year's tax on the ranch.

If we are already in the negative, how are we going to pay the taxes? If the rustlers aren't stopped soon, we won't have the cattle to sell later this summer to pay the taxes.

The ramifications of their situation made her heart sink.

She quickly closed the books, returning everything to its rightful place and blew out the candle before returning to her room. After she slipped back into bed next to the sleeping Michelle, a thousand thoughts ran through her mind. What will they do if they can't pay the taxes?

I can't allow my parents to lose their home. Silent tears rolled from her eyes. *I have to do something.*

The next day, she rode over to the Rocking W in search of Jeff. She needed to talk to him about what was happening with the rustlers and her parents' ranch. Surely he would be able to help her.

Riding into the yard, she spotted Jeff working in the corral with a mustang, and oh Lord, he'd stripped off his shirt in the heat of the day. She gasped silently at the sight he presented. His bare chest was tan from many hours in the sun and just the right amount of chest hair spattered across the expanse of muscles, leaving a small trail of hair running down his flat belly to the waistband of his trousers. With her eyes glued to the man in front of her, she quickly dismounted and tied her horse to the railing.

Tearing her eyes away from the picture in the corral, she saw the horse he was working with for the first time. She had heard he had brought in one a few weeks ago.

She's beautiful.

The tan coat, flaxen mane and tail of the mare in the corral, had Elizabeth gasping in appreciation. She was a very large mare from what Elizabeth could see. Withers peeked above Jeff's shoulder, indicating the mare stood several hands high.

He hadn't noticed her presence, while he stroked the nose of the mare and whispered to her in soft tones. The horse stood stock-still listening to the rumble of Jeff's words and quivering under his hand when he moved to stroke her neck.

When Elizabeth got close enough to hear the soft words he spoke, his voice fluttered across her skin making the hair stand up on her arms. It almost felt like he whispered to her and stroked her.

"That's it beautiful lady." His large hand moved gently over the mare, working his way around to the other side of the horse. He lifted his eyes when he noticed her standing not far away. The heat of his look while he continued to whisper softly to the horse or was it to her, made her quiver. "Easy, girl. I'm not going to hurt you."

Their eyes held for a long time while he continued to stroke the horse, calming her under his experienced hand and Elizabeth became more heated by the minute.

After a few minutes, he said, "To what do I owe the pleasure?"

"I, uh..." She wiped the sweat forming on her lip under the heat of his eyes. "I need to talk to you. I'm hoping you can help me with something." She stepped a little closer.

"Of course, Elizabeth. Would you like to go up on the porch where it's a bit cooler?" he asked, tying the mare to the fence and grabbing his shirt.

"Uh...yes, please. It is a bit warm out here."

"You could say that," he said with a sexy quirk of his lips.

Damn man! He knows exactly what he's doing to me.

They stepped on the porch and retreated to the rockers placed there in the shade.

"What can I do for you, sweetheart?"

The endearment caught her by surprise. She swung her gaze around to meet his and said, "Well, um...I've realized that my father is having trouble with the ranch and its finances. Is your father having the same types of difficulties? I mean with the rustlers and all."

"I'm not exactly sure. Father doesn't confide a lot of the finances with me, which is unfortunate should anything happen to him."

"Is he sick?" she asked, concern lacing her words.

"No, not that I know of, but accidents happen, you know especially working with horses and cattle," he said, eyeing the mare in the corral.

"Yes, I suppose so." Thoughts of the normal dangers of ranch life flittered across her mind. "I have a question for you."

"Shoot."

"What were you doing riding near the pond the other day?"

"Doing what I always do when I'm out riding the range. Why?"

"I was just curious. Father said we have been losing quite a few cattle especially out of that pasture lately. I thought maybe you had seen something when you were out there," she replied, trying to read his eyes. He had been out there about the same time the cattle had disappeared, and he *had been* wearing all black that day.

"No, I didn't see anything except you with that damned easterner," he said with anger in his tone.

"Well, that's none of your business."

"I told you then, and I'll tell you again now. I'm making it my business."

"Too bad." She jumped to her feet and headed back toward where her horse was tied. "I'll say it again. You are not my brother, nor are you my husband, so I'll thank you to keep your opinion to yourself."

"No, I'm not your brother, nor your husband, Elizabeth," he growled, after he'd gotten up and walked quickly to her.

He grabbed her around the waist and hauled her up against his chest. His lips swooped down to lock with hers in a kiss. The feel of his mouth was nothing like the last kiss they'd shared. She pushed against his chest for a moment until she gave in to the heat raging through her at the touch of his lips on hers. The passion between them almost raged out of control until they both heard his father clearing his throat behind them.

Jeff lifted his head at the sound behind him but didn't release her immediately. "You'll do well to remember what's really between us," he whispered when he let her go, and she almost stumbled.

Whirling on his heel, he headed back to the corral and the waiting mare while she attempted to mount her horse on shaky legs and her lips tingling like they had been seared.

"Damn him!" she said out loud while she rode back to her parents' ranch fuming at the audacity of how he had treated her. "How dare he!"

By the time she got back, she was furious! She rode into the ranch at a full gallop and came to a sliding halt at the barn, much to the surprise of Ray, who was working around the ranch that morning.

"What's wrong with you?" he asked when she flung herself off the horse almost at his feet.

"Nothing," she snapped, pacing across the yard. "Absolutely nothing!"

"Where did you go this morning? You took off before any of us were even up."

"I went to the Rocking W."

"Ah...that explains it."

"And just what is that supposed to mean?" she demanded.

"Nothing, sis," he said with a smirk.

"Men!" She flung her arms in the air, swung around, and headed for the house.

* * * *

Back at the Rocking W, Ernest approached Jeff as he went back to working with the mare in the corral.

"Jeff."

"Hey, Dad."

"Um...you want to tell me what's going on?"

"Not sure I know what you mean." Shrugging, he continued stroking the mare.

"John came by the other day. He's concerned about what's going on between you and Elizabeth. He wants me to keep you a little closer to the house for a while."

"Let me get this straight. He wants me to stay away from Elizabeth," Jeff said, his anger flaring with every word.

"That's pretty much it, son. 'Course that might be a little hard to do if she's coming around here."

"I hate to say this, Dad, but Elizabeth and I are both adults. We can make our own decisions concerning whatever is between us. At this point, I don't even know what that is, so if you expect me to explain it to you, you're out of luck." His fingers cut a path through his hair. "Hell! One minute she's having a picnic with that easterner and the next, she's over here and I can't keep my hands off her."

"Well, son. Let me give you a piece of advice. Don't be beddin' her and then droppin' her like a hot rock for the next pretty filly that comes along. She ain't that kind of a woman and you'll do well to remember that

"I know, Dad, I know." A frustrated sigh spilled from between his lips. "I just wish I knew what I was going to do with her."

"I'm sure you'll figure it out soon enough, son. Just be careful, or you'll lose your heart to that little filly."

"That's what I'm afraid of." Jeff muttered to himself before he turned back to the mare standing beside him.

CHAPTER 10

Gregory languidly stretched when he awoke and pulled the sheet down to his waist, exposing the scant hair on his chest. He rolled over next to the woman in bed with him, skimming his hand down her curving waist.

"You can't stay here anymore. It's too dangerous. You might be seen, and that just wouldn't do."

"Are you throwing me out again?" she said, rolling over and grabbing for her chemise on the floor.

"Aubrey, you know I love having you here, sweetheart, but I just can't let you be seen with me. Word might get back to Elizabeth and your precious Jeffery. What would he say if he knew you weren't a virgin on your wedding day, or before he actually beds you?"

"You're a bastard, Greg, you know that."

"Actually no, darling, I'm not," he said with a satisfied quirk of his lips when her shapely backside was exposed for his view. He bent over to pick up his own clothing from the floor.

"Well, you certainly act like it." The dress in her hand slipped over her head with a whoosh. "We need to come up with a plan to make things go as we wish them to, you with Elizabeth and me with Jeffery."

"I'm working on Elizabeth now, my dear. No problems with that end of things. She's coming around, trust me."

"Well, then you need to help me with Jeffery. We had been seeing each other for a long time until little Miss Elizabeth came back to town. Now I hardly see him at all."

"Maybe if you had given him which you so readily gave me, sweetheart, he might have come around a little quicker."

Aubrey came up off the bed in a flash and, with a hardy swing, slapped him clean across the face.

She pulled her arm back to hit him again, and he grabbed her wrist in a deathly grasp and said with a voice laced with steel, "I'll give you that one, my dear, but make no mistake, you'll never do that again or you will live to regret it. Next time, I'll kill you."

He flung her onto the bed, grabbed his hat, and headed out of the room.

When he walked out of the hotel on to the boardwalk, he noticed Elizabeth coming into town with her brother. The wagon stopped near the hotel entrance.

"Elizabeth. It's so nice to see you. I didn't realize you were coming into town this morning."

"Gregory, you look quite refreshed this morning. Sleep well?"

"Yes I did, in fact. Would you care to join me for breakfast?" He took her hand to help her down from the wagon.

"Actually, no. I can't. I've already eaten, and I have some business to take care of for my father at the bank."

"Something I can help with? I'm quite good with business matters, you know."

He continued to hold her hand after she had alighted from the wagon.

"Yes, I'm quite aware of your prowess in the business realm. I know you have many dealings, but I think I can handle this myself. Thank you though." She removed her hand from his.

"Are you going to be in town for a while? Maybe I can convince you to have lunch with me?"

"Maybe. I'm not sure how long this will take, and I know we need to pick up some things for Mother at the general store. Where can I find you later?"

"I should be around somewhere. If you check with the hotel around noon, I should be there. I have a few things I need to take care of this morning."

"All right then. If I'm still in town at noon, I'll find you at the hotel."

"Wonderful. I hope to see you then." He watched her walk off toward the bank.

I need to find out what she's doing for her father. I might be able to use it to my advantage.

Gregory slipped around the back of the bank to the window that he knew belonged to the banker in order to hear what was being said. His investments in the area were panning out rather well, but he could always use some inside information in order to continue with his endeavors.

* * * *

Jeff decided to make an unscheduled trip into town. He needed to go by the bank to see how things with his own finances were shaping up. He had plans after all, and they didn't include working for his father for the rest of his life. He wanted his own money, and if his plans worked out like he hoped they would, he would have plenty to finance his own dream. When he strode into the bank, he saw Elizabeth talking with Mr. Simpson.

"Thank you, Elizabeth, for bringing this to my attention. I'm sure I can work something out for your father without too much difficulty. Just tell him to come in and see me so we can make the arrangements."

"Thank you for your help, Mr. Simpson. You have no idea how much this means to me." She leaned over and the older man on the cheek.

"Yes, well," he mumbled as he turned a deep shade of red and retreated to his office.

"Elizabeth," Jeff said, tipping his hat to her before he proceeded to Mr. Simpson's office. He needed to talk to the banker. He had a plan, and he would need some help with it.

* * * *

"Jeff," she muttered in return and was surprised when he turned his back to her and stopped at Mr. Simpson's door.

He's ignoring me. How dare he! After the way he treated me earlier? Well, two can play that game. She turned on her heel and left the bank.

Retreating down the boardwalk toward the general store, she mumbled to herself, "He kissed the tar out of me, and now he ignores me. I just don't understand him at all."

"Sis, are you okay?" Matt asked when she reached the wagon.

"Yes, I'm fine. How are things coming with the supplies?"

"We still have several things to load and we have to wait for the eleven-o'clock train with the additional supplies on it before we can leave. It should be here shortly, but it will take time to unload it before we can load our things and head for home. Why?"

"I am going to meet Gregory for lunch at the hotel. Can you come find me there when we are ready to go?"

"Sure, sis. Are you sure you really want to continue to see that guy? I don't trust him."

"I'll be fine, Matt. I can handle Gregory. You know where to find me."

When she got to the hotel, she stopped at the hotel front desk and asked if Mr. Webster had been seen.

"Yes, ma'am. He said he would be in the dining room if someone was looking for him."

"Ah, I see him. Thank you," she said and started in his direction.

"Liz! I'm glad you could make it." He stood when she reached the table and pulled out the chair.

"Thank you. It was going to be a little bit before the wagon would be loaded to head for home, and since you had so graciously invited me to lunch, here I am."

* * * *

"Jeff! I haven't seen you in such long time," she whined with a little bit of a pout and Jeff had to grit his teeth.

"Aubrey. Nice to see you," he said politely, his eyes making a path down her body. "What are you doing today?"

"I was going by the dress shop to see if the new fabrics had come in that were ordered last week. Care to walk with me?" She wrapped her hand through his arm, though it wasn't extended to her.

"Uh...sure. I'm headed that way anyway."

"You haven't been in town for awhile. I've missed you." She batted her eyes at him while they walked.

"I've been really busy out at the ranch lately."

"We haven't even had dinner together for a while. I know! How about we have lunch? I haven't eaten yet, and since you are already here, that would be a wonderful idea!" She said it with so much enthusiasm, he couldn't quite refuse.

As they entered the restaurant, they stopped at the door. His eyes met Elizabeth's with a questioning rise of the eyebrow on both their parts.

She's here with that easterner again.

"Aubrey, my love. Let's get a table over there," he said loud enough for Elizabeth to hear as he pointed to a table close by and escorted Aubrey in front of him.

"My dear?"

"I'm sorry. Did you say something?"

"What would you like to eat, sweetheart?" Gregory queried.

"Oh...um...let's see. How about the roast? That sounds wonderful."

"Perfect. I'll have the same," he told the waiter. "Now, is there something I can help you with concerning your father's ranch and the business you had at the bank this morning?"

"No. Everything is fine, really. It's just with the rustlers that have been plaguing the area, we have lost several head, and it's making things a bit tight financially. That's all. Father has worked things out with the bank, so it's all taken care of now." Her eyes kept wandering to where he sat with Aubrey nearby.

"I'm sorry to hear your family has taken it so hard. I wish there were something I could do to stop the rustlers myself. I would do it for you if nothing else, Elizabeth, to help your family."

"It will all work out, I'm sure," she said as their meal arrived. "This looks wonderful."

"They do have very good food here." He picked up his knife and fork and dug into his food with gusto.

Jeff watched the other man dig into his food while Elizabeth wrinkled her nose.

"Maybe I'll make a trip out to your parents' place again so I might be able to talk to your father. I'm sure if nothing else, I could offer him a small loan to help him out until things get straightened out."

"Sure, that would be nice."

He took Aubrey's hand in his and almost laughed when Elizabeth's eyes narrowed. Every glance in his direction played on his mind.

Maybe the easiest way to get her out of my system is to see some-one else, like Aubrey. Her interest had always been clear. Maybe I'll start spending more time with her and get over this infatuation with Elizabeth.

"Aubrey." He took her hand in his. "I know we haven't been able to spend much time together lately. I think I'll have to remedy that. I've just been so busy lately with roundup and breaking some of the horses I've brought in that I've neglected you something terrible."

"I'm so glad you said that, Jeff. I've missed you terribly, and I would love to spend more time with you."

"I have some things to do today out at the ranch, but how about if I come into town tomorrow? We can go for a buggy ride and maybe have a picnic."

"I would love to."

"Good. I'll drive in about eleven o'clock, and we'll have our picnic."

This should be just what I need, a distraction from the chestnut haired beauty sitting at the other table.

"I can't wait! It will be so much fun." Aubrey giggled.

She continued to chatter away though Jeff's attention was drawn to Elizabeth while she and Gregory finished their meal and prepared to leave.

When they headed for the door, they had to pass the table where he and Aubrey sat.

"Jeff?"

Gregory's hand rested on the small of her back and Jeff ground his teeth together, resisting the urge to punch the man.

"Elizabeth?" he questioned with a raise of his eyebrow.

"I couldn't help but overhear Aubrey talking about your picnic tomorrow. I was under the impression you were coming over to the Double J to help Ray with rounding up some of the cattle out of the south pasture to bring them closer to the house? Was I mistaken?" She eyed Aubrey before her eyes traveled back to him.

"Actually, Elizabeth, you were correct. Would you be a dear and tell Ray I won't be able to help him until a little later in the afternoon tomorrow? I should be back from my picnic with

Aubrey by three o'clock or so, and we should still have enough daylight left to be able to do what needs to be done."

"Of course I'll tell him. I'm sure he wouldn't want to spoil your day with Aubrey tomorrow. If nothing else, I'm sure it can wait until the day after tomorrow." She turned to leave. "Have a good time."

"We will I'm sure, won't we, Aubrey?" he responded with a little too much enthusiasm.

* * * *

Gregory escorted her back toward the general store. Matt waved from the wagon, indicating that he was ready to leave.

"I believe we are ready to depart, Gregory. Thank you so much for lunch."

"You are most welcome, my dear. I would love do it again soon."

"Yes, yes, of course. That would be wonderful." She allowed him to help her into the front of the wagon. "Aren't you going to be going home soon though?

"I've decided to stay here a little longer. I'm still working on those investments my father is looking into here. I'll probably be here another month or so at least."

"Really? Well I'm sure we'll be seeing each other again soon then," she said when Matt jumped onto the other side of the wagon seat. "Good-bye."

"Good-bye, Liz. I'll probably out to your place in the next couple of days to see your father." He finished with a wave as the wagon began to roll away.

"What's he talking about?" her brother asked, steering the wagon out of town.

"He wanted to come out and talk to Father about helping with some of the financial difficulties we are having, that's all."

"How did you…"

"I looked at Father's papers one night, so I know we are in a bad way with finances. I don't know the extent of it, but I want to help. If that means being nice to Gregory so he can help us, then so be it."

"You are not selling yourself to that easterner. I won't allow it and I'm sure Dad and your other two brothers won't allow it either. Hell! Jeff would have something to say about it too, I'm sure."

"Jeff? He has no say in what I do, and technically, neither do the rest of you. Let me tell you something about Jeff. He only cares for what he wants and nothing else. I wouldn't be surprised if he's involved with the rustlers. After all, he was out in that pasture awhile back when the cattle went missing. I saw him myself, and he was wearing all black that day too. When I went over to the Rocking W to talk to him yesterday about how his dad's place is faring with the rustlers, he was very defensive about my asking. I even asked him what he was doing out in the pasture that day."

"He was? You did? You never mentioned this before. I just can't believe he would be involved though. He's been like a brother to all of us and like a son to our parents. He wouldn't do something like that," Matt said with disbelief.

"I thought the same thing, but now, I'm not so sure. He doesn't care about me, so I'm not going to care about him. He avoided my questions about what he was doing out there."

With a very passionate kiss. Heat from her thoughts crept up her neck.

"I'm not so sure of that." He kept his eyes forward watching for trouble along the trail.

"What's that supposed to mean?" she asked, looking at Matt.

"I think he cares more about you than he's even willing to admit to himself, Liz. I've never seen him look at a woman like he's looked at you lately."

"It doesn't matter anyway. He made his intentions clear today in the restaurant."

"What do you mean?" He

"He was there with Aubrey when I was having lunch with Gregory. He made his intentions of seeing Aubrey quite obvious."

"I'm sorry, sis."

The rest of the ride home was made in silence

I won't let him hurt me anymore. I don't care if he's seeing Aubrey again. What he does isn't any of my business so why does the thought of him kissing Aubrey like he kissed me bother me so much and tear at my heart.

* * * *

After his lunch with Aubrey, Jeff retrieved his horse and headed home. The thought of having a picnic with Aubrey tomorrow bothered him. He really didn't even like her anymore.

She had gotten to the point where she seemed cheap to him these days, but he needed a diversion and she was available. She'd always been available to him it seemed, ever since they were teenagers. When Elizabeth had caught them behind the barn four years ago, it was just a matter of convenience for him, but the anger Elizabeth had displayed, surprised him. She had been furious, and he smiled at the memory. Her beauty had stunned him, even then. Elizabeth had been so pleased with herself after pushing him into the horse trough. Aubrey had been so upset that she had taken off to find her mother right afterward, and Elizabeth's brothers had thought it was hilarious! They had teased him about it for quite some time, even after Elizabeth had been shipped off to school. He hadn't realized how much he'd missed her until he found her at the pond the day after her return. Of course, he hadn't realized it was *her* at first, but when he had figured it out, he hadn't been able to get her out of his mind since. She was under his skin, and he needed to get her out of his system and quick, before he did something stupid like fall in love with her.

With a frown, he kicked his horse into a gallop trying to erase the vision in his mind of a totally naked Elizabeth emerging from the pond.

Damn! This has got to stop. He pulled off his hat and raked his fingers through his curls as if to dislodge the image.

I can't let her get in the way of my plans. Aubrey is a safe diversion. I just need to focus on that right now.

He rode into the front of his dad's ranch. Everything was set, and if he didn't keep his wits about him, he would totally mess things up. That wasn't an option for him. He needed the money this deal would bring in to be able to get out of his dad's place and make his own way.

* * * *

The next day, Gregory arrived at the Double J to speak with Elizabeth's father. He knocked on the front door and half expected Elizabeth to answer, but Carmen met him there instead.

"*Señor.* Can I help you?" Carmen asked eyeing the squinty-eyed gentleman at the door.

"Ah, yes. Carmen, isn't it?"

"*Si.*"

"Is Mr. Johnston at home please? My name is Gregory Webster."

"*Si.* I will get him." Carmen motioned him into the front room.

"Carmen?" John asked, eyeing the man.

"I was just coming to get you, *Señor* Johnston. Mr. Webster is here to see you."

"Ah yes. Thank you." John stopped next to the settee. "Gregory, isn't it? Nice to see you again. What can I do for you?" John inquired, holding out his hand.

"Mr. Johnston." Gregory took John's hand in a firm handshake. "I had the pleasure of seeing Elizabeth in town the other day, and she mentioned she had been conducting some business for you at the bank."

Giving the man a dubious look John said, "I'm not sure I know what you are talking about, Mr. Webster."

"Well, you see, Mr. Johnston, my family has some very diverse holdings, and we are looking at business opportunities in the area. Elizabeth mentioned the rustlers have been causing some hardship to your family, so I thought I would stop by today. I thought we might be able to discuss some business and come to some sort of agreement that would benefit us both."

"Why don't we go into my office, Mr. Webster? I don't discuss business in the living room." Once they'd retired to his office, John asked, "Now, what do you have in mind sir?"

"You know I'm very interested in your daughter, Mr. Johnston. I've made no secret of that."

"Yes. I'm well aware of your interest, but if you think she's for sale, you are sadly mistaken, sir. I would not give you my daughter in exchange for saving this ranch," John said, with anger flaring in his eyes.

"Of course she's not, sir. I wouldn't degrade her in that manner. She's a lady after all, and I wouldn't think of treating her any differently. All I'm asking is that you give me your blessing to pursue her affections. I'm sure, given enough time and energy; I can make her love me as much as I love her."

"You love my daughter?" John asked with a questioning raise of his eyebrow.

"Yes I do. I have for some time now. When she was in Pennsylvania, I asked her for her hand in marriage, but she refused. Her reason, she said, was that she didn't love me. As you know, though, we have grown much closer since my arrival here in Texas."

"And if I give you my blessing?"

"If Elizabeth learns to care for me as I care for her, I'm sure that as your son-in-law, I could see fit to help with any financial difficulties that my new family was having." Gregory took out his wallet. He wanted Elizabeth's father to understand his willingness to contribute financially.

"I'll have to think about this. I will also talk to Elizabeth to find out her feelings where you are concerned. No blessing will be given without her knowledge of this conversation."

"I completely understand, sir." Gregory closed his wallet and returned it to his breast pocket.

"I will be in touch."

Gregory raised an eyebrow at the dismissal as he got up from his chair. His anger flared.

Dismiss me, will you! We'll see about that.

He took himself out of John's office and out the front door to the waiting buggy.

CHAPTER 11

That day, Jeff arrived at Aubrey's with the buggy. She stood near the window when he drove up and came bounding out the front door, her skirts flying behind her.

"There you are. I've been waiting for you." The bright smile on her painted lips did nothing for him. Her pretty but simple gown with its very low neckline, caught his attention, but only because her bosom almost spilled out of it.

She is kind of pretty, but not the natural beauty that Elizabeth is. Damn! I've got to get her out of my head.

He shook his head to try to dislodge the image of Elizabeth's smoky gray eyes. They had such fire in them after their passionate kiss in front of his parents place and he wanted to see it again.

"Everything all right?" Aubrey asked, drawing his attention back to her.

"Fine. Are you ready to go? I've already stopped at the restaurant and retrieved our lunch."

"Yes. I've been looking forward to this since yesterday," she said as he helped her into the buggy.

Once he went around to the driver's seat, he picked up the reins and flicked them over the horse's rump. The buggy headed out of town toward a small grove of trees, a perfect place to have a picnic.

He really needed to forget Elizabeth, and a day with Aubrey might just do the trick.

The woman next to him chattered all the way to their picnic spot without even realizing he hadn't heard a word she said.

"Jeff?" She placed her hand on his arm.

"I'm sorry. What did you say?"

"I said, 'What did you have them pack for lunch?'"

"Oh…cold chicken, bread, and some potato salad."

"That sounds wonderful."

Maybe I just need to bed Aubrey and that will do the trick. It had been awhile since he'd been to bed anyone. Celibate didn't do a man any good. Maybe that was the reason he had this ungodly attraction to Elizabeth lately. All his plans and the problems with his dad's place kept him too busy. It wasn't just Elizabeth. *I'd be attracted to any woman right now.*

After grabbing the basket with their lunch and the blanket for them to sit on, he walked over to the big oak and spread out it out.

"This looks wonderful. Thank you for inviting me."

"Sure. It was nothing really. I thought we could spend some time together."

"I would love that. We hadn't seen each other for awhile now and I've been terribly lonely for the company of a man." She handed him a plate and looked at him through her eyelashes with what he thought of as her attempt to be coy.

"Have you?"

This might be just the ticket.

"Yes, of course. There aren't very many handsome young men in our little town, you know. I've always favored you, which I'm sure you are very aware of." She picked at her food.

"Well, we'll have to see where things go then, won't we?"

"I think you know exactly what I mean."

"Um...maybe I do."

Two hours later, he dropped Aubrey off at her parent's place after their afternoon together.

The wanton had been more than willing to give herself to him under the oak tree, but even while he made love to Aubrey, he couldn't help but think of Elizabeth. It was her whom he imagined he was making love to, her lips he tasted, her eyes full of passion for him, her breast under his hand, and her cries of passion in his ear.

Damn her! What do I have to do to get her out of my mind?

Obviously being with Aubrey hadn't help matters at all. He was just going to have to think of something else.

* * * *

Allen Simpson came out of the bank and around the back of the livery to meet his contact.

"So what's the story?" the man asked from the shadows when Allen approached.

"The cattle will be delivered to a remote area on the railway tomorrow. We've kept them penned up on the very outside border of the Double J. Stupid men haven't even noticed them there. They have been right under their noses, and they didn't realize it."

"Have they changed all the brands already?"

"Of course. They've all been altered to read our brand, Circle W. The brands on the Rocking W were the easiest to alter. The Double J was a little more difficult, but we managed. We'll make a haul off this load. There has to be almost five hundred head there," Allen said.

"Just see that no mistakes are made. I have plans for the money this will bring in."

"The men we've hired are all trustworthy. They are looking for a nice pay day as well so there will be no mistakes."

"I'm trusting you, Allen. But, no mistake, if there is a problem, there will be hell to pay."

* * * *

"Elizabeth, sweetheart, I need to talk to you," her father said when she came into the house from working in the garden with her mother and Michelle.

"Of course, Father. What is it?"

"Why don't you come into my office so we can talk privately?" He motioned for her to precede him with a wave of his hand.

She walked inside and took a seat, while he closed the door softly behind them. Propping himself on the corner of the desk, he studied her intently.

"Sweetheart. How do you feel about Mr. Webster?"

"Gregory?"

"Yes."

"He's nice enough, I guess. Why?" she asked, squirming in her chair.

My beautiful Elizabeth. She can't even look me in the eye.

"He came by the house earlier."

"Really?"

"He also told me you had mentioned to him we were having financial difficulties with the ranch. Elizabeth? How did you know this?" She fidgeted even more, refusing to meet his eyes. "Elizabeth Caroline, you will tell me this instant."

"I wasn't snooping, Father. I didn't really mean to do anything wrong, but you wouldn't tell me what the problems were, so I came in here one night after everyone was in bed and looked at your ledgers."

"Elizabeth, sweetheart." His anger deflated. Bending down in front of her, he took her hands in his. "I didn't tell you because I didn't want you to worry about things. It's not something you need on your mind right now. There shouldn't be anything in that pretty head of yours except what dress you'll wear tomorrow or whatever young man has taken your fancy lately, not financial problems with this place."

"I only wanted to help, Father," she whispered, tears sparkling on her lashes.

"I know, sweetheart. You always were looking out for everyone else but yourself."

"What did Gregory want?" She wiped the tears from her cheeks.

"He wanted my blessing to court you." He stood and walked back behind his desk.

"He did? What did you say?"

"I told him we would have this conversation and I would find out your feelings concerning him before I gave my blessing."

"I'm not sure what to say. Gregory is nice enough but..."

"You don't love him, do you, sweetheart?"

Contemplation worried her brow and he knew without her saying, Webster didn't hold her heart.

"I wish I did, Father. It would make things so much easier."

She got up from her chair and began pacing the floor.

"My guess is there is someone else that holds the key to your heart. Am I correct?"

"No," she answered too quickly.

"Elizabeth?" John stood in front of her and lifted her chin to look into her eyes. "You know you cannot lie to me. You've never been able to."

"All right, Father. Yes, there is someone I care for very much, but he doesn't care for me that way, so it doesn't matter. In fact, he's seeing someone else, so you may give your blessing to Gregory."

"May I fathom a guess as to who holds your affections? Is it Jeff?"

"Yes."

"Oh, sweetheart. I was afraid of that." He hugged her to him and stroked her back.

"Why?" she asked, when he released her.

"Because I don't think Jeff is the right young man for you, at least not right now. He is still young and isn't settled enough to be able to commit to any relationship. I'm afraid you would just be getting your feelings hurt."

"I know. He's made his lack of feelings for me very clear. I have to move on with my life. If that means being with Gregory even if I'm not in love with him, then so be it."

"If that's what you want, sweetheart, then I will give my blessing to Gregory."

"Thank you." She kissed him on the cheek. "Now, I'm off to freshen up for dinner."

* * * *

The next day, the rustlers detoured the train with a little bribe to the conductor to pick up the cattle they had stored. The cowboys worked quickly and efficiently to herd the cattle onto the cattle cars without too much difficulty. The ringleader sat atop his horse under a nearby tree and watched the loading with a satisfied smirk to his lips. He would be quite well off after this load, but he needed more, wanted more. Money was the only way he could precede with his plans. They would have to rustle more if they were to make the money he had in mind. He would just have to push them to continue.

Allen rode up to the man. "What do you think?"

"It looks very profitable to me."

"I'm glad you are satisfied." Allen beamed with pleasure.

"Oh, don't be so quick. I'm not satisfied. This is just the start."

"What do you mean?"

"We need more. You'll all need to step it up."

"We are already rustling about twenty to thirty head a week from these ranches. If we try to take more, they come after us with both barrels of the nearest shotgun," Allen said with a bit of a frightened look on his face. "No one can know that I'm involved. How would it look if the son of the local banker had a hand in many of the ranches in the area losing their places while my father holds the mortgage?"

"I don't care whether they know about you or not, I'm after two things in this town and one of them is money."

"What's the other thing?"

"None of your business." The man turned his horse to ride back toward town.

I need to make arrangements. It was important that things go as planned. If something went wrong, he would have to hurt people and he really didn't want to do that. He wasn't a violent man by nature, but he knew what he wanted and if people got in the way, they would have to be eliminated.

* * * *

"Damn!" John sat at his desk going over the cattle numbers again. "This has got to stop!"

The rustlers had taken another large number of his cattle again over the last couple of weeks, and now it seems his prize bull was missing!

"I've got to find that bull! John! Matt! Ray!" he shouted out the door of his office. He needed them to drop everything and find the bull.

All three of the boys came rushing in to find out what had gotten their father in such a state. He never raised his voice before, so they had to know something was definitely amiss.

"Dad? What's wrong?" John Jr. asked.

"Boys, sit down. We have a major problem." He indicated for his sons to sit with an absent wave of his hand. "Our prize bull is missing."

"What?" Ray said, shocked.

"How did that happen?" Matt asked.

"What the hell?' John Jr. said as they all talked in unison.

"Easy, boys. The biggest issue we have right now is finding the bull. If we don't have him, we don't have a ranch, you all know that. He's the most important part of this herd. I need you three to spread out and find him, now."

They all jumped out of their chairs, with John Sr. right behind them, and scrambled out of his office hell-bent on finding the animal no matter what it took.

They all saddled their horses and split up as they left the barn headed in four different directions.

* * * *

The women stood on the porch wondering what was going on.

"Mother, do you know what that was all about?" Elizabeth asked.

"No. Your father didn't mention anything to me about them all leaving," her mother said shielding her eyes from the sun. "Michelle?"

"I'm not sure if what I heard is what is going on or not, but I heard Mr. Johnston mumbling about a bull."

"Mother, I'm going to check something. I'll be right back." Elizabeth started walking in the direction of the pen behind the barn.

A few minutes later, Elizabeth returned with a frown, "He's not there."

"Who?" her mother asked.

"The bull, Mother, the bull is missing. If we don't have him, we can't replenish the herd." Spinning on her heels, she headed back toward the barn.

"Elizabeth? Where are you going?" Margaret and Michelle asked in unison.

"I'm going to go out and help look. I'm sure that's where they have all gone. One more pair of eyes will be good," she shouted, reaching the barn doors to saddle her horse.

About thirty minutes later, Elizabeth rode up to her father near the border between the Double J and the Rocking W where he had stopped to inspect a piece of downed fence. His anger shouldn't have surprised her.

"Elizabeth. What are you doing out here? You should have stayed at the house with your mother and Michelle. It's too dangerous out here for you to be riding around alone." His eyes narrowed and he planted his hands on his hips in the stubborn manner she knew broached no argument. "Now you get your behind back to the house."

"No, I'm not, Father. The more sets of eyes, the better. I'll just ride near you." She dismounted from her horse to inspect the broken spot in the fence. "Do you think someone might have taken him through there?"

"I don't know. He was in the pasture next to this one, so if the fence was down between them, he might have gotten out and headed over to the Rocking W."

"How about if I ride over there and find out if they've seen him? That way, I'm safer between the two ranches."

"All right, fine but keep your eyes open, and if anyone looks suspicious, you avoid them at all cost, young lady."

"Yes, Father. I'll be back as soon as I can." She remounted her horse and kicked him in the direction of the Rocking W.

And Jeff.

Running into him again wouldn't be easy on her heart. The last encounter had been quite enough. All she could think of the rest of that and the day after was how Jeff's picnic with Aubrey had gone. She hated the thought of him with another girl, much less Aubrey Dillon.

Well, I'm just going to have to come to terms with all this. After all, Father is giving Gregory his blessing to court me, which means I can't have my cake and eat it too.

When she rode into the yard of the Rocking W, Jeff was again working with the mare in the corral near the barn.

Heavens to Betsy! He's got his shirt off again.

Her cheeks started to heat from the sight.

He really needs to stop doing that!

Pulling her eyes from the sight, she rode up to the rail near the porch and dismounted.

Jeff's mother, Donna, must have heard her ride in because the door swung open and she stepped out onto the porch. "Why Elizabeth! It's so nice to see you, dear. It's been forever I believe. How have you been?"

Elizabeth could feel the heat of his gaze on her backside and she had to fight the shiver rolling down her back.

"Well, hello, Mrs. Walker. It's nice to see you again too. It has been a while." Elizabeth walked onto the porch and gave Jeff's mother a big hug.

"What brings you by on such a beautiful day?"

"We are missing our bull and I wanted to come by and ask Mr. Walker or Jeff if they had seen him?"

"You can ask Jeff yourself, dear, since he's right over there in the corral." Donna pointed to Jeff standing by the fence pulling his shirt on.

His chest is way too nice for my health.

"Thanks. I think I will," she replied, shielding her eyes from the sun while she watched him pull his shirt on and button it up the front. With a fortifying breath, she walked toward the corral.

"Jeff," she muttered when she reached his side.

"Elizabeth."

"We are um...missing our bull. Have you seen him?" She licked her suddenly dry lips.

"Can't say that I have, but you are welcome to look around."

"Thanks. Would you care to ride out with me to look?"

Good Lord, what am I thinking! How am I supposed to concentrate on finding that bull if I'm riding along side of him? I'll just have to not look at him, or I'll never get through this.

"Sure. I guess I can take some time for a ride. Let me go saddle my gelding."

"No problem. I can wait." She turned and walked back to where her horse stood tied to the porch railing.

He brought the gelding out a few minutes later and walked over to where she sat talking with his mother on the porch. "You ready?"

"Yes. Which way shall we head?"

"Why don't we check the pasture between the two ranches first? He might have just gotten over here because some of the cows are breeding."

"Very true. Lead the way," she said with a wave of her hand.

They both mounted their horses and set out side by side.

CHAPTER 12

"How was your picnic with Aubrey?" she asked, then mentally kicked herself for asking. *I really didn't want to know. I'm not sure why I even asked.*

"Uh...it was very nice. We picnicked under the oak tree just outside of town."

"I'm glad you had a good time then." She kept her eyes forward so he wouldn't see the pain she felt at the thought of him with Aubrey.

"We did. Thanks."

They continued to ride and Elizabeth tried to make small talk so the silence wouldn't stretch on. The two of them had never been uncomfortable around each other before and she didn't want it to start now.

When they stopped near the break in the fence her father had seen earlier, she told him her father's theory that maybe the bull had come over into Rocking W pasture.

"That's possible," Jeff replied. "But we don't have in cows in this pasture right now."

"Well, that's strange then. I'm not sure what to think of it. Any ideas?" She looked into his eyes for the first time since they left the house and felt the heat of his gaze all the way to her toes.

"Not right off hand. Why don't we ride a little farther up and see what we find?"

One shoulder lifted in a shrug. "Sounds good to me."

"How are things between you and that easterner?"

"Um...you mean Gregory?" He nodded stiffly. "Fine, thanks." She rode up so she was along side of him. "He came over to the house the other day to talk to my father about some business."

"What kind of business?"

"Well, he had heard with the rustlers, we were having some financial difficulties, so he wanted to talk to my father about it." She then added, "He also asked my father if he could court me."

"He what?" Jeff asked, surprise evident in his voice.

"He asked Father if he could court me," she repeated, not looking his way.

"And what did your father say?"

"He didn't give him an answer right away. He wanted to talk to me first to find out my feelings on the matter."

"And?"

She looked away before answering. "I told him that it was all right with me if he gave Gregory his blessing."

"I see."

Uncomfortable silence stretched between them.

If he'd only tell me not to — if he'd say he wanted to be with me, I wouldn't even consider Gregory. If he'd tell me our kisses meant as much to him as they did to me, Gregory wouldn't even figure in the picture. If he'd tell me, he cares about me more than friend, even a little...

But he said nothing.

The sky began to darken to the west when they continued to ride in silence along the fence line between the two ranches and kept an eye out for the missing bull.

Lord! Why did I suggest we make this ride? This was about the stupidest thing I could have suggested.

She kept an eye on the darkening sky while they rode. A summer thunderstorm could catch them off guard quickly and a flash flood could mean certain peril. Jeff seemed worried too. Mentally calculating the distance between line shacks placed along the pasture fence, she knew they might have to take cover in one until the storm passed. They needed to make sure they were within a quick ride to one should they need it.

"Wait!" she said, pointing to a black dot on the horizon. "That could be him."

"Shall we go see?"

Jeff kicked his horse and took off at a gallop across the rolling hills with her hot on his heels. The wind through her hair was exhilarating! She hadn't ridden like this in a long time, and to be riding alongside the gorgeous man beside her at a full gallop was like nothing she'd felt before. The horsemanship bred into him from years of working a cattle ranch, came out with each pounding of the horse's hooves beneath him. It showed in the way he handled the powerful gelding, at the same time, keeping him under complete control.

She felt the wind pulling at her hair and working it loose in a few places when they rode toward the dot in the distance.

The darkening sky caught her attention. He began to pull back, indicating to her they needed to break off and head for shelter. The line-shack was still a fair piece away from where they were and she was afraid they wouldn't reach it before the downpour.

Moments later, the sky opened up and rain cascaded down, soaking both of them almost instantly. Elizabeth pulled back, and Jeff motioned to the line shack to their right. She couldn't hear anything he said over the pounding rain, but she knew where he pointed. She took off at a full gallop toward the shelter. There wasn't anywhere to protect the horses so when they reached the cabin, they both jumped off and let the horses go. Both animals were well trained and would make their way back to one or the other of the ranches after the rain let up. Running for the porch, she pushed open the door of the cabin and rushed inside. Jeff slammed it and slid the bolt behind them.

In the dim light, they stood there, dripping rainwater on the floor around them.

"Let me see if I can find a candle. I'm sure there is probably one around here somewhere."

Elizabeth nodded as she tried to pull the braid out of her hair and finger comb it. Hopefully it would dry some before she had to put it back up.

Her clothes were soaked, when she looked down at her pants and shirt, but she only shrugged.

Once the braid was loose, she sat on one of the wooden chairs in the single room cabin, to pull off her wet boots and socks.

I hope these dry some before the rain lets up. The last thing I need is a blister from wet socks.

Jeff located a small candle and placed it on the table next to where she sat, found some matches, and was able to illuminate the inside of the small cabin moments later.

"Well. It looks like we'll be here for a little while anyway." Jeff sat and started pulling off his wet boots and socks, too. "I'll start a small fire so maybe our clothes will dry a bit before we can leave."

"That would probably be a good idea. Can I help?"

"Why don't you see if there is anything to eat in here? I don't know about you, but I missed lunch."

"I'm sorry. I didn't know. You could have eaten before we left if you had said something. Let me see what I can find in the cupboards."

"It's all right. I just didn't expect to be out that long and now stuck in this line shack with you. It wasn't quite the way I had planned my afternoon," he grumbled with a bit of a scowl.

"I hadn't planned on this either, you know," she said sharply, before she walked over to the cupboard to see what she could find.

She turned around after looking inside and said, "I found a can of beans and another can of beans. Which would you pref..."

The wet shirt came off, revealing the broad chest she remembered so well with its smattering of black hair. Air rushed from between her teeth is a soft hiss. "What are you doing?"

"Taking off my shirt." He replied looking at her with a mildly amused twinkle to his eyes.

"Yes, I'm perfectly aware of that, thank you, but why?"

"So I can dry it a little when I build the fire. Do you really have to ask?"

"I, uh...um...well, yes, I see," she stammered when she placed the cans of beans on the table. "Oh Lord!" she whispered, watching the muscles of his chest and back work under his taunt skin while he moved. The muscles bunched and rolled, fascinating her with their movement, when he stacked the wood in the fireplace.

As the flames licked at the dry wood, the orange glow from the fire played along the skin of his back like the fingertips of a lover.

It's getting really warm in here. One hand began to fan her face, and unsteadily took a seat near the table.

* * * *

After building the fire, he turned and the look in her eyes. What he saw made his toes curl and his whole body come to attention.

Firelight played across her wet shirt, making it almost transparent. The paleness of her skin beneath the fabric had his fingers tingling to touch. Her nipples stood up like twin peaks when his gaze raked over them and she sighed as if he had actually touched her. When his gaze met hers again, the look in her eyes told him the passion raging inside of him, raged through her as well.

With measured steps, he moved toward her, captivated by the look reflected in the gray depths. He stopped directly in front of her and drew her to her feet. His fingers swept into the hair near her temple and she closed her eyes.

"Look at me, Elizabeth," he commanded, framing her face with his other hand.

He couldn't help himself. Kissing her was a need insistent on being fulfilled at this very moment. His lips met hers ever so softly and she melted against him until he could feel the tips of her breasts searing his chest, through her shirt. At the feel of her, he almost lost all control. He needed to go slow. Teeth clenched while he tried desperately to control the passion running crazily through his body at the contact. This was Elizabeth, not Aubrey and he knew his Elizabeth was innocent to the feelings she caused in him.

The kiss deepened to the point where he almost ravished her mouth the way he wanted to ravish her body. Lord he was on fire! When he began to explore her back through her wet shirt, her arms came up around his shoulders in an attempt to pull him even closer.

"You need to get out of these wet clothes," he whispered in her ear once his mouth left hers to run along her neck. "We both do."

His hands dropped away so she could reach the front of her shirt. Shaky fingers unfastened the buttons before it fell away, revealing her shear chemise.

Fingers reached for him, sliding through the hair on his chest and he closed his eyes at the feel of her hands on his skin. Muscles went rigid at the touch. The need for this woman drove him past resistance.

When she wrapped her hands around his shoulders and pulled herself against him, he grabbed her chemise by the edge and lifted it over her head.

I want her bare skin against mine if it's the last thing I ever do.

When the chemise was off and her naked breasts pressed against his chest, he wrapped his hand in her hair and took her mouth with his almost desperately. A soft whimper left her mouth under his onslaught. He softened his kiss and brought his raging passion under control.

"No, don't stop," she whimpered when he ripped his mouth from hers.

When he felt her hands on the waistband of his trousers, he was surprised.

"Are you sure you want this, Elizabeth, because if you don't, we had better stop this right now before I am completely unable to."

"I'm not sure what I want right now," she whispered and looked into his eyes. "Just don't stop."

"Oh God."

As he ravished her mouth with his, he expertly undid the button on her pants and slid his hands under the waistband to work the trousers off her hips and down her legs. When she stepped out of them, he wrapped his arms around her, lifted her, and carried her to the bed pushed up against the wall of the cabin.

It isn't much, but it'll have to do.

He quickly shed his wet clothes and joined her.

Firelight danced on her skin. Passion raged through her body, and when his hand skimmed over her breast, she arched her back, moaning low in her throat.

Her eyelids flittered shut.

His mouth replaced his fingers and she tossed her head from side-to-side as she whispered his name. She wiggled under him while her body reacted to the feel of his mouth.

One hand slipped down her flat belly to the mound between her legs. Thighs clamped together in an attempt to stop his exploration.

"Easy, girl. I'm not going to hurt you," he murmured softly while looking deeply into her eyes.

She slowly relaxed under his hand, allowing his fingers to slip over her sensitive tissues. A soft whimper left her lips when he continued to stroke and touch, bringing her ever higher.

"Jeff, I ..."

"Oh, sweetheart. Do you have any idea how much I want you right now?" he said while he worked magic on her body with his hands.

"Ohhhh..." Elizabeth moaned when his fingers slide inside to prepare her for what lie ahead.

He rolled partly on top of her and kissed her eyelids, her cheeks, and her nose. Lips parted in desire and he slipped his tongue over the soft surface. Fingers slid in and out, bringing her close to the peak of completion before sliding away. He wanted her to come with him on the journey.

Continuing to ravish her mouth, he nudged her legs apart and centered himself between her thighs. His mouth worked its way from her lips to her throat, and she arched her neck to give him better access to the soft skin under his lips. He took her mouth in a desperate kiss as he pushed inside her warmth. With feet planted on the mattress beneath them, she lifted her hips and arched to meet his thrust.

Keep it slow. Can't rush this.

Teeth ground together while he fought for control.

She's a virgin.

Conscious thought fled when she wiggle beneath him and whimpered softly.

Passion escalated out of control when he increased the tempo of their lovemaking, and her cries of excitement echoed in his ears with each thrust of his hips. Vaginal walls started to quiver as she raced toward completion.

Moments later, she fell over the abyss, taking his final bit of power to forestall the end, along with her.

When their breathing slowed, he rolled off and lay beside her, pulling her into the crook of his arm so her head could rest on his chest.

"Are you all right?" He softly kissed the top of her head.

"Yes." Fingers slid through the hair on his chest.

"Elizabeth?"

"Yes?" she asked, continuing to play with the hair under her hand, but refusing to look directly at him.

"Sweetheart, look at me." He placed his fingers beneath her chin and lifted her face so he could look into her eyes. "Are we all right?"

"I'm not sure what you mean. You'll have to help me out here. I'm not sure what is supposed to happen now."

"Well, I, uh...." he stammered.

I know what I'm supposed to do with other women, but I don't quite know what to do with this one.

His father's words came back. "She's not the love 'em and leave 'em kind."

Where do we go from here? Her brothers will kill me if they find out I bedded their little sister.

When his grip loosened, she rolled away and got up. Reaching for her damp clothing, she pulled them on as he sat up behind her.

"The rain has stopped. We should start walking toward home if the horses have taken off."

Trousers slid over her nicely rounded backside and he had to stifle a groan. The shirt came next, hiding her exquisite breasts from his view when she buttoned it up and tucked it into the waistband of her pants. Crossing the room to the bench, she grabbed her socks and pulled them on.

With a heavy sigh, he snatched his clothing from the floor and pulled on his still wet pants over his hips before he headed to the fireplace to retrieve his shirt.

While he buttoned up the front of his shirt, he watched Elizabeth bend down to pull on her boots.

Now, what the hell am I going to do with her? I couldn't keep my hands off her before we made love. I know how it feels to hold her, kiss her lips, hear her sigh while I make her body come to life. It will be nearly impossible to stay away from her.

Slim fingers combed through her thick mane of hair to give it some semblance of order before they left. Lord help them if anyone found out how they had spent the afternoon in this small cabin.

Lost in thought, he didn't hear the knock at the door or the rattle of the handle until they heard her father's voice.

"Hello? Anyone in there? Elizabeth?"

Terror filled eyes met his. "What are we going to do? He can't find out what happened here? He'll kill you!"

"We have to let him in. Just act normal, and he'll never know," he replied as he pulled on his boots. "Now. Get the door."

Elizabeth tentatively walked to the door and slid the bolt.

Mr. Johnston barreled through the door and slammed it shut behind him. "Are you all right? God! You had me scared, girl. I saw your horse grazing nearby, and after the storm let up, I came to find you."

"I'm fine, Father. The storm caught us by surprise, so we headed in here to wait it out."

Her father's suspicious eyes rested on him with a questioning expression.

"That's right, sir. We just sat here talking until the rain let up. We were just going to head out to see if the horses had stayed nearby before we started walking."

"Well, I can see you are both fine. I caught both your horses, so I brought them here with me and they are tethered outside."

"Any sign of the bull?" she asked, pulling her father's attention back to her before he could see the guilt on Jeff's face.

"No, not yet."

"We thought we had seen him on the ridge right before the storm hit, but that's when the rain came down in sheets, so we headed here instead."

"Well, it's going to be getting dark soon anyway, so we'll have to suspend the search for tonight." John said, scanning the cabin.

"I suppose we should be getting home then." Elizabeth started for the door with Jeff on her heels. "I'm sure Mother will have supper ready soon."

"Yes, I suppose you're right," her father replied, following them out of the cabin and pulling the door behind him.

"I'm sorry we couldn't catch him for you sir."

"I'm sure we'll find him tomorrow, son. Thanks for keeping my little girl safe." John looked from one to the other.

"Uh...you're welcome, sir, though I really didn't do anything."

A quick glance at Elizabeth revealed nothing.

"You are a trustworthy young man. I would trust you with my daughter no matter what the circumstances. If you'd like to help us look for the bull again tomorrow, come by the house in the morning," John said after he had mounted his own horse and turned him in the direction of the Double J.

His eyes locked with hers for a moment before she glanced away and turned her horse in the direction of home. Jeff sat there for a few minutes watching her ride away with her father before he turned his horse toward the Rocking W.

CHAPTER 13

"Are you all right, Lizzie?" her father asked while they rode along.

"I'm sorry, Father. I was a bit lost in thought. What did you say?" Her thoughts had been occupied by one sexy, brown-eyed cowboy.

"I asked if you are all right. You seem a bit preoccupied."

"I guess I am. I was just thinking about where the bull might be." Her father didn't need to know where her real thoughts were, back in the cabin lying naked with Jeff on the bed.

"It's hard to say at this point. The storm could have caused him to bolt anywhere. We'll have to look again tomorrow."

"I just hope we find him soon."

"Me too sweetheart, me too."

They rode into the yard, where her brothers stood waiting next to the hitching post.

"What happened to you?" Ray asked, his eyes sweeping over her disheveled hair and wrinkled clothing.

"I got caught in the thunderstorm that rolled through a little while ago."

"I found her in the small line cabin between the Rocking W and our pasture waiting out the storm," her father explained. "She and Jeff had taken shelter there."

"Jeff?" Ray asked inquisitively with an arched eyebrow.

"Yes with Jeff," she said, ignoring his questioning look and heading for the house.

"Liz?" He came up behind her. "Are you all right?"

"Yes, Ray. I'm fine. Other than being wet clear to the skin."

"Just wanted to make sure."

"You don't have to worry about anything. Everything is just fine, I promise," she said shooting him the best innocent look she could come up with. She could never let her brothers know what happened between her and Jeff in that cabin, not even Ray. If they ever found out, there would be hell to pay, for both of them.

* * * *

The next day Jeff came by to help with the search for the missing bull. He really felt like he needed to talk to Elizabeth after what happened yesterday in the cabin. Knowing she had been innocent until he'd taken her virginity, he felt like a heel. He was the experienced one, and he should have stopped it before it had gotten as far as it had. To apologize would be the best thing he could do.

Elizabeth stood outside near the fountain when he rode up. Once he tethered his horse near the house, he headed in her direction.

The look in her eyes told him she wasn't sure. Pink stained her cheeks when he stopped next to her and took her hand.

"Elizabeth? Can I talk to you?"

"Now is probably not a good time. I'm really busy."

He took her arm before she could brush past him. "Elizabeth, please. I want to apologize for yesterday."

"Apologize?"

"Yes. I should never have let what happened between go so far. Things got out of control, and I shouldn't have let them. I'm the experienced one here, and I should have stopped it before things got so out of control. I'm sorry."

Her eyes spit fire.

Oh Lord, now she's mad.

Pulling her arm out of his grasp, she snapped, "You should have stopped things? If I'm not mistaken, we were both there, and since we are both adults, I had just as much to say about what happened as you did. If you really didn't want to make love to me, then you should have said so."

"What? No! I mean, yes. I mean I should have stopped it. You were a virgin."

"Yes I was. I chose to be there with you, and I'm not sorry that I did, but if you really didn't want to be with me, then I am sorry you put yourself out like that."

"But I did!" Jeff yelled, raking his fingers through his hair in frustration. Lord she's making this difficult. All he wanted to do was say he was sorry and she's twisting it all around.

"Well, I'm not sure what there is left to say. If you'll excuse me."

"Damn it!" He followed her back to the front of the house.

Right after the door slammed, Ray came out of the barn and walked briskly in his direction.

Aw hell! What if Ray heard the whole argument?

"Jeff."

"Ray."

"What were you and Elizabeth arguing about?"

"Sorry. That's between me and Elizabeth."

"You bastard!" Ray yelled as he swung and hit him square in the jaw, knocking him to the ground. "You had better come clean with me before I kill you."

Pulling himself up off the ground, he rubbed his jaw where Ray and hit him. "What in the hell has gotten into you?"

"I heard your argument in the garden. Your little afternoon romp with my sister was quite clear. You'll be lucky if I don't kill you. I can't speak for the rest of the men in our family."

"Listen. It shouldn't have happened, I know that, but it's done. I can't take it back even if I wanted to."

"What do you plan to do about it?" Ray clenched and unclenched his fists at his sides.

"I'm not sure what you mean."

"You have defiled my sister. Exactly how do you plan on fixing this? She can no longer go to another man pure."

"Exactly what do you expect me to do, Ray?" Jeff asked while he continued to rub his jaw.

"Do you plan to marry her?"

"I, uh..."

"Wrong answer," Ray growled before he punched him again, knocking him to the ground a second time.

"Damn it, Ray!" Jeff yelled, lying on the ground. "I doubt she would have me even if I asked."

"Well, you had better be finding out before I let the rest of the men in this family know what you've done. I should just kill you and get it over with. God help you if she's with child because of your carelessness. Now get the hell out of here before I do what I want to."

Ray left Jeff lying there in the dirt and went into the house. Jeff pulled himself up, brushed off his trousers, and shot a glance at the door half expecting Ray to come back out and beat the hell out of him.

* * * *

From inside the house, Elizabeth watched Jeff mount his horse and head back toward the Rocking W. She had heard him and Ray arguing outside and she hoped her mother hadn't heard. It was bad enough Ray knew what happened between them, but she didn't need anyone else to know.

"Liz?"

Ray came up behind her, and she about jumped out of her skin when she swung around. "Ray! I didn't hear you. You about scared the tar out of me."

"I need to talk to you."

"I would, but I need to help Mother right now. Maybe lat—"

"No. Now!" Ray said firmly, taking her arm and leading her outside.

"My goodness! What has gotten into you?" she asked as they approached the barn. He had practically dragged her across the yard.

When they reached the interior of the large structure, he let her go and he turned so he faced the wall.

"Liz. I overheard your argument with Jeff in the garden."

"Oh." The disappointment in his voice broke her heart. If there was anyone in this world who she didn't want to hurt or to be disappointed in her, it was Ray.

He raked his fingers through his hair. "Why, Liz?"

"It just happened. I don't know what else to say."

"I'll kill him!" he shouted, all his rage returning.

"No, listen to me. It wasn't entirely his fault. I could have stopped it but I didn't, so you need to blame me, too."

Ray took her shoulders in his hands. "The hell I will! He should have known better. He's a man after all."

"I'm an adult. I can make my own decisions, and if I chose to make love with Jeff, then so be it. I will accept the consequences of my actions."

"What will Dad say when he finds out?"

"He can't find out. No one else must know what happened. It has to stay a secret, and don't worry."

"How can you be so sure?"

"Jeff didn't want to make love to me in the first place. I'm sure of that so I'm just as sure it will never happen again. Please, Ray. You need to keep this a secret, please? For me?" she said, desperately.

"I'll keep quiet for now, but I'm not as sure as you are. I've already talked with Jeff, and he knows where I stand on this." He hugged her, and then let her go.

"Thanks, big brother. I'll deal with Jeff in my own way."

Elizabeth stayed in the house the rest of the day. She needed to figure out what she was going to do about Jeff. The last thing she needed would be for her father and other brothers to find out what had happened between them. For Ray to know was bad enough!

"Elizabeth?" Michelle called, pulling her out of her pensive musings.

"I'm sorry. My mind is a bit preoccupied. Did you say something?"

Vegetables sat in piles on the table, waiting for the flash of the knife in her hand.

"I asked if anyone had seen the missing bull yet."

"No. I saw him yesterday or we think we did, but the thunderstorm caught us off guard so we had to take shelter."

"Us?"

"Um...yes, us. I had rode over to the Rocking W to see if they had seen the bull, and Jeff rode out with me to look for him. We got caught in the storm and had to take shelter in one of the line shacks." Elizabeth avoided looking at her friend. She was afraid if she looked at her, Michelle would be able to tell that she and Jeff had been more than just staying dry.

"Ah. I see."

I hope not. It wouldn't be good if her friend found out either. As close as Michelle and John had become, she would surely tell him, and then where would she be! "I'm done with mine. How are you coming with yours?" Elizabeth asked, trying to change the subject.

"I'm finished, too. Shall we take these into the kitchen?" Michelle asked, gathering up the vegetables in her skirt.

The next day, the men went out again to look for the still missing bull. Elizabeth had met Ray in the barn before they'd left. "Ray? You won't say anything to anyone, will you?"

"No, Liz. I promised I wouldn't, but only for now. I want to see how Jeff handles this before I have to kill him."

"Ray! You will do no such a thing!"

"Okay. Maybe I won't kill him, but I want to right now even if he is my best friend." He drew his sister into a hug. "I love you, Lizzie, and I just don't want you to get hurt."

"I know, Ray, and I love you too. It will be all right, I promise." She pulled out of his arms. "Now go find that bull!"

"I'm riding with Dad today, so I'm sure we will. We are going to be checking out that outer pasture where you said you had seen him yesterday."

"I'm sure you'll find him."

* * * *

That afternoon, Ray and John Sr. rode in the outer pasture and thought they saw the bull grazing on the hillside.

"Over there. That looks like it might be him," John said, pointing to the black spot on the horizon.

"I see it. Let's go!" Ray replied, kicking his horse into a full gallop toward what they thought was the bull.

When they got closer, they could see what appeared to be several more cows off to the right of where the bull grazed. The cows appeared to be in a makeshift corral of some sort so they slowed their approach.

"What the hell?"

"No wonder the bull is up here. There must be over a hundred head in that pen, Dad. Several are probably breeding, so he came looking for them."

"Let's stop here and take a look. I don't like the looks of this," John said, nodding toward a grove of trees where they could hide the horses and walk in for a better look.

They stopped and tethered their horses, before they slowly approached the corral keeping a close eye on the surrounding area.

"What do you make of this?"

"I'm not wondering if this isn't where they've been keeping all the rustled cattle. I can't see the brands though."

"We need to get a bit closer. I want to see whose brand is on those cows." John scurried from behind the boulder and slipped silently to the next.

When they were close enough to see the brands clearly, Ray said, "Those are Rocking W cows over there, and it looks like some on the other side are Double J. There is even a couple from the Flying C that I can see."

"Appears we've stumbled on the branding point of where our cows have been disappearing. It makes sense. They could easily herd them to the rail line that crosses about two miles from here."

"What are we going to do, Dad?"

"We need to let the rest of the ranchers in town know we've we found, so we can get the law out here. Let's work our way back to the horses so we can get out of here before we're seen."

They attempted to silently slip back near the horses when they heard riders coming from the other side of the corral. Their horses nickered to the approaching riders in greeting.

John cursed as they saw the riders they notice their horses near the trees. "Damn!"

When the riders stopped, it gave them a chance to make a break for the horses. "Run, Ray!" John shouted as he took off running toward their horses with Ray right beside him.

"After them!" one of the rustlers shouted.

They had just reached the horses and managed to mount when shots rang out with several whizzing over their heads. "Ride! Ride like hell and don't look back!" John shouted, jamming his heels into the side of his horse. If they could just reach the borders of the ranch yard, they would be safe. John shot a look behind him as they sprinted toward home and his eyes met the brown eyes of the leader who was now too close for comfort.

* * * *

Damn it! Why hadn't they brought rifles?

More shots rang out and he leaned lower onto the back of his horse, trying to make himself the smallest target possible.

Ray rode into the ranch yard at a full gallop. He turned to locate his father before he realized his father wasn't there. The horse reared back on his haunches when he pulled it up hard.

Shivers ran through him as he headed back in the direction they had come.

"God please let him be all right," Ray said aloud, scanning the horizon for his father.

Luckily, the rustlers had rode back in the direction of the cows and not followed them as far as the ranch house, but when Ray crept along looking for his father, he had a terrible feeling. It wasn't like his dad to not stay close behind him if they were riding hell-bent for leather.

His father's horse near a tree they had passed on the way in, so he turned in that direction. When he got close the horse, it moved to the right and he could see his father lying on the ground.

"*No!*" Ray screamed, leaped off his horse, and scrambled towards his father's still form.

He knelt on the ground near the slumped man and noticed the bloodstain on the back of his dad's shirt. With shaking hands, Ray rolled John on his back.

Thank God, he's still alive.

"Dad?"

"Ray?" John said quietly, struggling to open his eyes. "What happened?"

"You've been shot, Dad. I need to get you home."

"You'll have to put me on my horse son and tie my hands to the pommel. I'll make it. We aren't far from the house. Make Jack lie down so I can mount."

"I'll get you home." Ray picked up his father and gently put him in his horse's saddle after he had gotten the gelding to lie down. Nudging the horse to stand, Ray steadied his father, tied his hands to the pommel, and led the horse near his so he could lead it home.

Ray tried to get the horses to ride as gently as possible, keeping a close eye on his dad. He had to get him home quickly. He had already lost too much blood.

As they rode into the yard, Ray yelled, "Momma! Lizzie! Help me!"

The women came running out of the house to be faced with John leaning dangerously over the pommel of the saddle.

"Liz, grab the horses while I get Dad down. He's been shot."

Elizabeth grabbed the reins of both horses to steady them, and Ray struggled to get the big man down from the horse. The other two siblings rode into the yard, moments later.

"Holy shit! What happened?" John Jr. asked, jumping down from his own horse to help Ray with their father.

"I'll tell you later. Right now, we need to get him in the house. He's in bad shape."

"I can see that. Matt, come help us."

The three boys gently carried their bleeding father into the house while their mother directed Carmen to get some hot water ready. Ray couldn't believe how calm their mother was.

"Now out! All of you! I need room to work."

CHAPTER 14

"How bad is it doc?" John asked as the doctor worked to staunch the blood flowing from the exit wound in his abdomen.

"It's bad, John. There isn't much I can do. The bullet got you in the middle of your back and exited clear through your stomach. I can't really tell if anything vital was hit, but by how much blood you've lost and the area of the exit wound, I'd say your liver has been damaged."

"Damn! This isn't supposed to end this way!" John cried, tears filling his eyes and shooting a glance at his beloved wife of thirty years. "Come here my love."

Margaret approached the bed with tears streaming down her cheeks. "You can't leave me, John. I won't let you," she told him in a cracked voice as she knelt beside the bed.

"Sweetheart. It is God's way. Only he has the power to say when, and it appears now is the time. You'll need to be strong for the children. They'll need you now more than ever to keep this place going." He took her hand in his and pressed it against his wet cheek.

"I can't go on without you, John. You are my life!"

"Mother, it will be okay. We'll be together again someday in God's heaven. Please be strong. Now, bring the children in. I need to say my good-byes."

She sat next to the bed holding his hand for a few minutes longer before she finally struggled to her feet and walked slowly toward the door. After a quick glance, she turned and opened the door to find all four of their children waiting on the other side.

"This can't be happening. Please tell me he'll be all right. Please?" Elizabeth asked.

"I wish I could sweetheart. I wish I could."

The boys moved closer.

"Your father wants to see you," she said to all of them. "John, you better go first."

Moments later, John Sr. saw his son come near.

"Son." He held out his hand for his eldest son to take it. "You'll be the man of the house now. You need to take care of your mother and your sister especially. I'm afraid Elizabeth is going to be a handful."

John Jr. smiled and laughed slightly and said, "She already is, Dad. You know that better than anyone."

"Very true son, very true."

"Dad? What do you want me to do?"

"Just take care of things. I've taught you everything I know about this place. It's yours now. Make sure it stays in the hands of a Johnston." John Sr. replied as he grimaced. "You might seriously consider marrying that cute thing that's here visiting. She'd make a fine wife for you I think."

"I know Dad. I've thought about it a lot lately actually."

"Good. Just be strong for the rest of the family. They'll need your strength in the coming months." John Sr. slowly closed his eyes. "Now, send in your brothers, will you? I'm not sure how much more strength I have left."

"Of course. I love you."

"I love you too, son."

John Sr. listened while his eldest boy said, "Dad wants to see you, Matt, and you too, Ray."

"What about me?" Elizabeth asked.

"I think he wants to talk to you alone, Liz."

Matt and Ray slowly walked through the door and closed it softly behind them.

"Come, closer boys. I need to tell you a few things," John said from the bed when his other boys came into the room. "Ray, take good care of your sister. She's going to need you. And make sure that you and your brothers get those rustlers and string them up in the nearest tree; every last one of them."

Ray stood at the side of the bed holding his father's hand in his. "For you, Dad, I'll kill 'em myself."

"Matt, you need to take care of the books. You are the best one to handle the finances. You're excellent with numbers, boy, so do them right and make this place grow."

"I'll make sure this place is the best damned ranch in the area, Pop." Matt replied while tears flowed down his cheeks.

"Good. You boys are my pride and joy. All of you kids are. I just wish I was going to be around to see my grandchildren, but the Lord has other plans for me and for this family. Take care of it for me while I'm gone."

"Sure, Dad." Matt said.

"Now. Send in Lizzie. I need to tell her something."

When Matt and Ray walked out of the door, Elizabeth was standing near the doorway waiting for her turn to say good-bye.

"Lizzie, my sweet daughter." John smiled and took her hand in his. "I'm going to miss you so much."

"You can't go, Daddy. Who's going to make sure I stay out of trouble?" She cried and laughed a little as she knelt beside the bed and put her father's hand to her cheek.

"Your brothers will take good care of you, sweetheart, but there is something I need to say before I go. Lizzie, you need to follow your heart, sweetie. I know you have feelings for Jeff. I've seen it in your eyes when you look at him. I had thought before that he wasn't the right man for you, but now I know I won't be around to guide you, I think you need to do what you feel is the best thing for you. I wish I had more time. God, I wish I had more time to help you with this, but I think you and Jeff would be good together. I think he has some deep feelings for you, but he's scared, sweetheart. I know I felt the same way with your mother. She scared the hell out of me when I first saw her. He's afraid of the feelings he has for you, but in time, he'll realize that he loves you as much as you love him."

"Daddy, please don't go. I need you. I love you. I don't know what to do."

"I know, sweetheart. I love you so much, and it hurts me to have to leave you. I wish I didn't have to go either, but it's my time. One more thing I need to know. That day in the line shack, did you and Jeff..."

She stared into her father's eyes, and she knew she had to tell him the truth. What did it matter now anyway? "I don't know what to say," she muttered and bowed her head, unable to look into her father's eyes for fear of seeing disappointment in them.

"Just tell me the truth, Lizzie. I won't judge you."

"Oh, Daddy. I don't want you to be disappointed in me." She returned her gaze to his. "Yes, Jeff and I have been together, but it wasn't entirely his fault. I didn't stop him, and I know I probably should have, but it just felt right."

"I thought as much. It's all right, sweetheart. I'm not disappointed in you, but if you should be with child, you need to marry him. There is something you need to know as well so you don't feel guilty about what happened between you two. Your mother and I had been together before we got married, too. When it's right, you just know it. You shouldn't feel bad about what happened." John slowly closed his eyes. "You had better send your mother in, sweetheart. I don't have much time left."

Not leaving her father's side, she yelled, "Mother?"

Elizabeth moved from her spot next to her father so her mother could be near him.

"John? John?" Her mother grasped his hand.

"Margaret, my love. I wanted you here near me, but I need to go now. I love you my wife and we'll be together again soon," he said, closed his eyes, and took his last breath.

"*No!* Daddy!" Elizabeth screamed as she knelt beside her father on the opposite side and took his hand. She put her head down on his hand and cried with such force, her whole body shook with sobs.

Elizabeth stood on the porch while the light faded beyond the horizon, unable to shed anymore tears. She felt empty, emptier than she had ever felt in her life. Her father was gone and he would never return. The ache filling her entire soul at the loss of her father spread through her, and she almost doubled over with the pain.

A whisper of a breeze blew around her. It sent a chill up her arms even in the heat of the evening and lifted her hair from her shoulder in the gentle touch. "Daddy?" she whispered into the breeze.

With no answer reaching her ears, she stood in the silence and, closing her eyes, imagined her father lifting the curl from her shoulder and playfully running it through his fingers. He had always lovingly tugged at her curls when she was young, so this made her feel a little more peace.

Now what am I going to do? His loving hand wouldn't be there to guide her anymore.

Her eyes came open with a start, and she almost took off at a run toward the barn. She needed to feel loved. She needed to be held so she could start to heal from the pain running through her before it swallowed her whole. There was only one person she knew who could help her through the long night ahead.

She quickly saddled her horse and, in the moonlit night, rode hell-bent toward the one person she knew would be there for her no matter what. She needed him, and she needed him now more than ever.

CHAPTER 15

The man stood behind the livery stable waiting to hear from his contact the fate of the owner of the Double J. Riding up on the two men that day had been a surprise. A surprise he really hadn't expected and unfortunately, a man might have paid with his life. A man he truly admired for his business sense and fairness in dealing with people. A man he had known for some time. He really didn't know how he would be able to handle this if it was known he was involved in the shooting. What would he do if Elizabeth found out?

A shadow approached from behind the barn. "He's dead."

"Damn it! That throws a wrench in the plans. We'll need to move out quickly now instead of being able to pad our pockets with more cattle. The whole county will be out looking for us."

"Us? I didn't kill anyone."

"Just because I was one of those who pulled the trigger doesn't mean you aren't just as guilty. You were shooting at them too. Who knows which one of our bullets found their mark? If the town found out you were involved, you'll hang, too. We'll load the last of the cattle at the railhead tomorrow at noon. Get the men ready to disappear."

"Yes, of course." The shadow blended back into the night.

The other man stood there for a moment before he, too, moved into the night and disappeared.

* * * *

Elizabeth rode toward the Rocking W at breakneck speed, not caring about the danger she put herself in riding so quickly across the rugged terrain separating the Double J from the Rocking W with only moonlight to guide her. She needed him to hold her like she had never needed anything before in her life.

She quickly pulled the mare to a stop, and rocks flew from around her feet. Elizabeth jumped from her back, and with a breathless stop at the front door, she started knocking very loudly. It was late, she knew that, but she knocked anyway.

A light appeared near the front window as she continued to knock, and a small face looked through the curtain next to the door.

"Elizabeth? My goodness, girl! What are you doing here at this hour?" Donna asked after she opened the door.

"I'm sorry to be here so late, Mrs. Walker, but I need to see Jeff."

"Let me go get him. I'll be right back."

After Donna left, Elizabeth stood looking around the familiar room of the Rocking W. She had grown up coming here with her father and playing with Jeff and her brothers in the front yard while the men talked business.

Now he will never come here again.

A tear started to roll down her cheek at the memories. When Donna came back into the room, Elizabeth quickly brushed it from her cheek.

"I'm sorry Elizabeth, but he doesn't seem to be here. His room is empty, and his bed hasn't been slept in yet."

"Oh." Elizabeth muttered and bent her head. "I'm sorry I bothered you then. I guess I'll have to see him tomorrow or something."

"He didn't tell me he was leaving, so I'm not sure where he is. I'll tell him you came by though," Donna said when they walked back toward the front door.

"Thank you, ma'am. I would appreciate it if you would tell him it's important that I talked to him as soon as possible."

"Of course," Donna replied while they stepped onto the front porch.

The two women were saying their good-byes when a rider approached from the direction of town.

"Elizabeth? What are you doing here at this time of night?"

"I came looking for you."

"Really." He dismounted from his horse and tied him to the front porch.

"Well, I'll leave you two alone. I'm going back to bed." Donna she went back into the house and shut the door behind her.

Elizabeth came off the porch toward him and, without another word, wrapped her arms around his waist, laid her head on his shoulder and began to cry.

He didn't say a word as he wrapped his arms around her. He was surprised she'd sought him out since they hadn't seen each other in some time, but he knew why she cried and he felt like a total ass.

"Sshh. Everything will be all right." He stroked her hair while the tears flowed.

"You don't know what has happened," she mumbled into his shoulder. "My father is dead!" She sobbed, pulling back in his arms.

"I know, sweetheart."

"You know? How could you know? He just died a few hours ago," she said with shock in her voice.

"I heard it in town."

"But that's impossible! No one has even gone to town tonight from the ranch." She pulled farther back in his arms. "Who did you hear it from?"

"One of the hands must have left when you didn't know it. Talk is running wild in town already about it."

"I suppose. What am I going to do Jeff?" She laid her head on his shoulder again. "I miss him so much already."

"It'll be all right. He was a good man and one who will be missed terribly by everyone. You know I'll be there for you and your brothers. You know I loved your dad like he was my own." One hand moved from the crown of her head and down her back.

"I know."

They stood locked in each other's arms for a long time, each taking comfort from the others presence. After a while, Jeff released her but took her hand and led her to the barn.

Elizabeth knew she wanted him to hold her, so she didn't protest when he took her hand and headed toward the barn. She needed to feel his arms around her, protecting her from the evils of the night and the loss of her father.

After walking into the dim interior, Jeff led her to the stairs leading to the hayloft in the top. The moonlight streamed through the open loft door, bathing the entire area in silver.

He walked to the loose pile of hay that was off to the side. There was a blanket that had been left hanging over the rafter nearby, so he grabbed it and laid it out on the hay.

"Hold me."

"All night, if you want."

* * * *

The next morning found the two of them still wrapped in each other's arms lying on the hay in the loft. When the sunrise crept into the room, Elizabeth opened her eyes to see Jeff's chest under her cheek.

This is nice.

Her thoughts drifted back to the line shack and their afternoon together. When she raised her hand from his chest, he took her hand and threaded her fingers through his. She hadn't realized he was awake. Her heart skipped a beat when she tipped her head and looked into his eyes.

"I, um...I didn't know you were awake," she said, almost embarrassed at where her thoughts had wandered.

"I've been awake for a little while."

She tried to squirm out of his arms, but he held on tight. "Why didn't you wake me?" she asked, gave up trying to work her way out of his arms, and just relaxed against his side.

"You were sleeping so soundly, I didn't have the heart to. I'm sure you needed the rest. I just figured I'd wait until you woke up on your own. Besides, it was nice holding you while you slept."

When she looked into his eyes again, she thought she'd see mockery or something, but all she saw was sincere, heartfelt concern, and it scared her. She didn't want to be dealing with her feelings for him, or his lack thereof, for her right now. She knew he didn't care for her the way she wanted him to.

Distance would be a good thing at this moment. I have more pressing matters to deal with, like finding my father's killers.

"I really need to get back to the ranch. My brothers will be frantic with worry if they realize I'm gone." She got up and began attempting to straighten her hair in some semblance of order.

"You're right. Let me ride back with you though. It's not safe for you to be out by yourself."

"I suppose. We better get going." She headed toward the stairs. "I don't need a hassle from my brothers about where I spent last night."

"We'll deal with that when we get there," Jeff said, following her down the stairs and out into the morning light to retrieve their horses.

When they rode into the yard of the Double J, all three of her brothers stood next to their horses preparing to mount up and head out looking. Relief washed over their faces when they saw her ride in with Jeff.

"Where in the hell have you been? You scared us to death when we realized you were gone."

Ray stood staring at the pair when they dismounted from their horses in front of the house.

"I rode over to the Rocking W last night."

"That's obvious, Liz," John grumbled.

"Do I need to send someone after the preacher, sis?" Matt asked from behind her, picking the hay from her braid.

"Preacher? What are you talking about?" She rounded on her brother until she noticed the hay he held in his fingers and she noticed the hay still clinging to Jeff's shirt.

"It's not what you think," Elizabeth and Jeff said at the same time.

"Nothing happened," Jeff said right afterwards. "She wanted me to hold her, that's all. I swear!"

"You spent the night together, did you not?" John asked.

"Well, yes but..." Elizabeth answered, heat crawling up her cheeks in embarrassment.

John turned to his sibling. "Then it's settled. Matt, ride for the preacher."

"What? John, you can't be serious!" she shouted.

"I'm deadly serious, sister. As the man of the house now, your virtue has been compromised whether anything actually happened last night or not. You two will be married this afternoon."

"Now listen, John. As Elizabeth said, nothing happened. There is no use jumping to conclusions here. No one knows we spent the night together but the five of us. It need not go any further."

"Are you saying you won't marry my sister?"

"Not at all. I'm just saying there is no use forcing us to marry if we don't want to. Nothing against Elizabeth, but I don't want to marry her. I don't want to marry anyone right now."

"Is there a chance she could be with child?" John asked, looking from Jeff, then to Elizabeth.

"Well, uh…" Jeff said.

"Um…well…" she started to say at the same time.

"Matt, go on." John motioned for Matt to head out.

"Jeff, I suggest you ride back to your place and let your parents know there will be a wedding this afternoon, that is, if you want them here. But be prepared that if you don't return, I'll come after you myself," Ray stated, approaching the pair, making his presence known for the first time.

"Ray, come on. Help me out here," Jeff said.

"Help you? Are you kidding me?" Ray scoffed. "Liz, you better head into the house and let Mother know what's going on."

"I can't believe you! All of you! This is my life, and I'm not marrying him!" she yelled, pointing to Jeff, and then turned on her heel to retreat to the house. "And you can't make me."

"What is all that shouting?" her mother asked coming out of the guest room down the hall.

"Elizabeth, you really don't have a choice in this matter," John said, trailing behind her.

"Yes I do, and I'm not marrying Jeff."

"Marrying who? What's this all about?" her mother asked again, looking from her to John and back while they continued to argue.

"I'm sorry. This really isn't the best time to be bringing this up, but there is going to be a wedding this afternoon between your daughter and Jeff Walker."

"What? How did this come about? Elizabeth? John?" She looked between the two. Michelle came out of Elizabeth's room with a worried look on her face.

"I don't really want to go into details at the moment, Mother. Let's just say it needs to happen, and it needs to happen today."

"John, this is ridiculous. You need to give me more details if I'm to marry off my only daughter on such short notice." Her mother looked at her, demanding an answer. "Elizabeth? Would you care to explain?"

"Mother, nothing happened. I was upset last night because of Father, and I went over to the Rocking W. I spent the night there. That's all."

"That's all?" Margaret asked, eyeing John.

"No, that's not all and you know it, Elizabeth. Mother, she spent the night with Jeff."

"You spent the night with Jeff?" her mother repeated. "Elizabeth Caroline!"

"It's not what you think."

"Then what is it?" her mother asked with a raised eyebrow.

"I...well...I...uh..." Elizabeth stammered. "Mother, can we discuss this in private please?"

Her mother looked at her a moment, then said, "Of course." She turned and headed into her father's study.

It had always been a place of comfort for Elizabeth, a place to feel the presence of her father in this room, but today, it just felt cold and empty without him here.

"All right, so what happened?" her mother asked after she had shut the door to give them some privacy.

"I needed to talk to someone, and I found myself heading over there. When I got there, he wasn't even home. I talked to his mother for a short time, and when I was getting ready to leave, he rode up. I was upset and started crying. He just held me in his arms and the next thing I knew, we were up in the barn hayloft, but nothing happened. I swear! He lay down with me in the hay and just held me while I slept."

"From what you've told me, there seems to be something going on between you two. A man wouldn't just feel contented holding a woman he wasn't very comfortable with. No matter the fact that nothing happened between you, you spent the night with him. Has anything happened like this before between you?"

Elizabeth looked at her mother, and knowing she couldn't lie to her, she whispered, "Yes."

"Then I'm sorry, but your brother is right. You need to protect your reputation, and if word got out that you had compromised yourself in such a manner, you would never be able to find a suitable husband. The marriage will proceed, and I hope you and Jeff can move past this rocky start and make a life together." Her mother wrapped her arms around her and hugged her. "Now, we need to find you something beautiful to wear. You are getting married after all."

"Mother, please! This isn't fair!"

I know, sweetheart, but I have to ask myself, what your father would do if he knew of this, and I think the answer is the same. You will marry Jeff this afternoon."

* * * *

Later that afternoon, Jeff returned with his parents in tow. He rode his horse back to the Double J and his parents' rode in the wagon. He wasn't quite sure what to make of his mother's lack of surprise that her son was being forced into marriage.

A shotgun wedding at that!

She didn't even bat an eyelash when he had told them he wanted them to come with him because he was marrying Elizabeth this afternoon. Of course, the thought really didn't bother him very much. He knew he cared for her and enjoyed bedding her, but marriage? Well, he didn't have much choice in the matter now, unless he wanted his head blown off by her brothers. Besides, he could see himself enjoying making love to her each and every night for the rest of their lives.

With a quirk of his lips, he rode into the ranch yard with his parents behind him. The yard was decorated with all kinds of flowers, and some kind of lace now hung on the porch railing. A quickly assembled trellis had been placed near the fountain in the garden, the same fountain he had first kissed Elizabeth at so long ago, or was it? It seemed like it had been forever ago, but in reality, it had only been a few short months.

"I'm glad you decided to return," Ray said when Jeff dismounted.

"I didn't think I had much of a choice in the matter."

"You're right, you didn't."

John and Matt stopped next the wagon as it came into the yard.

"Good afternoon, Mr. and Mrs. Walker. It's so nice to see you again."

"Good day, John," Mrs. Walker said when he helped her down. "I'm so sorry about your father. He was such a good man and will be greatly missed. When will the services be?"

"I'm not sure, ma'am. Probably tomorrow since we are having the wedding today."

"And everything looks so beautiful. I'm sure your father would be proud." She touched his arm in condolences. "Now, where is your mother so I can chat with her?"

"She's in the house, ma'am. Go right in."

"Thank you."

* * * *

"I'm not doing this, Mother. I don't want to marry Jeff." Elizabeth protested with everything she had when her mother bullied her into the beautiful white gown that fit her like a glove. It was one of the dresses they had sent to her while she was away at school, but she had never found a reason to wear it until today.

"Yes you are, Elizabeth, and I'll hear no more about it."

Her mother forced her to step into the several petticoats that went with the dress in order for it not to drag the floor. The dress was pure white with small red flowers scattered throughout the full skirt. The neckline was square but swept across her full bosom with a small ruffle that only accentuated what was held inside, while the waistline hugged her full curves.

"Is there a problem?" Donna asked when she poked her head into the room. "What's this about not marrying my son?"

"I'm sorry, Mrs. Walker, but neither of us really wants this. My brothers are forcing us to marry."

"And why would they do that, my dear?" Donna replied.

"Well, after you went back to bed last night, Jeff and I spent the night in the barn together."

"Oh, I see!" Surprise widened Donna's eyes.

"No! Nothing happened, really!"

"Even if nothing happened, my dear, your reputation needs to be upheld, and if word got around, it could be devastating to you," Donna said with an understanding look in Elizabeth's direction. "Unfortunately, I agree with your mother and your brothers."

"I don't believe this!" Elizabeth yelled and flung her arms in the air. "Michelle? Help me."

"I agree with them, Liz. You need to do this whether you really want to or not," Michelle said coming to her side. "May I speak to her alone for a moment, ladies?"

"Yes, yes of course. Donna? Would you care to join me in the kitchen to check on the food?" Margaret asked, retreating to the door. "We'll be back in a moment."

When the door closed behind them Michelle said, "Elizabeth, I know you are saying you really don't want this marriage between you and Jeff, but let's be truthful here for a moment. I know you care for him as more than just a friend. This will give you the opportunity to have what you really want, which is to be with him for the rest of your life, isn't it? Correct me if I'm wrong."

Elizabeth stood staring at her friend for a moment before lowering her eyes and nodding. "I just never wanted it to be this way. What kind of a marriage can we have, Michelle, if he doesn't really want to be married to me and doesn't love me?"

"Love can grow in time. You may have to be patient. Now, shall we finish getting you really to meet your new husband?"

"Husband? I'm not so sure about this," Elizabeth said, sitting down at the mirror.

"Everything will be fine. You'll see." Michelle piled the long chestnut curls on top of Elizabeth's head and pinned them into place.

Her mother and Donna returned a few minutes later.

"You look beautiful sweetheart. Your father would be so proud of you. Now, it's time."

When they all walked into the living area of the house, Elizabeth felt a sense of panic overwhelm her.

I can't go through with this. I can't do this!

Donna opened the door, and when the bright sunshine streamed in, it blinded Elizabeth for a moment before her mother ushered her outside.

The two older women moved off to join the families, and Elizabeth stepped to the edge of the porch to be met by her brother John. He would be giving her away this day since her father wasn't able to be there.

Thoughts of her father raced through her mind, and a small tear rolled down her cheek. She lifted her eyes to the blue sky above and said a little prayer that she hoped he could hear. She asked for his guidance in what she should do and in her ear she heard his voice, "Follow your heart."

With what she felt was her father's blessing, she faced this new challenge with all the pride and stubbornness her father had instilled in her.

CHAPTER 16

John took her hand and looped it through the crook of his arm. "Are you ready, sis?"

"Yes," she whispered, before they slowly walked toward the garden where the new trellis stood with the preacher and her soon-to-be husband waiting.

Elizabeth lifted her gaze to meet Jeff's across the expanse of space separating them and when she did, she was surprised to see a smile on his lips.

I didn't think he wanted this marriage, but he sure doesn't seem to be too upset about it.

John took her hand, kissed her on the cheek and then placed her palm in Jeff's outstretched one.

"Don't you dare hurt her," John said.

Jeff nodded knowingly and John stepped back, leaving Elizabeth standing at his side.

"Who give this woman to this man to be married this day?" the preacher asked.

"Her father and I do." her mother replied and she looked heavenward.

"Then we shall begin." the preacher said.

Elizabeth and Jeff stood side by side, and while the preacher droned on with the vows and prayers, Elizabeth's mind wandered to the time ahead. Soon they would be man and wife, and then what? Her minded clouded with feelings. She just couldn't quite fathom in her heart how she would be able to live with this man for the rest of her life.

Elizabeth hardly heard a word said, but she apparently said I do in the appropriate places because before she knew it, Jeff bent his head and softly kissed her on the lips.

Quickly, they were surrounding by her family and his with the congratulations being said all around, lots of hugs and kisses as well as slaps on the back for Jeff.

"Shall we eat?" Ray suggested before he started toward the house. "I'm starving."

"Aren't you always, little brother?" Matt said with a huge smile and hardy slap on the back.

Everyone in the family had made their way inside while Elizabeth and Jeff continued to stand in the garden facing each other with that now-what look on their faces.

"Care to join me, Mrs. Walker? I don't believe your brothers are waiting for the bride and groom to start eating," Jeff said with a sweeping bow and a sexy smile.

Without waiting for her reply, he took her hand, slipped it into the crook of his arm, and escorted her into the house and to their waiting families.

The families ate and celebrated with tons of merriment and lots of whiskey for the men. Elizabeth quietly stood off to herself.

Mrs. Walker. I'm now Mrs. Jeffery Walker. How did this happen? Where on earth did I lose complete control of my life?

Her father had died just yesterday and now she was married to a man she'd known all her life but really didn't know? She would be expected to cook his meals, take care of his home, and bear his children, and the thought scared the hell out of her.

"Elizabeth?" he said softly, bringing her out of her musings. "Are you all right? You have the look of a scared doe in your eyes."

"What? Oh, I'm sorry. I was just thinking."

"Thinking about what?" One arm leaned against the mantle near her shoulder.

"Oh, nothing. Are you having a good time?" She tried to draw his attention away from what she hoped didn't look like terror on her face.

"I suppose. Your brothers are already half drunk and having a good enough time for all of us, I think. If you are ready to leave..."

"*No!*" she said, startled at her own vehement reply to his unfinished statement. "I mean, not just yet. The party has really only just started, and we'll be all sad tomorrow since we'll have to say good-bye to my father. We should stay a little longer."

"Sure, sweetheart. Anything you want is fine with me. We'll leave when you're ready."

For the next two hours, she gave him every excuse she could think of not to leave. They hadn't cut the cake yet. She hadn't packed yet.

He'd obviously had enough of her stalling tactics when he said, "Elizabeth, it's time to go."

Her trunk sat at her feet and she couldn't think of another excuse.

"No, we can't leave yet—"

"Yes, we can and we are."

"But...."

"It's time to go. We just need to load your trunk into the wagon and we're gone. Say your good-byes until tomorrow." He hefted her trunk onto his broad shoulder and, expecting her to follow, led the way outside.

When she balked at his insistence they leave, her mother said, "Go on, Elizabeth. It's time for you to be with your husband now. We will all see you tomorrow in town."

Elizabeth opened her mouth to protest but closed it again when she saw the look in her mother's eyes. The look that said, "I'm proud of you." With a quick nod, she turned her back on her mother and obediently followed her husband to the waiting buggy.

Jeff loaded her trunk on the back, and then came around to help her up. He took her hand in his and guided her into the buggy. For a moment, their eyes locked and she could see the strongly leashed desire in his eyes as well as feel the electricity raging between them. During that moment, the world slipped away and it was only the two of them locked in a storm holding them spellbound. The horse whinnying and jerking against the rigging of the buggy broke the spell. Elizabeth quickly stepped in, which caused Jeff to let go of her hand. Arranging her skirts around her, kept her hands busy while Jeff came around the other side, jumped in, and grabbed the reins.

"Ready?"

"As ready as I'll ever be I guess," she replied, tightly folding her hands in her lap.

After flicking the reins over the rump of the horse, Jeff expertly turned the buggy around in the yard and headed for town with their families waving and saying good-bye in the background. Elizabeth sat up on her knees and waved vigorously to her family as they disappeared from sight. When she couldn't see them anymore, she turned back around and sat down heavily on the seat.

"Where are we going? This isn't the way to your parents' ranch. This is the way to town."

"You're right. We are headed to town." He kept his eyes on the road in front of them.

"But why?"

She looked at him for what seemed like the first time and noticed how snugly his shirt fit across his broad chest, how strong his hands were holding the reins with expert precision, how the hair curled against the collar of his shirt making her wish she could runs her fingers through them just once to see if they were as soft as they appeared.

"I've made arrangements for us to spend tonight at the hotel in town. I thought it might be nice to not spend our wedding night at my parents' place." He gave her a sideways glance. "You know, you look mighty pretty today."

"Thank you. Since I didn't have time to have anything made for a wedding, I had to wear something I already had. You look pretty handsome yourself, you know. I don't think I've seen you all dressed up that way since the night of the spring dance when you ended up in the water trough," she said with a devilish grin, remembering how he had looked standing in the middle of the road after she pushed him in. He had been very handsome that day, too, but today, it was almost a sin how good he looked.

"I wouldn't have been in the water trough if you hadn't pushed me in there, you little minx." He shot her that oh-so-sexy grin again that made her heart stop. "It was your fault I ruined one of my best set of dress clothes. My mother was not happy when she saw them."

"My fault? How do you figure?"

"You pushed me in there," he said, teasing her.

"Well, if you hadn't been back there slobbering all over Aubrey, I wouldn't have pushed you in," she replied with indignation, turned back around on the seat, and folded her arms over her chest.

"Slobbering? I don't call kissing her slobbering, and I doubt she would either."

"I really don't care what she would call it. For that matter, I don't care what you would call it either. It was just disgusting, that's all."

"Not jealous, are you?"

"Me? Jealous? Of course not. Besides, I was only sixteen at the time. I couldn't care less how many women you've bedded in your lifetime including Aubrey." She turned back around as they approached the outskirts of town.

He pulled the buggy to a halt in the middle of the road, turned to her, took her chin in his big hand. "You are the only one who counts."

Then he kissed her full on the mouth, parting her soft lips with the tip of his tongue making her melt against him. When he finally released her, she almost couldn't sit up anymore. She leaned against him and he put his arm around her shoulders and started the buggy rolling again with the other hand.

* * * *

The lone man stood on the porch of the hotel smoking a cigar while the heat of the night surrounded him.

God I hate this place. I need to get my business taken care of quickly, so I can get the hell out of here and back to civilization. The backwards town will be the death of me.

Moments later, he noticed a buggy rolling into town with what appeared to be two people snuggled on the seat. They didn't appear to see him standing there when they stopped at the livery to leave the buggy for the night. He stepped off the front porch of the hotel, curious about who had just rolled in. The buggy looked familiar to him, and he wanted to find out who was in it. He stayed in the shadows so he wouldn't be seen by the pair while they walked arm and arm toward the hotel, the man carrying a trunk on his shoulder. They passed not far from his hiding place, and when he realized who it was, his eyes narrowed when rage whipped through him.

The pair moved into the front lobby of the hotel and stopped at the desk to register while he watched from outside the window.

What the hell is Elizabeth doing here with him?

They took the key to their room and start up the stairs. After they were out of sight, Gregory approached the front desk. The clerk left the desk for a second, giving him time to flip the register around so he could see the signature of who had just registered at the hotel.

Mr. and Mrs. Jeffery Walker.

The rage filling him was all consuming, and he was almost surprised at the intensity.

How dare she give herself to that cowboy. She's mine and mine alone.

* * * *

When they reached the door to their room and Jeff unlocked it, Elizabeth started into the room ahead of him, but he stopped her with a hand on her arm. She turned with a puzzled look until he set the trunk on the floor, swept her up in his arms, carried her over the threshold, and gently placed her on the floor. With a quick kiss to her mouth, he returned for the trunk.

The lamps flared to life, filling the room with light.

Her eyes got bigger and bigger when she looked around and noticed all the beautiful flowers placed everywhere.

He stopped behind her, slipped his hands around her waist, and whispered, "Do you like it?"

"It's beautiful. I can't believe you did this for me. How?"

"It doesn't matter. I just wanted you to have something special to remember today by." He seated her on the bed, sat next to her, and took her hand in his. "I know marrying me wasn't probably what you had in mind when you thought about getting hitched eventually, and how this all came about wasn't the most romantic thing, but I didn't want today to be all bad."

"Thank you for this. It means a lot," she said a bit shyly.

"Elizabeth," he whispered. He slid his hand along her neck and into her hair, held her head at the nape, and slowly dipped his head to take her soft lips with his.

God I love how her mouth tastes, how soft her hair is when it wraps itself around my hand like a living breathing entity.

The pins holding her hair in place fell to the floor and scattered on the bed around them. He needed her with everything in his soul. His body cried out for release, but he held himself in check.

This night was for her.

He continued his play on her mouth with nibbles to her lips. Fire burned out of control between them with each passing touch, each lingering kiss.

A small whimper left her mouth when he finally pulled away. The heat raging a battle within her reflected bright in her eyes. Her passion was so alive, it had become visible in the glow of the lamps and it took his breath away. This girl, this woman who was now his wife, appeared to want him as much as he wanted her. She completely amazed him at every turn these days from her daring escapades to the way she had made love with him before, recklessly in the line shack without worry or care in the world. How could he have not seen this beautiful woman who had been one of his best friends his entire life, as more than just a friend.

She's the perfect partner for me.

Accepting the gift of her body, he finally took her mouth with his with all the pent up passion inside, and laid her back on the soft bed beneath them.

When he lifted his mouth from hers, her hands wandered up his chest to the buttons on the front and began to unfasten each one, slowly, to reveal the soft chest hair beneath. The tails of his shirt gave to her insistent tugging. Fingers entwined in the hair as she ran her hands up and encircled his neck before she pulled his mouth back to hers. He worked the buttons of her dress loose in order to reach inside.

One hand cupped her breast through her chemise. Her nipple stood taut against his palm, begging for his touch.

A small smile lifted the corners of his mouth when she bowed her back, pushing the round flesh further into his hand. Her eyes close with her passion. Joy lifted his heart while he watched her body come to life beneath him. Her innocence made him want her even more, but this need to give her pleasure engulfed him, and his own passion to almost spiral out of control. He kissed her neck, sliding his lips over the soft skin before he moved toward the enticing bud waiting for his mouth. A nudge against the material and the rosy tip came into view.

Squeezing his eyes shut, he fought for control.

"Jeff, please."

The tip of his tongue flicked against the hard flesh.

"Tell me."

"I need…" She started but couldn't finish. "I want…"

"What do you need, sweetheart? Tell me," he murmured against her eyelids, kissing her there, and then moved down her face, kissing her nose and cheeks. "Tell me what you want."

"Make love to me please," she whispered, almost embarrassed by her need.

"My pleasure, sweet wife." He removed his weight in order to continue to divest her of the rest of her clothing and his own.

When he stood to finish removing his pants, she didn't turn her gaze away.

He crawled back onto the bed, moved over her, grazing her skin with his, setting them both ablaze with need.

Lips, teeth and tongue, licked, sucked and nipped at each piece of skin he touched. He kissed her everywhere, her thighs, her soft belly, each breast in turn. When he finally settled on her mouth again, she whimpered beneath him

"Please."

Placing his hands next to her shoulders he lifted his chest and centered between her legs. The tip of his manhood pressed firmly against her nest of curls. The tongues danced an age-old rhythm as he pushed into her wet heat. Holding himself in check, he waited for her to accept his full length, but when she started to wiggle beneath him, he almost lost all control.

"Elizabeth, please. Hold still a minute, sweetheart, or this will be a really short ride," he growled low in his throat.

"I'm sorry. Did I do something wrong?"

The fear and sadness in her eyes tore at his heart.

"No." He groaned. "Just give me a minute."

Heat licked at his balls, tightening them to painful proportions against his body. With a slow glide, he began to move and she lifted her hips to meet each thrust. Slender legs wrapped around him and brought him closer to the ultimate fulfillment waiting just beyond the peak.

Breaths grew faster and faster, hers panting in his ear. Her sex quivered, drawing the last of his control away when she cried out in climax, taking him over the edge with her.

CHAPTER 17

Gregory stood outside of the room he had seen the couple walk into—no, that Jeff carried her into—listening at the door. He heard the rumblings of voices, but couldn't hear what was being said as he pressed his ear to the wooden panel, trying to hear. Frustration grew when he couldn't make out what they were saying. A short time later, he heard nothing but silence.

"Damn it! Damn it to hell!" He whirled on his heel and headed back down the hall to the stairs. He stopped momentarily, looked back at the door, and then punched the wall near him. The impact caused an old portrait to fall. Without a backward glance, he continued down the stairs, taking them two at a time.

I need to find out what's going on and I need to know now!

Almost running out the front door of the hotel, he headed directly for the livery to retrieve his horse and ran smack into Aubrey on the boardwalk.

"Gregory! Lord! You almost ran me over. What is your hurry anyway?" she asked when he grasped her shoulders to steady her.

"Aubrey," he said, realizing whom he was holding onto. "I'm sorry my dear. I didn't mean to run into you. I just didn't see you."

"That's obvious. What's gotten into you?"

"Aubrey? Yes, Aubrey. Have you heard anything about Elizabeth and your cowboy?" he asked hurriedly, pushing his fingers through his hair.

"What do you mean?"

"Have you heard anything about them being together? Or married?"

"Married? Are you serious? Of course not! They can't be married! Married? What on earth gave you that idea?" Her own tone rose is agitation.

"They just signed in at the hotel under Mr. and Mrs. Jeffery Walker. That's where I got the idea."

"Oh my. This can't be true. He's mine. Mine!" she yelled. "He couldn't have betrayed me like this."

"I'm not sure what's going on, but I intend to find out." He continued on his trek to the livery for his horse with Aubrey following close behind.

"What are you going to do?"

"I'm going to ride out to the Double J and find out, that's how."

"Now? It's pitch-black out there. You'll get yourself killed trying to ride out there. Besides, you don't even know how to saddle that horse."

"What else do you suggest then?" He pulled the saddle off the horse's back and flung it across the stable in his rage.

"Let me see. I need to think about this a minute." She started to pace. "I know. How about if I go by the preacher's house and casually ask him? I could feign some kind of need this evening to talk to him, and he wouldn't be the wiser."

"Yes. Yes, that might just work."

"Of course it will work. I grew up in this town, don't forget. Everyone here knows the preacher and uses him to confess their woes and sins. It won't be unusual at all for me to go to his home and talk with him for a few minutes." She started off in the direction of the church. The preacher's house stood behind the building, obscuring it from view of the boardwalk. "I'll be back in say thirty minutes."

"All right. I'll wait at the hotel."

About twenty minutes later, Gregory stood on the porch of the hotel waiting for Aubrey when Jeff and Elizabeth came out the front door.

They didn't see him at first after they walked out the door with their arms around each other like two lovebirds until he asked, "Liz? Is that you?"

"Gregory. What a surprise."

"Yes, well, I am still staying here. What brings you into town?" He ignored Jeff altogether and the fact that he stood there with his arm around Elizabeth's shoulders.

"I, uh..."

"We were married today, so we are here for our wedding night. Now if you'll excuse us."

"Married? My goodness. I didn't even know you were seeing him," Gregory said, not looking at Jeff but drilling Elizabeth with his gaze.

"Well, it's a long story and one I'm sure you don't really care to hear. Let's just say that yes, we're married and leave it at that, shall we?"

"All right then. I guess congratulations are in order. I'm sure you'll be very happy." He stepped forward and kissed her on the cheek.

"Yes well. We should be going now. I'm sure we'll see you sometime again," Jeff added.

Gregory's eyes narrowed and watched the pair disappear into the night. Aubrey came up behind him and, out of breath. "I know what's going on."

"I do too," he said, not looking at her. "They were married today, although I'm not sure why."

"What? How did you find out?" she asked, standing next to him holding her side.

"I just ran into them as they came out of the hotel a moment ago."

"You did? What did they say?"

"What I just told you. They were married today."

"The preacher said he married them, and that it was a hurried wedding. Something about them spending the night before together. I can't believe he would do this to me!"

Gregory didn't answer, but he heard every word she said.

They had spent the night before together, had they? Well, obviously she is soiled now. Not worthy of his family name but that doesn't mean I don't desire her still. A smile spread across his lips when a plan began to form in his mind.

"What are you smiling about?" Aubrey asked when she saw the look on his face. "This isn't the least bit funny, you know. Now what are we going to do?"

"I have something in mind, don't you worry. Right now, we need to just let things be as they are." Gregory turned back to the woman standing next to him. "Shall we see how we can keep ourselves entertained until then?"

"Well, I'm sure we can think of something."

"I thought you might see it my way." He slipped his arm around her shoulders and ushered her into the hotel lobby. "I'm sure I can keep you busy for a few hours anyway."

"I'm sure you can." She followed him up the stairs to his room.

* * * *

Jeff and Elizabeth returned a short time later, thankful that Gregory wasn't still hanging around the front of the hotel. The run-in with him had definitely soured the mood between them while they had sat at the café eating pie.

"I really don't know what you saw in that easterner, Elizabeth," Jeff said as they walked in the moonlight.

"I really didn't like him all the well. I knew him when I went to school, and he had made his intensions known even then, but I had never thought he would come out here and stay so long, my goodness! I really didn't seriously consider him as husband material." She snuggled up next to Jeff with a small smile. This marriage thing might work out after all.

"You didn't, huh?"

"No, I didn't, but then again, when I found out Father was having such trouble with the finances of the ranch, I had considered it. I mean his family is rather wealthy."

"You would have considered marrying him to save your family's place?"

"Well yes, of course," she said, surprised that he even asked. "Why wouldn't I if it meant keeping my family safe? I would do anything for them."

"Even marrying someone you didn't love?"

"Yes, even marrying someone I didn't love. Why do you seem so surprised?"

"I don't know. I just never really thought you'd marry him, I guess, when your brothers told me he was here to see you after he first got here," he replied when they began walking again.

"I really didn't want to, but for a while, I thought I might have to. I'm glad that decision has been taken out of my hands though."

"Are you? Are you really?" The worried expression on his face, made her wonder.

"Yes, I am." Up on her tip-toes, she pressed a quick kiss to his lips and asked, "Now, shall we return to our room, Mr. Walker?"

"It would be my pleasure, Mrs. Walker," he answered with a smile and he opened the door for her. "Shall we?"

The next day found them completely exhausted from the night before, but it was a very sobering morning. They would bury her father today. When she opened her eyes to find herself snuggled next to Jeff in the big bed in their room at the hotel, she smiled to herself thinking about how they had made love most of the night before they'd finally fallen into an exhausted sleep. After a moment the smile left her face and sadness returned.

"What's wrong, sweetheart?"

"I was almost able to forget what today meant," she said, when a lone tear rolled down her cheek.

"I know. I'm sorry. I know today will be very difficult for you." He kissed the top of her head where it rested on his shoulder.

"I'm sure it will be fine. I just am going to have a hard time accepting he's gone."

"I won't say I know how you're feeling because I obviously don't, but know this; I'll be here for you from now on."

"Thank you. That means the world to me." She smiled and then kissed his chest in butterfly kisses that had him completely aroused again.

"All right, little wife. We'll have none of that now. We have things to do, so we need to get up and get moving."

"Already? I thought we could just stay here for a little while longer. I mean I learned so much last night that I wanted to try out. I thought for sure you'd be a willing participant." She chuckled and continued to rain small kisses along his chest when she noticed his manhood had come to life beneath the sheet.

"You little minx! I think I've created a monster!" He laughed at the twinkle in her eyes while she ran her hands and lips all over his skin. "Oh, Lord," he said with a groan that rattled deep inside, before he lifted her up off his chest, flipped her onto her back, and began to rain kisses all over her, too.

"Um...that's nice," she murmured, then groaned when his mouth settled on her breast.

* * * *

Sometime later that morning, her mother arrived at the hotel, and when she approached the desk and asked which room belonged to Mr. and Mrs. Walker, she was met by the laughing pair descending from upstairs.

"Mother!" Elizabeth raced out of Jeff's arms and ran into her mother's embrace.

"Lizzie! You look radiant, sweetheart. Marriage must agree with you."

"I can't complain," Elizabeth said with a smile at her new husband.

"I was just coming to find you to let you know the services will be in the church at about one o'clock. The preacher has already made the arrangements, and I've already been to the undertaker's."

"Oh." Elizabeth muttered, sobering with the thought of burying her father soon.

"We'll be there, Mrs. Johnston," Jeff said, putting his arm around Elizabeth to comfort her.

"Mother. Please call me Mother, Jeff. You are one of my children now."

"Of course. Whatever you wish, but it might take me some time to get used to that."

"That's all right. I'm sure whenever you are comfortable is fine." Margaret smiled. "I must go and make sure everything is ready. I'll see you two after while."

Elizabeth watched her mother walk away and then turned to Jeff when he pulled to his side. "I don't know how she can be so strong."

"She probably feels she has to be for you and your brothers. She's the matriarch now."

"I know, but I never imagine my parents not together. This all just doesn't seem real." She gathered her strength. "Something needs to be done about the murder of my father. I can't just let it rest."

"Elizabeth, I know you are upset about this, but you need to leave this to the law, sweetheart. The sheriff will take care of it, I'm sure."

"We'll see," she growled as she narrowed her eyes searching the streets around her. Someone in this town or surrounding area murdered her father, and she would die before she let him or her get away with it.

* * * *

Jeff watched when the entire town filled the church for the funeral of John Johnston. John was almost like a founder of this town and had been very well liked, so the news of his death spread like wildfire on a hot summer day.

The preacher went on about John and how he had made a successful business of his ranch and how he had raised four beautiful, loving children along with his wife of many years. Each of the children got up and said a few words of their own in remembrance of their father, of how they would miss him, and of how he had enriched their lives with his presence and spirit.

When Margaret got up to say a few words, complete silence filled the church. "My loving husband. How on earth will I go on without you? You've been my soul mate, my confidant and lover for so many years now. We've raised our children together to be strong, faithful and loving, but now I must go on without you in this life and I'm not sure I can. My soul is lost without your guidance and love with me, but I can feel you here, even now and I know that some day we will be together again. Until then my love, I must say good-bye."

A pin being dropped would have been heard when she stepped down from the podium near her husband's casket. There were silent tears shed by many a member of the church, but Margaret held herself with dignity and grace. She would shed her tears in private later. Today, she needed to be strong for her children.

The congregation moved to the cemetery, and the boys carried John's casket to the graveyard in preparation for burial. The preacher said a few more words when they lowered him into the ground, and Elizabeth cried as she stood near her mother.

Jeff stood on Elizabeth's other side, and when he pulled her to him, she buried her face in his shoulder.

She'll need me more than ever now.

He kind of liked the thought of her needing him. It felt really nice for her to want to be with him like this. He never thought he would want someone clinging to him as she was doing now in her grief, but the thought of her heart breaking sliced through him like a razor, and he didn't like it at all.

All this because of a few damned cows!

* * * *

After the services were over, the family made its way home to the ranch with many of the mourners following them. There would be a feast this afternoon to honor the head of the Double J, and families from many miles away would be welcome in their home. Carmen had already been cooking since dawn in preparation for this.

John would want it this way. He would want everyone to have a good time and celebrate his life and the marriage of his daughter. Although most of the people here didn't know about that yet, they soon would.

"Folks. Can I have your attention please?" The crowd turned expectant eyes toward her. "Thank you all for coming today. I know you all will miss John and his kindness, but this is also a bit of a celebration, too. Not just for John but for our daughter Elizabeth." She waved her hand. "Elizabeth, Jeff, can you come here please." When the two made their way up near her and stood next to her, she continued, "We also hope you all will help us this afternoon to celebrate the marriage of our beautiful daughter to the son of our best friends. They were married yesterday here in the garden of our home, and we hope they will have a marriage as long and loving as ours has been. Be happy you two."

Elizabeth hugged her as the tears started down her cheeks, and many congratulations were hollered from the crowd.

"I love you, Momma," Elizabeth said in her mother's ear.

"I love you too, sweetheart."

The newlyweds were swallowed up in the crowd as many of the town's people came to congratulate them on their marriage with hugs for Elizabeth and handshakes for Jeff.

* * * *

With a gentle push, Jeff managed to get her away from the crowd and into the house for a few moments.

"Are you all right, sweetheart? It's been a pretty crazy couple of days, maybe you should lie down?"

"Lie down? You're not serious?" she asked, a little exasperated when he all of the sudden wanted to coddle her. "I'm fine, and I hope you don't start getting all maternal on me. I'm not a helpless female who you need to take care of. If we are to make this work between us, we need to get one thing straight. I'm a complete partner in this, and that means everything. I will not be sent off to the house to cook, clean, and raise babies while you are out working all the time. Understand?"

"There isn't anything for you to get all fired up about. I didn't mean anything by it, really. I know the funeral and burial were hard on you because you were really close to your father, that's all. And as far as a partner in this, I'm sure you are, but you will be the one responsible for the house and such, you know. If you want to help outside, then so be it. I won't stop you."

"Good. I wanted to make sure you understood." She started for the door again. "Now, there is a party out there and part of that is a celebration for us, so I intend to enjoy it."

"Of course, little wife, but one thing first." He grasped her hand before she could slip away, and he pulled her into his arms. His mouth swooped down on hers in a fiery kiss that left her panting against him. "Just remember whose bed you'll be going home to."

When they returned to the yard, she knew her cheeks had to be red and her lips more swollen. Several matrons twittered around them, their voices loud enough, she knew everyone heard.

"I am completely surprised at this marriage. I wonder if she's with child," Martha Ollinger said to her neighbor. "I mean really. This was awfully sudden."

"I know, but I've always said those two should be together. I think it's perfect."

"Well, we shall see in a few months, won't we?" Martha added.

"Oh stop it, Martha! Leave those two alone will you? It wouldn't be the first hurried marriage around these parts and I'm sure it won't be the last."

The party began to wind town about dusk as people started to head for home before it got too dark on the road back to town. Friends and neighbors helped her mother and her with the cleanup. After everything was inside, they said their good-byes and "I'm sorry's" to her mother and left the family alone.

"We should be getting back to my parents' place," Jeff said, when darkness began to descend on the ranch.

"Your parents' place? I didn't realize we were going there."

"Where else would we go? Your parents' ranch is already full with your brothers and your friend here. My parents' place is not as big, but I do not have to share my room except with you."

"Yes, well. I suppose you're right." She turned to her mother to say her good-byes. "Mother, we should be going too. We will be staying at the Rocking W until we figure out what we are doing from here, I guess."

"Of course, sweetheart. You should be with your husband, and there is more room over there. You two be careful going home." Her mother kissed Elizabeth's cheek and hugged her before she did the same with Jeff.

"Thank you for the party, Mrs. Johnston. It was very nice of you to include our marriage in your celebration."

"Mother," she corrected. "Of course I would include you. Even if it wasn't the best of circumstances, we should still celebrate your marriage. It is still something to celebrate. Now, you two go on."

They walked outside to retrieve the buggy they had brought from town.

"How long do you think we'll have to live with your parents?" Elizabeth asked while they bounced along in the buggy.

"I'm not sure. I have some things that I've been working on that have given me some money in the bank. Not a lot, but some. It's funny, you know. We've never really talked about what my dreams are and what yours are. I guess we should do that if we are to spend the rest of our lives together," he said was a soft smile in her direction.

"Yes, I guess we should at that."

Spend the rest of our lives together. I hadn't really thought of it like that but I guess he's right. Marriage is forever no matter how it started and maybe someday, he will fall in love with me.

CHAPTER 18

The coming days found things settling down in both households. She and Jeff settled into a routine around the Rocking W, with him working with his father, managing the cattle, and spending his extra time working with the wild Mustangs he seemed to bring in daily. He often disappeared for a few days at a time, without really any explanation to his whereabouts to her. He would just say, "It's for our future. Nothing you need to worry about. Just trust me."

The nights were spent cuddled together in what had become their room, in the big bed that seemed to dominate the entire space.

Many nights, he would fall into exhausted sleep after coming in late into the night. Elizabeth didn't quite understand his burning desire to train these horses, and sometimes, from the house, she would watch him softly running his hands over their coat, coaxing their compliance with his whispers. He seemed to have a way with them that allowed them to keep their spirit while he gained their compliance with his training.

Michelle would often ride over for visits during the day, and they would talk about what she would do now. She really loved Texas, and she was beginning to care deeply for Elizabeth's brother.

"I need to go home," Michelle said one afternoon while they sipped lemonade on the porch at the Double J. "I've been here for quite some time, and it's probably time, but I really don't want to.

"What about John?"

"I don't know, Liz. I thought he cared about me and all, but he's never said anything. I just don't know if there is anything there beyond what my heart desires. He's never even tried to kiss me."

"Well, I'll just have to have a talk with him then," Elizabeth said getting up from her place to seek out her oldest brother.

"No! Don't you dare!" Michelle squealed. "I would be too embarrassed."

"You want to know, don't you?"

"Of course but..."

"Then I shall ask him. Wait right here."

Elizabeth started for the barn where her brother worked on repairing some of the stalls. She walked into the dimly light interior, waited for a moment so that her eyes could adjust to the darkness, and then saw him nailing some railing in place in the corner.

"John, I need to speak to you."

"Hello to you too, little sister." John smiled and kissed to her cheek.

"Sorry. I didn't mean to be curt, but I need to ask you something."

"What would that be? Having trouble with your husband, are you?"

"No. Things are just fine there, thank you," she said a little whimsically, thinking about their previous night of lovemaking.

"Ah! So what else can I do for you?"

"What are your intentions with Michelle?" She narrowed her eyes. "I mean, do you intend to have a relationship with her or not?"

"Are you serious?"

"Of course I'm serious. You have played with my friend's feelings long enough, big brother. She will be going home soon so I want to find out what your intentions are before she does or are you going to let her walk out of your life?"

Running his fingers through his hair and giving her a sheepish grin, "I'm not sure what to say. I mean, I care for her, I care for her a lot, but..."

"But what? If you love her, then you need to make those feelings known, otherwise she intends to return home next week."

The little white lie wouldn't hurt anything. John needs a bit of a push in the right direction. I think the two of them would be fantastic together, but he's not the forward type.

"She does? I mean, she is?" he asked with a worried expression furrowing his brow.

"Yes she is, so you better figure things out and quickly otherwise you will lose her for good."

Elizabeth turned on her heel and headed back to the porch.

"Well?" Michelle asked when Elizabeth sat back down next to her.

"I gave him some food for thought. I'm sure he'll be letting you know his feelings in a day or two. Oh, by the way, I told him you were leaving next week."

"Next week? But I hadn't decided when I would leave."

"I know that, but he doesn't need to know. Let him stew just a bit over the fact that you are leaving soon."

Later that afternoon when Elizabeth rode back in the direction of her home, that is, the home she now shared with her husband, she noticed a rider over the hill just sitting there like he was watching her. She felt a shiver of apprehension run down her spine. She kicked her horse into a slow canter in order to make it back to the ranch house a little more quickly.

The horseman continued to stare, making her more uneasy with every step of her horses' hooves. He never attempted to approach, but she could feel his eyes boring into her when she crossed the plain. She would have to ask her husband if there were any of the Rocking W hands out that day in the area. If there were and they were acting this way, she would have Jeff talk with them.

Around the dinner table that evening, she asked Jeff and Ernest if there had been any of the ranch hands in the area where she had seen the mysterious man.

"No, I don't believe so. Why do you ask?" Ernest inquired.

"When I was riding back from my parents' place, I saw a lone rider on the hill between the two ranches. He didn't approach me, but it felt like he was watching me. That's all."

"Why didn't you say something sooner?" Jeff asked. "I would have ridden over to see if I could find him. You won't be going out alone anymore."

"Don't get all protective on me," Elizabeth quipped. "It was fine. I was just curious to see if there were any of the Rocking W hands over near there. I'm going to ask my brothers if there were any of the Double J hands in the area."

"Like I said, you won't be riding out alone from now on, do you understand?" Jeff asked, his eyes narrowed, making her pull her shoulders back in defiance. "It is obviously not safe."

"Excuse me? Last time I checked, you aren't my master, so don't tell me what I can and cannot do." Her anger started to rise, causing her cheeks to flush.

"No, I'm not your master, but I am your husband, and I'm telling you right now, I forbid you to ride alone."

"And I'm telling you I don't care what you forbid me to do. I'll do as I please." She rose from her place, and turned her back on the family, before she walked in the direction of their room.

"Damn woman!" He growled in frustration, quickly following her down the hall. "Elizabeth!"

Jeff stopped her when she was just about to reach the back door to the ranch house.

"Just where do you think you are going?" He grabbed her arm and swung her around.

"Outside, thank you," she replied flatly, wrestling her arm from his grasp.

"Oh no you're not."

He bent over, put his shoulder into her stomach, and lifted her off the ground like a sack of potatoes, and headed back toward their bedroom.

"Damn it. Jeff! Let me down!" Trying to get him to let go of her, she slapped him on the back.

"That language is not the least bit ladylike, you know." He smacked her on the bottom.

"Ouch!"

After walking through the doorway, he kicked the door shut with his foot, and then unceremoniously dumped her on the bed. Standing next to it with his hands on his hips, he said, "Now, then. Shall we discuss this in private?"

"There is nothing to discuss." She swept her hair out of her face. "You are being a bully and just downright unfair in your treatment of me, and I'll not stand for it."

"A bully and unfair, am I?" He watched her try to work herself out of the middle of the bed.

"Yes. And if you don't stop treating me like this, I'll..."

"You'll what, sweetheart? Tell your brothers?" he asked with a grin.

"Yes. That's it. I'll tell Ray, and he'll stop you."

"Stop me from doing what, Elizabeth? I'm only trying to keep you from getting hurt. Besides, your brothers won't come between us. They'll just say I'm your husband and you need to listen to me."

"No they won't," she said quite unconvincingly. All this wrestling had gotten her thinking of something else, and she had lost most of her fight already.

"Yes they will, and you know it. I'm not saying you can't go riding, sweetheart." He sat on the bed next to her. "I just don't want you going alone. They killed your father, remember? They obviously have no regard for life in the least sense of the word. They would kill you too, given the chance, I'm sure."

"How can you be so sure? Besides, how am I supposed to find out who killed him if I don't go out alone? Having a bodyguard would just complicate things. They would never suspect a woman to be out hunting them," she protested almost absently while she noticed how the shirt stretched across his chest.

"Elizabeth, please. Do not go out alone, and leave the manhunt to the law. Besides, I'm sure I can keep you busy here at the house."

"Can you now? Doing what, pray tell?" She turned so that she was on her knees in front of him and began to unbutton his shirt.

"Well, let's see. There is always helping my mother with canning." He ran his fingers along her arm, and she continued to slowly unfasten each button.

"No. I don't think that would be very much fun."

"There is mending to do, I'm sure, and the barn could use a good cleaning, too," he said, slightly breathless when she pulled his shirt from the waistband of his trousers and slipped it off his shoulders.

"Nope. Doesn't sound fun either, but I have an idea of how you could keep me busy," she teased with a smile gracing her lips. She pushed him back on the bed, and sprawled over him.

"Um...I wonder what that would be." He feigned innocence and attempted to take her lips with his.

She kept avoiding his seeking mouth, nibbling along his jaw line and skimming her way down his chest, nipping as she went.

"Oh let's see. Maybe a little of this," she whispered as she took his nipple in her mouth and grazed it with her teeth. She often wondered if he had the same reaction as she did when his mouth was on her. When he inhaled a sharp breath through clenched teeth, she got her answer.

"Woman, you'll be the death of me," he murmured, before he swiftly rolled her onto her back. "God I need you."

She gave him a sweet, innocent smile, even though she knew the fire that burned in him. Those same flames licked at the blood racing through her veins.

"I want you to make love to me," she said with all the passion she felt. "Now, right now."

He didn't say another word but quickly stripped out of his clothing and she from hers, then climbed into the bed beside her. He softly ran his hand across her cheeks and her nose before his thumb grazed her lips.

I love him—I love him so much it hurts. A small tear slipped from under her lashes.

"What's wrong?"

"Nothing." She slid her hands up around his shoulders. "Make love to me."

When the sun rose the next morning, Elizabeth rolled over to find her husband gone from the bed with a note attached to his pillow. "I'll be gone for a few days. Stay close to the house," he had written.

"I'll be damned if I'm staying close to the house," she growled, furious that he hadn't even woke her before he left and then having left orders like she was some hand on the ranch he could boss around.

Jumping from the bed in a fit of rage, she grabbed her clothing and pulled them on in haste.

"We'll just see about that, dear husband. I've never been one to sit idle when there are things to be done, and he should know enough about me to realize that," she muttered, swinging the door open and finding a huge burly man standing in front of the door.

"Going somewhere, missus?" he asked with a large toothless grin.

"Yes, as a matter of fact, I am. Now, if you'll excuse me." She tried to wiggle by the man.

Lord, but he's enormous!

"And just where might that be, missus?" He didn't move from his post at her door.

"Out for a ride if you must know. Just exactly who are you and what are you doing standing in front of my door?"

"Mr. Jeff, ma'am. He told me to watch you and make sure you didn't leave the house without me, ma'am."

"Did he now? And what else did he tell you?" She crossed her arms over her chest as her anger began to boil out of control. How dare he!

"Just that if I valued my job, ma'am, that if he found out you had left the house and I wasn't guarding you, I wouldn't have one no more, ma'am."

"I'm sorry. What did you say your name was?" she asked sweetly, changing her approach because she could see this man was loyal to a fault, and unfortunately, it wasn't to her.

"Jackson, ma'am, Harold Jackson."

"Well, Mr. Jackson, I appreciate your concern for my welfare, I really do, but there is no need for it. You see, I'm only planning on going for a ride over to my parents' place. You know, the Double J?" She poured on the charm. "So I'll be perfectly safe. I've ridden that trail too many times to count since I was a little girl."

"I know that, ma'am, but Mr. Jeff told me..." He stammered, unsure of what he should do.

She conceded with a huff when she realized her attempt at charming the man wasn't getting her anywhere. "All right! All right. Fine. Follow me over there then."

"Yes, ma'am."

This is just ridiculous. I am perfectly safe riding over to my parents' place without this shadow hanging over me. I can't believe he is being so silly about this. I am perfectly capable of taking care of myself and he knows it.

Once her horse was saddled, she jabbed her in the ribs and took off at a full gallop in hopes of losing her bodyguard. When she turned her head took look back, she was astonished to find the man right behind her, at a full gallop himself. Obviously he was one of the ranch hands if he could ride like that, as big as he was. She realized that there would be no way to lose him, so she slowed her horse to a canter and let him pull up on her side.

I guess I'll just have to put up with it for now, but my beloved husband will certainly hear about this when he gets home. He'll be getting an ear full from me!

When she rode into the ranch yard of her parents' place, she was met by her brother Ray, who was outside heading for the barn.

"Hi, sis. What brings you over this way so early in the day? I thought you'd be sleeping in," he said with a distinctively devilish grin and a raise of his eyebrow. "Who did you bring with you?"

"Ray, this is my new shadow, Harold Jackson. Mr. Jackson, this is my brother Ray," she said a bit sarcastically.

"Shadow?" Ray asked as the man tipped his hat to him.

With a quick nod, she said, "Courtesy of my husband you could say."

"I don't think I understand, sis. Maybe you could explain."

"Let's go up on the porch where it's cooler. It's going to be a hot one again today, I'm afraid."

"You're right about that."

"I was riding back from here yesterday and I saw a rider on the hill between here and the Rocking W. I didn't recognize him, but he was a long distance off so I couldn't really tell, though the horse wasn't familiar either."

"He didn't approach you?"

"No. He just sat there watching me ride past. It was kind of strange, but he never moved but I could feel his eyes on me the whole time. I don't know Ray, maybe it was just my imagination or the heat, but I asked Mr. Walker about his ranch hands last night, and when I said something, Jeff forbade me to ride alone. Forbade me! Do you believe that?" she said with some indignation.

Ray let out a hearty laugh that continued, seemingly, with no end in sight. He laughed so hard, he almost fell off his chair and tears rolled down his cheeks. Elizabeth sat there watching him like he was crazy.

What has gotten into him?

When his guffaws settled to an occasional snicker, she demanded, "Just what is so funny?"

He snickered again before replying, "I can't believe he actually got away with forbidding you to ride alone. I think it is hilarious! My independent, steadfast, bullheaded sister has been forbidden by her husband to do something, and he actually got away with it!"

"This isn't funny, Ray."

"Yes it is! I'm sure John and Matt would think so too. Michelle as well, I'm sure," he insisted with a bit of a laugh under his breath.

"I should have known better than to ask for help from you," she grumbled, got up from the chair, and started back in the direction of her horse.

"Now, Liz, he is only trying to protect you, so stop being so stubborn. There are too many unwanted people running around these hills of ours for you to be out alone. That's why he's put a guard on you. Don't forget, he's known you all your life. I'm sure you tried sneaking out of the room this morning too, didn't you?"

"Well..."

"I thought as much."

"I wasn't sneaking. He was already gone when I awoke this morning to a note on his pillow saying he would be gone for a few days. I didn't make any secret of going riding this morning.

Just maybe where I was going to ride to," she finished under her breath.

"See. He knows you better than you think he does. Just let us handle things around here before you go get yourself into trouble. We are working with the law to figure out exactly what's going on and who killed Father. You have to be patient."

"I'm not good with patience."

"I know, but you better learn. Now why don't you go in and visit Mother and Michelle? I'm sure there is something they can give you to do to keep you out of trouble for the day." He rose from the chair and started in the direction of the barn again.

"We'll just see about that," she muttered, staying right where she was until he had ridden out with a wave in her direction.

Now, how can I get rid of my shadow?

She squinted, watching her brother ride over the hill.

CHAPTER 19

Elizabeth sat rocking on the porch. She could ask Michelle for help, but no, if she knew what she was up to, she would never agree. Just about the time she was going to give up, a rider came into view up the long road to the house. She didn't quite recognize the rider until he got closer, and she realized it was Gregory.

Of course! He could help me.

"Gregory! It's so nice to see you. What brings you out this way?" she asked brightly when he approached the ranch house.

"Liz? I'm almost surprised to see you here. I thought you'd be with your husband," he said, dismounting in front of her.

"Oh that. He's going to be gone a few days so I came over to see my mother and visit Michelle."

"I see."

"Is there something I can do for you?" she asked when he didn't answer her question.

"I just came over to offer my condolences to your mother and you, of course. When I heard about the death of your father, I was shocked! Who would want to shoot him?"

"The rustlers. Ray and Father had come across their hiding place for the cattle they had stolen, and when they saw them there, they rode after them, shooting my father in the back, the dirty cowards."

"Rustlers? Really. I hadn't really understood that it was to the point of killing people over it."

"They're stealing our livelihood, Gregory. They have to be stopped, and if I find out who shot my father, I'll kill him myself."

"Liz, really. I can't imagine you shooting anyone."

"Trust me, when I find out who it is, they'll be sorry they messed with the Johnston family."

"Well then, I'll be sure to warn them to stay away from you."

"Warn them? Do you have some idea who is behind all this? If you do, I suggest you tell me and tell me this instant!"

"No. I certainly do not. If I did, I would be telling the sheriff all the details."

"Are you sure?"

"Of course I'm sure. I don't know anything about the rustlers. I don't even like cows except when they're sitting on my plate as a nice, big steak."

She eyed him for another moment before deciding he was telling the truth. "Would you like to go for a ride with me?"

"Are you sure your husband wouldn't mind?"

"Of course not! We've known each other way too long for Jeff to bother with us riding together. Just let me talk to this man over here about where we are going then we'll be on our way." She started in the direction of Mr. Jackson.

"Mr. Jackson, you can stay here while I ride with my friend over there. He'll protect me from anyone that might try to hurt me," she told him while he stood leaning up against the barn.

"Now, Mrs. Walker, you know that Mr. Jeff told me not to let you out of my sight."

"Yes I know, but he didn't know Gregory would be here. I've known this man for quite a few years, and I'm perfect safe with him. Jeff would be fine with it, so you can stay here and keep an eye on things here until I get back." She walked back to Gregory. "All set, let's go."

Gregory mounted his horse, Elizabeth did the same, and they rode off toward the eastern hillside.

They rode along the creek bed now dry in the summer heat.

"So, how are things with your business ventures here in town?"

"They are blooming very well," Gregory replied.

"Will you be traveling home to Virginia soon then?" she asked as they crossed and rode into the tall grass.

"I'm not sure. I've got a few things that I'm still working on, so I can't leave quite yet. I have a plan for something that will become very pleasurable for me, I'm sure, but I haven't quite been able to nail things down."

"Something pleasurable. I wonder what that could be. Maybe a woman?" She turned to look at him. "Someone has caught your eye then, Gregory?"

"You could say that, yes. I've been seeing someone while I've been here, but I want to make sure things are set in motion before I move forward, if you know what I mean."

"Well, I'm sure she'll be thoroughly entranced by your charm and fall headlong in love with you if she isn't already."

"I believe she already is, but I need to move somewhat slowly. She's a bit gun-shy in the area of relationships, but I'm sure she cares for me as well."

"Someone I know?"

"You could say that, but I'm not going to tell you who just yet. That's my little secret for now, but you'll know soon enough."

"She's one lucky girl then. I'm sure you'll make her very happy." They rode under a tree. "How about we sit for a bit?"

"Of course. A nice bit of shade would feel good right now." He pulled his horse to a stop next to hers and dismounted, looking for a place to tie up.

Elizabeth found a big rock on which to sit, and Gregory sat next to her.

"It's really nice here. I love it when the stream is running. It's nice to walk in it with bare feet and cool off before the summer heat dries it up for a while."

She wanted to keep him off guard a bit so that she could make a break for her horse and be gone before he knew what she was about. His riding skills weren't nearly as good as hers, so she figured she could be mounted and gone before he could stop her.

"Why do you like Texas so well, Liz? I mean it's rather barren, dry, dusty and hot, isn't it?"

"It is hot in the summer, yes, but it's so bright and pretty with the flowers in bloom and the wild grasses swaying like they are dancing to music. The wild horses are so magnificent when they run across the land in a flow of horse flesh as far as an eye can see with the stallions nipping at the mares to keep them running. The colts are so beautiful when they are born and being all legs, they look so funny! I guess for me its home. It's always been home, and I love it here. Unfortunately, someone is trying to take that away from me and I won't stand for it anymore so if you'll excuse me—"

She jumped up, almost catapulted herself into the saddle, and rode off in the direction of where Ray and her father had seen the corral as fast as the horse's legs could carry her.

Racing across the plains with the wind through her hair felt exhilarating! Oh, how she loved to ride like this. It almost felt like she could fly.

She wasn't surprised to see Gregory hadn't even attempted to follow her, and she was sure her bodyguard was still back at the house.

Freedom. Free to ride as she had when she was a child, without a care in the world.

With that thought, she slowed her horse to a canter. She wasn't free of a care; she needed to find her father's killer. The drive to find out who, and why they had shot him, gave her purpose. They'd shot him in the back like a bunch of yellow-bellied cowards.

Riding near the abandon corral, she could see it had been used fairly recently, but wasn't anymore.

Damn! After Ray and Father had found it, the rustlers must have moved their operation. Now what? I think I'll follow what's left of the cattle trail and see where it gets me.

She got down from her horse to study the prints in the dirt. Squinting in the direction they appeared to have moved the cattle, she remounted and began walking her horse in that general direction in hope of seeing signs of where cattle had been taken.

She had ridden for what seemed like a long time when she saw the train railhead come into view.

So, they were loading the cattle from here onto the train and taking them out of town that way. Very clever. They could be moved fairly quickly that way without too much trouble and too many people the wiser. Obviously the leader behind this operation had connections with the railroad or the money to pay off the conductor to load the cattle before he took the train on into Houston.

When she reached the small area where the cattle were penned near the railhead being loaded onto the train, she stopped and dismounted to look around. She wasn't sure what she was looking for, but she knew there had to be a clue to the identity of one of the men around here somewhere. She walked around, kicked at the dirt in the pen, scuffed it with the toe of her boot, and tried to think of who might be connected to this.

Someone higher up in the gang was probably connected in town. How else would they have the connections to the railroad company in order to secure transport for cattle at what, to most people, would be an odd time of the year for roundup. They must have felt threatened by Father and Ray finding out where they were holding the cattle to the point that they shot Father.

She continued wandering through the pen, kicking at the dirt until something reflecting the sunlight caught her attention. It lay not far from where she stood and she walked over to see what it might be. When she squatted down to pick it up, she was surprised to find what appeared to be a piece of a branding iron that had broken off from the rod. She turned it over and over in her hand, trying to figure out what it might represent until she grasped it by the end that would normally have been attached and held it facing her. At that moment, she finally understood what the brand represented, and her heart sank.

Holding the piece, she plopped down on the ground. She sat there for a long time turning the piece over and over trying to understand what it meant. How could this be? Surely there must be some mistake. She knew she had seen it before. There were no brands in the area like this one, so it had to be an unregistered brand mark, but it was distinctive enough she who it belonged to.

As the sun began to dip in the sky, she decided she needed to get back to the ranch house before it was completely dark. Almost in a daze, she put the piece in the pocket of her trousers, remounted her horse, and rode solemnly in the direction of the Double J. Tonight, she would stay at her parents' place. She felt as if she couldn't return to the bed she shared with Jeff tonight. Besides, he wouldn't be there anyway.

When she did ride back into the yard, the stern faces of her three brothers met her.

"Just where in the hell have you been?" Ray said when she dismounted. "We've been worried sick. You know you weren't supposed to be off riding by yourself, sis. You could have been hurt if you'd come across any of those rustlers."

"Well, I didn't and I'm home safe and sound." She started for the house, ignoring her brothers' exasperated looks.

"Liz, I don't think you understand how dangerous it is for you to be out riding alone." John said. "I obviously need to have a talk with your husband about your behavior."

"Excuse me?" She whirled on her heels to face him. "I'm not a child, and I will not be coddled like some dimwitted, no-brain woman who doesn't know how to take care of herself. My husband already put a guard on me this morning and I still managed to get away from him enough to be able to ride alone, with the help of Gregory of course."

"Gregory? You mean that easterner?" Ray asked. "What was he doing out here?"

"He said he came to give Mother his condolences, and then he went riding with me."

"You are a married woman. You shouldn't be keeping company with any man, much less a man who made no mistake about his fascination with you," Ray said.

"He was the perfect gentleman, thank you," she replied, defending Gregory's involvement in her escape.

"I don't care if he acted like a saint, Liz, you still shouldn't have been out riding with him and since he couldn't keep up with you, he was worthless as a protector if something did happen."

"Pardon me, sirs," Mr. Jackson spoke up, approaching from the barn. "I'm Harold Jackson, and I was Mrs. Walker's guard today."

"And just where in the hell have you been? Obviously you weren't guarding her very well if she was out alone and you were here."

"Actually, I was near her the entire time. She just didn't know it. I saw her take off from that dude she was riding with, and I followed her. I kept an eye on her just to make sure she didn't get into no trouble. She just didn't know I was there, that's all."

"You did?" The four of them asked in unison.

"Yes, ma'am," he said, addressing Elizabeth. "I saw you near that corral and then rode behind you as you went down by the railhead.

"Railhead? Liz? What is he talking about?" Matt asked.

Elizabeth glared at Mr. Jackson, and the fact that he had given her away in her secret ride.

"I found the pen where Ray and Father had seen the cattle corralled before they had moved them. No. It wasn't being used currently. I followed the tracks of the cattle, and it appears they were driving them down to the railhead at the northeast corner of our property where the railhead crosses right before the fork heading to Houston. They apparently were driving the cattle there and loading them onto a cattle car to be transported into Houston to be sold." The piece of the branding iron in her pocket remained a secret. She wasn't quite ready to reveal that piece of the puzzle just yet.

"We need to let the sheriff know what she's found, but we'll do it in the morning since it's now getting dark." John motioned for them to retreat to the house. "Liz, no more riding out alone. You could have been hurt today even if your bodyguard was closer than you thought."

"You sound like Jeff," she grumbled, completely exasperated at her overprotective husband and her brothers.

"He's only doing what's best for you, so stop trying to cross him at every turn. We all want to keep you safe, because after losing Father, if something happened to you..." Ray trailed off as he got slightly choked up.

"Nothing is going to happen to me, Ray. I'm perfectly capable of handling myself and taking care of myself. I've been doing it for years now." She hugged her brother.

"Maybe, but I don't want to take the chance, Liz, and I'm sure neither does your husband nor John and Matt," Ray replied with John and Matt chiming in their agreement. "Please don't go out alone again."

"All right. I won't." She crossed her fingers behind her back. "I promise."

When they had all filed into the house and were met by her mother and Carmen, the thought of the events of the day left their minds, all except Elizabeth and the piece of metal that lay heavy in her pocket.

CHAPTER 20

Later that night, she slipped out of her bedroom as quietly as she could so she didn't wake Michelle and wandered out to the front porch. The moonlight spilled across the ground in front of her making the night almost as bright as day. She could see everything around her, but the music of the crickets, the bawling of the cattle, and the occasional nickering of the horses filled her heart with dread. It didn't give her the peace it normally did when she was growing up. Tonight, something lay heavily on her mind.

She took out the piece of metal she had found and held it up to the moonlight so she could clearly see the brand. A large circle W stared back at her, mocking her, telling her she should never have trusted him.

How could he betray me like this?

All he would tell her was his disappearances were for their future when, all along, he'd been behind the cattle rustling and possibly her father's death? All the time she had known him, she really hadn't. Surely it wasn't as it seemed, but her heart battled with her head. Surely there was an explanation for this her heart said while her head argued, "No, the brand is his. You know this because you've seen this brand on the rump of the horses he's been breaking, the Mustangs he's brought in."

"No," she said aloud and shook her head to dislodge the disturbing thoughts. "This can't be true. He can't be involved."

"Who?"

A shadow stepped out from the side of the house and she jumped. "God, Ray. You scared the hell out of me!" She quickly stuffed the metal in her bathrobe pocket.

"Who can't be involved, Liz?"

"No one. I was just thinking to myself who might be involved, that's all," she said, avoiding directly answering his question.

"That's not what it sounded like to me. It sounded like you knew someone who might be involved and you were questioning yourself to that reasoning. If you know something Liz, you need to tell me."

"I don't, honest. I couldn't sleep so I came out here to clear my head. Since I had found the corral and the trail to the railhead, I was trying to reason out who might be involved. I got to thinking though that it had to be someone connected to the railroad or someone who had enough money to pay them off, right?" she asked, trying to divert his attention from what he heard her say before.

"Could be. We didn't know about the trail to the railhead, but now that we do, we need to get this information to the sheriff so he can check it out," Ray replied. "Where did you say Jeff went?"

"I didn't because I don't know. He's been doing this for a while now evidently. He's gone for a few days at a time, and when he comes back, he's exhausted and almost sleeps the day through," she murmured a little absentmindedly.

"Gone for days? Really? That's rather odd, I'd say. Have you asked him about it?"

"Of course I have. He just says it's for our future and not to worry about it, but I am worried, Ray. What if he runs into the rustlers and is hurt or killed? We wouldn't even know where to look?" she said a little concerned now that she thought about what could happen.

Or what if—he was caught.

"Let me know when he gets back, all right? I think I need to ask him a few questions myself."

"Why? Do you think he's involved?" she asked, breathlessly waiting for his answer.

"I don't know sis, but if he is, I'll kill him myself or hang him from the highest tree I can find."

"How can you say that, Ray? He's your best friend and my husband," she said a little defensively.

"Friends don't steal from friends, Liz, and husbands don't steal from their wives' families either. If he has reasonable explanation for his whereabouts, then there isn't a problem, is there."

"I know he's not involved, I just know it. He can't be," She continued defending Jeff even though the piece of metal in her pocket pulled at her conscious.

"I wish I could be as sure as you are. He's just been acting really strange the last six months or so, which is just coincidently about the time the rustling started too."

"Just give him the benefit of the doubt, please?"

"You really care about him, don't you?"

"Yes." She bowed her head to hide her emotions from her brother.

"Are you in love with him, sis?" He lifted her chin with his hand.

"Yes," she replied looking him square in the eye. "Yes, I am. That's why I can't believe he would be involved in this, but I'm not so sure myself sometimes. Let's just have a little more patience, and I'll talk to him when he comes home to see what I can find out."

"All right. I'll let you handle this for now, but if he doesn't give you the answer we want to hear, then I'll take care of it from there. Now, I'm going to bed and you should be too. It's been a long day, and I'm tired."

"Me, too. I'm hoping he'll be home tomorrow. Sometimes he's only gone for a day or so, and sometimes, he's gone three days or more." She sighed and followed her brother back inside the house.

"Are you going back to the Rocking W tomorrow?"

"Yes. I'll leave in the morning. I know there are things around there that I can keep busy with until he gets home," she replied as they reached the door to her room. "Night, Ray."

"Night, sis. Be careful."

"I will, brother. I will."

When she closed the door behind her, she pressed her back against it and a small tear slid down her cheek.

He just can't be involved, and I'll just have to prove it. I want to see the brand on some of those horses he's brought in and then I'll know. If it was the same as the piece of metal she had, then he would need to explain and she wouldn't settle for "it's for our future." Not this time.

The next morning found Elizabeth up and dressed with the dawn as the sun slowly rose in the morning sky. She stopped in the kitchen early morning and found Carmen already up and making breakfast.

"Well, good morning, *chica*. You are up early this morning. Where are you off to so early?"

"I'm going back to the Rocking W this morning, Carmen. I have some chores I need to do around there, and I'm hoping my husband will be home today."

"Where did he run off to so soon after your marriage? He should be staying home with his new bride," Carmen said with a frown.

"He's been rounding up wild mustangs and training them. It's been keeping him really busy."

"Ah! Good! That will keep him out of trouble then. Come. Eat something before you go, eh?" Carmen put the plate of eggs, ham, and potatoes in front of Elizabeth.

"You were always such a good cook. I need you to teach me some of your recipes so I can cook for Jeff at some point."

"Of course, *chica*. You come over any time and I will teach you everything I know."

After Elizabeth finished eating, she grabbed her boots, slipped them on, and stomped to wedge her foot in tightly before she headed out the door to saddle her horse. The man who had been her constant shadow stood silently by the door of the barn as if he hadn't slept at all and was just waiting for her.

"Don't you ever sleep, Mr. Jackson?" She asked, approaching him with a smile. She had really begun to take to the man, even if he could be a nuisance sometimes.

"Yes, ma'am, just not as much since I've been watching you." He grinned in return.

"Well, you'll be happy to know we are heading home this morning and I won't be going anywhere else today from there. I'll be spending the day helping my mother-in-law with some of the work around the house."

"Thank you, Lord!" he said with a large grin.

Elizabeth chuckled as the big man raised his hands in praise and raced into the barn to saddle his own horse for the trip home. Home. It really had become home to her even in the short time she and Jeff had been married. Living with him and his parents had been a much easier transition than she had thought possible. His mother had been so gracious and patient with her, teaching her how she ran their home with quiet efficiency and kept Ernest and Jeff in line at the same time. She laughed again when she remembered how one day while Donna had been cleaning, Ernest had come inside tracking dirt through her freshly swept kitchen and she had chased him out with her broom! Elizabeth had almost doubled over, laughing so hard, while she stood in the corner watching the whole scene. The best part though was when Ernest had gone back outside, taken off his dirty boots, walked into the kitchen, bent Donna over his arm, and gave her a big kiss right on the mouth. Donna had turned as red as a beet when he had finally let her go and walked off into the front room without a backward glance. Elizabeth knew they were still very much in love, and she hoped someday she and Jeff would have the same kind of a relationship.

Sobering at the thought of possibly facing her husband with what she knew, she turned to finish saddling her own horse so they could be on their way. She hoped he would be able to explain away her fears and they could go on with their lives.

When they arrived at the ranch house, she noticed the mustangs penned in the corral near the barn. They were so beautiful and she could easily understand why her husband was so enthralled with training them. She loved to watch him work while he ran his hands over their coat to calm them with his voice. He worked his magic on them just like he did with her in their bed.

The thought of him making love to her, made her feel all warm and liquid.

Had it been that long already? No, it had only been a one day, but Lord, how I want him again!

This lust for her husband was a startling discovery for her. She would never have thought the mere sight of him could cause this unbridled passion to well up inside of her, but it did, and she rather enjoyed his lovemaking after all.

"Elizabeth?" Donna said. "I'm glad your back. I really could use some help with this canning today. Can you help me, dear?"

"Of course. I'll be right there." She dismounted and took her horse to the barn.

When she came back out, one of the horses that Jeff had brought in was near the fence and she could clearly see the brand on her rump. The large circle W stared glaringly at her, and all of the sudden she started seeing spots in front of her eyes and her head began to swim.

She awoke to the sound of her husband calling her name.

That's strange. He isn't home, why is he calling my name?

"Elizabeth? Sweetheart? Open your eyes please?" Jeff said as he held her in his arms with her head resting on his chest.

"Jeff?" She tried to open her eyes, but her eyelids felt so heavy.

"Yes, sweetheart. It's me. Open your eyes for me," he said while Donna placed a cool cloth of her forehead and then stood by, wringing her hands.

When Elizabeth opened her eyes to the glare of the sun, it was hard to see anything in front of her. Spots were swimming within her vision again. She started to sit up only to hear him say, "No. Lie still for a moment. You fainted."

"Fainted?" she asked. "I never faint. That's ridiculous, but why am I lying on the ground outside of the barn?"

"I don't know, sweetheart. I was hoping you could tell me," he said with a small smile gracing his lips.

"I'm not sure, but I don't feel very well. I think I need to go into the house." She tried to rise again only to be swept up in her husband's arms and carried inside.

"You rest. I'll be right back." Jeff gently laid her on the bed and placed the cloth over her eyes.

* * * *

He strode into the front room to find his mother nervously ringing her hands.

"Is she all right, son?"

"I'm sure she'll be fine, Mother, but I'm going to send for the doctor just in case." He went out the front door only to find Mr. Jackson anxiously standing on the porch.

"How's the Missus?"

"I'm sure she'll be fine, but just to make sure, will you ride to town and fetch the doctor for me?"

"Course I will. I'll be back in a jiffy."

Jeff went back into the house, and noticed how worried his mother appeared. She needed of something to keep her occupied, he figured. "Why don't you make her some tea, Mother? I'm sure she'd appreciate it."

"That's a good idea, son. I'll start the water right now."

Having given everyone something to do, he walked back to their room and opened the door quietly so he wouldn't disturb her if she had fallen asleep. He walked up to the side of the bed at looked down at his beautiful wife. He had left yesterday morning with dread, but knowing he had left Mr. Jackson to watch over her had made it a little easier. Mr. Jackson was one of his best hands, and he was also loyal to a fault. If given a job to do, he'd do it, and that's what Elizabeth needed. He was sure she'd tried to shake her guard on several occasions yesterday, but obviously the big man had come to care for his wife in the short time. He hated leaving her at all, but having to leave her still sleeping in their bed while she cuddled up to him in her sleep drove him crazy. He knew what he had to do to make things right for them, but every time he left, it got harder and harder.

While she lay there softly snoring, he watched her. He loved to watch her sleep. She was a firebrand when awake, always testing him, teasing him, and driving him crazy with wanting her, but while she slept, she was like his guardian angel. His only hoped was this whole messy business with the cattle rustlers would be over soon. He wished he could tell her the whole truth, but it wasn't the right time. Soon he would be able to tell her everything.

"Soon, sweetheart, very soon," he said softly to his sleeping wife before he turned and left the room so she could rest.

About an hour later, the doctor arrived and found Elizabeth propped up in the bed with Donna hovering over her like a mother hen.

"You just need to rest dear until the doctor gets here and checks you out. You've probably been doing too much and got too warm or something."

"I'm fine! Will you all just please leave me be?" Elizabeth asked, exasperated when they all kept looking at her worriedly, even Mr. Jackson.

"Let's see now. Elizabeth, my dear, how are you feeling?"

"Fine!" she almost yelled, but she quickly apologized for her rude behavior. Being snappish with folks wasn't her way at all, and it came as a surprise to her that she was behaving this way.

It must be time for my menses.

"Well, your husband here was worried because he said you fainted outside. He wanted me to check you over, so just be a good girl and let's see what's happening with you." He sat on the edge of the bed. "Now, I think your company here needs to wait outside while I examine you."

Donna and Mr. Jackson made a quick retreat to the door, but Jeff didn't move.

"You too, son. I'd like to talk to my patient in private for a moment," the doctor said to Jeff.

"But..." Jeff started to say, but the doctor pointed at the door and he complied, unwillingly, leaving the room and shutting the door quietly behind him.

"Now, young lady. What have you been up to that might cause you to faint?"

She told him what she'd been doing the last few days while he scratched a few notes on a small pad of paper he held and mumbled, "I see."

"So what do you think, Doctor? Is there something seriously wrong with me? I never have fainted before in my life. Maybe the heat? But I've lived here all my life. Surely the heat wouldn't get to me now, would it?"

"Let me be the doctor, Elizabeth, all right? I've had a bit of training in that department you know," he said with a grin.

She blushed when she realized what she had been doing. "So tell me. What do you think it could be?"

"It could be several things actually, but let me ask you one little question that might shed some light on the subject. When did you have your last menses cycle?"

"Well, let's see. It's been...maybe a couple of months ago. I can't remember exactly with everything that has been going on with my father dying and all. Why do you ask?"

"I think the reason you fainted today was a combination of things. You've been under a lot of stress with the death of your father and your rather sudden marriage to Jeff, but more than that, I think you are with child."

"With child?" she almost shouted. "But, that can't be."

"I'm assuming you and your husband have consummated your marriage. Correct?"

"Well, yes but…"

"Then it's very possible, and I'm quite sure, that's what is currently causing your queasiness and your fainting spell today. You'll need to come by and see me in a month or so if you haven't started your menses by then. I want to monitor you closely if you are indeed pregnant. I'm sure you'll want to break the news to your husband yourself, so I'll take my leave now, and congratulations."

A few moments later, Jeff came back into the room. "Elizabeth? The doctor wouldn't tell me what's wrong. He said you would tell me. Please tell me everything will be all right? When I found you on the ground by the barn, it scared the hell out of me." He took her hand in his. "Elizabeth?"

Startled, because she hadn't heard him reenter the room or anything he just said. "I'm sorry. I didn't hear you come in. My mind was somewhere else I guess."

"Well, what did the doctor say?"

Scooting to the edge of the bed, she stood and began pacing, trying to decide what to do. She really wasn't sure whether she should tell him the truth or not. She suspected he was involved with the rustlers, now that she had seen the brand on the horses outside, and she wasn't sure what to do.

"What is it, sweetheart? Whatever it is, we can handle it together." He pulled her in his arms, and she rested her head on his shoulder. "You can tell me."

She stepped back in his arms enough so she could see his face. "We are going to have a baby."

"Wha... A baby?" he asked, dumbstruck.

"Yes, at least that's what the doctor suspects." She squealed because he hollered out loud, picked her up in his arms, and swung her around in circles until she was almost breathless.

"A baby! I can't believe it! We are going to have a baby!" He yelled when he had set her down on the floor again and hugged her tight against him.

When he had finally let her go, he kissed her square on the mouth and said, "I love you."

He quickly disappeared out the door and she could hear him excitedly telling his parents about their coming grandchild.

She stood with her mouth hanging open wide enough to catch flies while what he'd said sank in. Her heart felt like it would shatter. He had said he loved her. Her fondest dream had come true, but she couldn't be happy. Not until she had answers to the burning questions in her mind. Where did he go when he left for days on end, and why did the piece of metal in her possession match the brand on the horses that now stood in the corral near the barn?

CHAPTER 21

Jeff's parents rushed into the room and enveloped her in warm hugs while saying congratulations in unison. They were smiling from ear to ear.

"You'll be a wonderful mother, Elizabeth," Donna said. "I can't wait to see you getting big with child. It will be such a joy!"

Elizabeth stood there in stunned silence while they hugged and kissed her. Jeff watched from the doorway with a proud grin on his face.

"All right now, Mother. Elizabeth needs to rest. She obviously is overwhelmed with the thoughts of having a child, and since she fainted earlier, it would be good if she rested now. Besides, I'd like to spend a little time alone with my wife." Jeff shooed his parents from the room. "You can talk with her more tomorrow."

Elizabeth spoke up after he shut the door behind his parents and returned to her side. "Jeff, we need to talk. I need to ask you some things."

"Not right now, sweetheart. You look exhausted and with a baby on the way, you need to rest." He tried to steer her in the direction of the bed.

"Damn it! Jeff, stop! We need to talk, and we need to talk now!" She pulled from his grasp and retreated to the window.

"All right. I'm sorry I upset you. If you'd like to talk, that's fine. What shall we talk about?" He took a seat on the bed.

She walked over to him, pulled the piece of metal from her pocket and placed it in his hand. "This."

"What's this?" He turned it over in his hand trying to make out exactly what she had handed him. "It looks like a piece of branding iron. Where did you find it?"

"Down by the railhead west of my parents' place."

"The railhead? What in the hell were you doing over there? When was this? Where was Jackson? Answer me, Elizabeth!" His voice rose when he stood and took her shoulders in his big hands.

"Stop it!" she almost shouted and pulled out of his grasp. "Yes, I went to the railhead. It was yesterday while you were gone. Mr. Jackson was still following me, although I hadn't realized it, keeping me out of trouble. I went searching for answers and what I found was that. Can you explain it to me?"

"What do you want me to tell you, Elizabeth, and I will. I've never seen it before."

"Explain to me why the same brand on that piece of iron in your hand is the same one that appears on the rumps of the horses you have in the corral outside. The mustangs you've brought in over the last few weeks bear the same mark. How did it get near the railhead?"

"What are you getting at?" He looked closer at the brand on the piece of metal.

"I found that after I had followed what appeared to be cattle tracks from the corral Father and Ray found the day Father died.

The tracks led to the railhead, which apparently is where the rustlers have been loading the cattle on a train car and taking them to Houston to be sold," she explained, sending an accusing glare in his direction. "Tell me the truth. Are you involved with the rustlers, and did you have anything to do with my father's death?"

"All right. I will tell you the truth. Sit down, sweetheart." He motioned for her to sit on their big bed. "No, I'm not involved with the rustlers. How that brand, which appears to be very close to the one I've been using on the mustangs, got near the railhead, I don't know. I haven't been in that area in some time now."

"Where do you go when you are gone then, if you aren't involved?" She asked, wanting to believe him with all her heart.

"I've been catching mustangs on a piece of land I bought adjacent to this ranch. I go up there quite often to work with the horses before I bring them down here closer to civilization. It seems to calm them more at first if they are still near the herd. I've also been working on a house up there. I knew we would need a place of our own soon, but it appears to be sooner rather than later now with the baby coming. I swear I had nothing to do with the death of your father. I could never hurt him! He was like another dad to me, and your brothers are like brothers to me, too. I could no more hurt your family than I could hurt my own. I don't know who is behind this mess, but I sure intend to find out because now they've gotten you thinking that your husband is a criminal, and I won't stand for it."

"I want to believe you, with all my heart I want to believe you, but it's hard. You've been disappearing for days on end, and you just happened to know about my father's death the night it happened and I did ask around. No one left the ranch that night to go to town, so how did you know?"

"I had been at your parents' place that night when the doctor left. I rode back into town with him and he told me that your father wouldn't make it through the night."

"How were you there and we didn't know it?"

"I had stopped over there to talk to you. We hadn't really had a chance to talk after what had happened in the line shack, and I wanted to talk to you about it. When I heard what was going on, I thought it wasn't a good time, so I just stayed in the shadows."

Her steps took her across the wooden floor she tried to absorb what he had told her.

"Elizabeth, I can show you the land I bought and where the other horses are penned. I can show you the house that I've started up there too. Our house. Please. You have to believe me."

"Why did you come back today in what appeared to be just the right time to find me on the ground by the barn?"

"Because for some reason, I felt you were in trouble. After I left yesterday, things just didn't feel right. I felt terrible for leaving again when all I wanted to do was stay here with you, but I knew I needed to keep working with the horses and selling them to make the money we needed for a place of our own. Then last night, it was like a shadow had come over me and I could hardly sleep a wink. I felt like I needed to be here, for you. I headed back first thing this morning and when I rode in, which obviously wasn't long after you, I found you on the ground. When I saw you lying there so pale and unconscious, it scared the hell out of me."

"Did you mean what you said earlier?" she asked in a whisper.

He stood, went to her, and took her in his arms before he answered, "Do you mean when I said 'I love you'?"

"Yes."

"I meant every word. It seems like I've loved you forever. Even when you pushed me in that trough so long ago, I think I loved you even then." He took her lips in a soft kiss. She opened for him and their tongues danced, igniting a fire in her belly that took her breath away.

Lord, I love it when he kisses me.

All thoughts fled when he his hands slipped down her back and over her hips to pull her closer.

Their lovemaking that night took on a whole new meaning. He loved her, her heart sang while they moved together to bring them both to the ultimate climax where the stars above them shone brighter and their rapid breathing mingled.

When their passion was spent, Elizabeth rolled over to cuddle next to him, and he wrapped his strong arm around her shoulders. She rested her head on his chest, and while their breathing slowed, he kissed the top of her head and whispered, "I love you."

A smile graced her lips, and she turned her head so that she could look at him. "I love you too. Even when you are stubborn and a bully and won't listen to me but when you love me especially."

"I'm glad." He smiled back at her. "I was afraid you didn't care for me as much as I care about you. Are you happy we are having a baby?"

"I haven't really had time to absorb the thought, but I guess I have nine months to come to terms with it. I don't know if I'm ready to be a mother yet, though."

"You'll be perfect." He kissed her on the forehead, then on the nose, and moved down to her lips, taking them in a passionate kiss. "Do you think it would be all right if we made love again? It won't hurt the baby, will it?

"I don't think so. I mean women have been having babies for centuries without too much trouble. I'm sure if the doctor thought there was a problem, he would have said something. Does that mean you want to make love again?" she asked with a devilish little grin.

"Always my love. Always."

He rolled her onto her back and took her mouth with his, and the world slipped away.

* * * *

The next day found Jeff staying at the ranch house and keeping a watchful eye on his wife. He couldn't believe she loved him too! His heart swelled with joy at the thought of her loving him and now pregnant with his child. He knew his stubborn wife all too well, and he also knew she would try anything to get him to let her go riding today.

"Please? I just want to ride for a little while. I'll even stay close to the house." She wrapped her arms around his waist and, burying her face in his neck, rained small soft kisses along his neck and his jaw line.

"Elizabeth, that's not fair and you know it, young lady," he said as she continued to rain kisses over to his lips, and he groaned.

"What's not fair? It's not fair for me to want to kiss my husband?" she teased.

She knows exactly what she's doing to me, the little minx! Well, two can play at that game.

He started returning her kisses in the same manner.

There would be no work getting done today.

She tilted her head back to give him better access, moaning low in her throat.

"We should probably take this somewhere other than here in the yard," he whispered as he reached her mouth.

"Um...I supposed you're right. The hayloft?" she suggested with a twinkle in her eye and a groan when he continued his onslaught.

"We might be able to get away with that." He loosened his hold on her, grasped her hand, and quickly headed into the barn toward the stairs while she giggled behind him.

* * * *

Several hours later, his father came into the barn looking for a shovel while he worked on loosening some of the dirt around a post holding up the front porch of the house.

Feminine giggles and male laughter coming from the hayloft made him smile before he retreated to the house without the shovel

It can wait until later.

He whistled as he went into the house and into the kitchen to greet his wife, wrapped his arms around her, and gave her a big kiss.

"Lordy, Ernest! What has gotten into you?" Donna said with a smile.

"I just came from the barn. That's all. I don't think we'll be seeing our son and his wife for a little while, Mother," he said with a large grin.

"What on earth are you talking about?"

"I went to the barn to get a shovel and heard them up in the hayloft. I don't think they'll be down for a while." He wiggled his eyebrows and grinned.

"I declare! Those two! It's no wonder they are having a baby so soon after they got married," Donna said, going back to cleaning her vegetables for supper.

* * * *

Jeff and Elizabeth lay wrapped in a blanket in the hayloft after their afternoon of lovemaking. She traced circles on his chest, and asked, "Where do you suppose that piece of branding iron came from?"

"I don't know, but I'm going to get to the bottom of this. Whoever is doing this is obviously trying to make it look like I'm involved. I can't let this go anymore." He pulled her more tightly against his chest.

"What are you going to do?"

"I'm not sure yet, but I'll think of something. If my name gets linked to them, we'll never be able to stay here because people will always think I was involved even if I'm not. I know one thing—you need to stay close to the house for your own safety. I don't want anything to happen to you or to our baby. I love you so much. I don't know what I would do if something happened. Please promise me you'll stay close."

"I will. I just wish I could help, but I know I need to behave to keep this baby safe." Her hand went to her still flat belly. It was hard to believe there was a little life growing inside since she didn't feel any different except for being tired and a little queasy. "It's probably time we got up and got dressed, don't you think?"

"I kind of like it this way." He rolled her on her back and started kissing her again, making his way down her throat to her breast.

"Um...so do I but...oh, that's nice." She sighed and closed her eyes. At the feel of his mouth on her breast, her passion started raging out of control again and thoughts of abandoning their sanctuary in the hayloft left her mind until much later.

When they finally got dressed and went back to the house, Elizabeth was embarrassed to see the huge smiles on both the faces of Ernest and Donna.

Jeff picked a piece of hay from her hair and twirled it between his fingers.

"Did you two have a nice afternoon?" Donna asked teasingly.

"I guess I can go get the shovel that I tried to get earlier now." Ernest said and heat crawled up her cheeks even more.

Jeff laughed and she dropped her gaze to the floor before she made a hasty retreat to their room.

* * * *

The next day Jeff left the ranch to see what he could find that might give him some idea who the rustlers were. He searched every inch of both the Rocking W and the Double J without too much success. He'd found a few clues like tracks from the old corral that Elizabeth had traced to the railhead, and then to a new corral farther up. He could tell it was more recently used, and he made a mental note to check back there in the next few days, though he would be bringing help with him. He didn't want to end up like her father. Going there alone wouldn't be beneficial to his health. He decided he would ride over to the Double J with his wife so, one, they could tell her family that she was with child and, two, so he could talk to the boys about what Elizabeth had found and about the new corral he had discovered.

Two days later found them riding in the buggy toward the Double J. He hadn't been able to go any sooner because Elizabeth hadn't been feeling well with the queasiness the pregnancy was causing and the work he had waiting for him at his parents' place.

"Are you excited to tell your mother about the baby?" he asked her while they bounced along in the buggy.

"Yes. I'm sure she'll be just as thrilled as your mother was when she found out. In fact, I'm surprised your mother hadn't made a trip over there to tell her yet, but I guess she wanted to leave it to us."

"I'm sure she did."

"Did you realize your mother is knitting booties and sweaters already?"

"I'm not surprised at all, sweetheart. She's more than excited about the arrival of her first grandchild."

"I realize that, but don't you think it's a bit early to be knitting already? My goodness. The baby isn't even due for several months."

"She's going to be a grandmother. You can't fault her for being excited. She'll calm down in the next few months, I'm sure. How are you feeling? Are you doing all right?" he asked with concern when he noticed she was a little pale.

"I'm fine. It's just the nausea returning a little. I'll be better when we get to the house."

A short time later, they arrived in the ranch yard to find her brothers outside saddling their horses. When they saw the pair coming up to the house, they waved in greeting and retied their horses to the hitching rail.

"Hi, you two," John said, waving. "What brings you out today?"

"Elizabeth wanted to visit her mother, and I wanted to talk to you three about a couple of things," he said to the brothers as he walked around the other side of the buggy to help Elizabeth. "Will you be all right for now, sweetheart?"

"I'll be fine. Go talk to those ornery brothers of mine," she replied with a smile in their direction and walked off toward the house.

"Is she all right? She appears to be not feeling very well. She's awfully pale," Ray said, watching her go into the house.

"I'll let her tell you all later, but right now, I need to talk to you about something Elizabeth found at the railhead the other day. She showed me this." He handed the piece of metal to John.

"What's this?" John asked.

"It's obviously a piece of a branding iron."

"I've never seen this brand before around here, have you?" John said, handing it to Matt.

"I haven't either." Matt handed it to Ray.

"I think we need to sit down. Why don't we retreat to the shade of the porch so we can talk?" Jeff suggested and walked toward the house.

"I've been keeping a bit of a secret from everyone, including Elizabeth, you all, and my parents. I've been rounding up the wild mustangs in the hills, penning them up on a piece of land I bought some time ago, training them, and selling them. I've used that brand on the horses."

"Then how did it get down by the railhead where it looks like the rustlers have been moving the cattle?" John asked.

"I don't know. I wish I did." Jeff raked his fingers through his hair in frustration. "I swear to you, all of you, that I haven't had anything to do with the cattle rustling. I'm just not sure what to make of that." He pointed to the metal Ray held in his hands. "It appears to be extremely similar to the brand I'm using, but I haven't been near the railhead in a long time. I did ride down where the corral was that you found and where Elizabeth tracked the cattle to the railhead from, but I found a newer pen being used more recently farther up the canyon. They obviously have moved their operation farther away but are still very much in business. I need you boys help me prove I'm not involved, not only for my sake but also for Elizabeth. Right now, she believes me when I say I'm not involved, but if I don't prove it to her by finding out who is, it could be bad for our marriage."

"We'll help you any way we can, won't we?" John said, eyeing Matt and Ray, who, in turn, had a doubtful expression. "Ray. Do you want to say something?"

"No."

"I think we should get started today then. We can ride up to where you found that new corral in the canyon and see what we can dig up out there. Who knows, maybe we'll get lucky and run into them. I'd sure like to take a few of them out, if you know what I mean," Matt said.

"Me too," John replied.

"Great. I think we should get moving then. What do you all say?" Jeff asked.

"I'm ready. Let's go."

Two of the Johnston boys headed, but Ray held back.

"Is there something you want to say, Ray?" Jeff asked when he saw Ray standing there eyeing him as if he had three heads.

"One thing. Right now, I don't trust you very much. But I'm warning you, if I find out you indeed had a hand in this whole rustling business and you hurt my sister, there will be hell to pay. For some strange reason, she loves you, and I won't allow you to hurt her."

"Let me tell you something. I have not had, nor intend to have, anything to do with this dirty mess. I love your sister, and I won't hurt her. You can bet your life on it." Jeff proceeded across the yard to borrow a horse from their barn.

"Good," Ray said, following him. "Let's keep it that way."

CHAPTER 22

After the boys had ridden out, Elizabeth wandered out of the house toward the barn. When they had arrived, she had walked in on her mother and Carmen in the kitchen, in the process of canning some fruits brought from town and some vegetables her mother had grown in the garden outside, for winter.

"Elizabeth! What a pleasant surprised, sweetheart. I didn't expect to see you today. Where is that handsome husband of yours?" her mother asked, coming over to give her a warm hug.

"He's outside talking with the boys." She sat down at the table near her mother. The smells of the kitchen were making her queasiness even worse.

"Are you all right, sweetheart? You don't look very well."

"I'm fine. I've just been rather nauseous lately." Elizabeth put her head in her hands.

"Really? You haven't come down with something have you? You probably should have stayed home in bed then dear. No use being out if you aren't feeling well."

"Mother, I have something to tell you. I wish Jeff had come inside with me even for a moment because we wanted to share this with you together, but I know he has other things on his mind at the moment. My queasiness isn't from being ill. Jeff and I are going to have a baby."

Her mother dropped the knife she was holding her hands and squealed with delight. She pulled Elizabeth up and wrapped her arms around her. "A baby? That's wonderful news! I couldn't be happier for you two, sweetheart. You'll be a wonderful mother."

"I hope so. I wish I knew more about babies and what to expect for the coming months so you'll need to sit down and tell me. I never had a little brother or sister to practice on."

"Of course darling. Now, let's see…" her mother started, and for the next few hours, she told her everything she knew about having a baby, finishing with, "then he or she will grow into a wonderful adult I'm sure."

"Thank you. I'm sure I'll have many questions for you and Mrs. Walker in the coming months. I hope this overwhelming feeling of being tired and sick all the time goes away soon. I hate being sick."

"I hope so too, sweetheart, but I never had it long with you or your brothers, so hopefully you'll follow in my footsteps and it will go away soon. I absolutely loved being pregnant, hence four children,"

Elizabeth fondly remembered her afternoon with her mother. It was nice to be able to sit and talk about woman things with her.

Now, while she wandered out near the barn, she turned to see a rider coming up the drive. She cocked her head slightly, confused at seeing Gregory riding into the yard.

I wonder what he's doing here.

"Well hello, Liz. I hadn't expected to see you here."

"Hello, Gregory. What brings you out this way?"

"John had sent me a message about a business venture he was interested in possibly investing in with me, so I came out to talk to him about it."

"Really? He didn't mention anything to me, but then again, I'm not here much anymore. He's not here, though. They all went riding earlier to check on something. Can I offer you a cold drink?"

"No. That's quite all right. But there is something you can do for me."

"Anything. What is it?"

"You can come with me. Very quietly, I might add."

He grasped her around the waist and put his hand over her mouth to quiet her. She struggled against his arm, kicking him and trying to bite his hand. When he took his hand away just before she bit him, she almost got a scream out but was silenced by him striking her across the face with his heavy hand and knocking her unconscious.

* * * *

"We've been out here for hours and nothing!" Jeff exclaimed, frustrated beyond compare at their lack of progress. "There has to be something!"

Ray had walked away from the rest of them to search the canyon opening. He'd told them he had a gut feeling something might lead them to whoever was behind this whether it be his brother in law or someone else. Searching the ground, looking for even the slightest hint, he finally caught a glimpse of something half buried in the dirt and reflecting the sunlight. He walked over, picked up the piece off the ground, and turned it over in his hand.

A cuff link? What the hell was a cuff link doing out here in the middle of nowhere? Surely it had to belong to one of the rustlers, and if it did, obviously whomever it belong too wasn't accustomed to riding across the prairie. Cowboys didn't wear cuff links.

"Hey. Look what I found." He walked back toward the others.

"What the hell is that?" Jeff asked, taking it from his hand.

"It's a cuff link," Ray replied. "But what I don't know is what it's doing out here."

"Who would be wearing something like that out here?" John asked. "Maybe some dandy who might have been out riding with a girl to find a place quiet and out of the way."

"Look. There is a letter on it that holds the clasp together. What does that look like to you?" Ray asked.

Jeff turned it over in his hand, studying the engraving on the clasp. "It looks like a *W*. Is that what it looks like to you?" he asked John, handing it to him.

"Yep. That's what it looks like to me, too. But who could it belong to? Who do we know that has a *W* for a first or last name?"

"Walker for one," Ray said, giving Jeff a look meant to say he didn't trust him.

"Damn it, Ray. It's not mine! I've never even owned those things before much less engraved ones."

"All right then. Who else do we know around here with that initial?" Matt asked.

"Well, there is Donald Webb, but I don't think he'd be wearing something like that either." John said.

"And Jack Wyatt, but he's not that type," Matt added.

"What about Carl Wade? He's kind of a dandy," Ray suggested.

"Hey, wait a minute! What about that Webster guy? You know, the one who came here from back east to visit Elizabeth," Jeff said, snapping his fingers. "He's definitely the type that would wear those things. I wouldn't be the least bit surprised that he was involved."

"If so, we need to get back to the ranch and warn Elizabeth. Who knows what he might pull if he's crazy enough to steal cattle right from under our noses," Ray replied before they raced back toward their horses.

* * * *

Jeff rode into the front yard of the ranch house, skidded his horses to a stop at the rail, and jumped down almost before it had stopped. He had taken off and such a fast rate of speed, he'd left her brothers lagging quite a ways behind him.

"Elizabeth?" Jeff called out as he bounded through the front door. "Elizabeth?"

"What in the devil is the matter?" Margaret asked when he started walking through the house yelling her name.

When he came back into the front room, he asked, "Where is Elizabeth?"

"Well I'm not sure. We had a nice chat earlier, and by the way, congratulations on the baby, and then she went outside. I haven't seen her in sometime actually. Did you check in the barn?"

"No. I'll go check there." He ran back out the front door and headed for the barn, yelling, "Elizabeth?"

When he didn't find her there and her brothers and finally caught up with him at the ranch house, he told them, "I can't find her. Where do you think she's gone?"

"I don't know. Let's see if Mother knows anything." John suggested, heading toward the house.

"She's not in there either. I already checked and your mother didn't seem to know anything."

What will I do if something has happened to her?

"Calm down. We'll find her," Ray assured him as he watched him pacing the yard, running his hands through his hair in frustration.

"What if we don't? What if something's happened to her? What if that dandy has gotten to her and taken her somewhere? He's behind this whole thing, I just know it. I knew we shouldn't have trusted him at all, but he's a friend of hers so I wanted to give him the benefit of the doubt. If he hurts her, I'll kill him!" Jeff growled continuing to pace.

"Everything will be fine. If he has taken her somewhere, we'll find them. Don't worry. We need to find out if anyone has seen him around here today," Ray said and went in search of any of the hands that had been hanging around the house earlier.

He came back about thirty minutes later only to tell them no one had heard or seen anything.

"What are we going to do now?" Jeff asked, really beginning to panic. The sun had started to go down and they still couldn't find her.

"I know this isn't what you want to hear, Jeff, but we will probably have to wait until morning. We can't track anything in the dark," John said.

"The hell I will! If that bastard has taken her, I'll find him, see if I don't." Jeff went to saddle his horse again, but Ray stopped him.

"Take it easy. We all want her back safe and sound, but getting ourselves hurt or killed in the process doesn't help Elizabeth at all. Let's search around the yard here to see if we can see anything out of the ordinary that might lead us to believe something is amiss. All right? It doesn't do anyone any good to go off half-cocked."

"I know you're right, but it's so frustrating! All I want is her safely back here with me."

"You really do love her, don't you?" Ray asked when he saw the torture in his brother-in-law's eyes.

"With all my heart, Ray, with all my heart."

"I'm glad to hear you say that." Ray smiled a little.

Matt shouted from the entrance to the ranch, "Hey! Come here. I think I've found something."

Jeff went running down the road to where Matt stood holding what appeared to be a piece of cloth.

"What? What did you find?" Jeff asked, taking the cloth from Matt's hand.

When John and Ray reached the pair, John took it from him saying, "I'm not sure. It could be something or it could be nothing."

"No. I recognize this. It's a piece of the dress Elizabeth was wearing this morning. I know because she had complained the whole time she was putting it on, saying it wasn't as comfortable as her trousers. He's taken her. I know he has! We have to find her!" Jeff panicked, and he headed back down the road toward the house to saddle his horse, but his brothers-in-law stopped him with a chilling note.

"Liz would not have gone willingly. We need to be careful. The man is crazy if he took her right out of our yard," John said, freezing Jeff in his tracks. "We have to do this right. We need to put together a plan to find her, and we can't do that if you go off half-cocked. Let's go back to the house and formulate something so we can find her as quickly as possible."

"So what's the plan?"

"For tonight, we wait. Tomorrow morning at first light, we'll head out after we've figured out which way they headed. A horse carrying two people can't travel as fast as one carrying only a single passenger. The hoof prints will be deeper and more obvious, but we can't see them in the dark so we need to wait."

"All right. We wait, but I can tell you one thing, I won't be sleeping tonight," Jeff muttered as they walked back to the house.

"Neither will we, brother. Neither will we." Ray sighed and put his arm around Jeff's shoulder in comfort.

Jeff knew tonight would be one of the longest nights of his life.

As soon as the sun had peaked over the horizon, the four men were saddled and ready to ride. They had taken every gun that John Sr. had owned in the house in preparation for what might be an ugly scene once they found Elizabeth.

The atmosphere was solemn this morning and Jeff knew each of them completed what they might find. He sent up a little prayer to God that he would find her safe and sound. The entire night had been spent praying nothing would happen to her or to their baby, but he just couldn't seem to shake the feeling of impending doom.

When the men reached the spot where they had found the piece of cloth the evening before, they all got down and looked around to see if they could figure out which way Gregory had gone.

Jeff found what appeared to be hoof prints that were indeed deeper than a normal print. He walked along looking for another clue. The prints appeared to double back. He kept walking until he reached a spot where the prints seemed to be confused like the horse was balking. He mounted his own horse, riding in the direction the prints seemed to go. Something was familiar about this path.

I know. This leads eventually to the pond, the same pond where I first saw her when she returned from school so many months ago.

"This way!" Jeff shouted to the others, and he took off at a full gallop toward where he hoped to find his wife. While he rode, he tried to think of where near the pond Gregory might have taken her.

Dread almost consumed him.

When they reached the clearing, Jeff dismounted with the others right behind him.

"Are you sure this is where they were headed?" John asked.

"Of course not, but this is the direction the tracks seemed to lead. There's got to be something here." Jeff searched the surrounding area for some sign.

Another horse whinnied in the distance

"Where did that come from?" Matt asked in a whisper. "Did you hear that?"

"I think it came from over there."

* * * *

Elizabeth had awoken from her brutal attack and found herself bobbing along over the saddle of a horse. When she tried to upright herself, she was pushed back down with a firm hand in the middle of her back.

"Lay still, my dear. We'll be there soon."

"What? Gregory? What's going on? Let me up!" She tried to push herself upright again, causing the horse to stumble and twirl in circles.

"If you don't lie still, I will have to knock you out again. Now stop being so difficult." He pushed her back down.

She could tell by the undertone of his voice, he was holding his temper in check, so she decided not to push things, but she needed to get off her stomach.

"Gregory, please. I won't be a bother if you'll just let me up. It's hurting me to lie over the saddle like this."

"Oh all right, but if you start to cause trouble, you'll be back over the side of this horse before you can say a word. Do you understand me?" he said in a menacing tone.

"Yes, yes, of course," she muttered when he stopped the horse and helped her up so she was sitting in front of him with his arms wrapped around her middle.

"Now. Behave yourself and we won't have any more problems. We'll be there soon."

"Where? Where are we going?"

"Some place private. Somewhere I can have you all to myself and it will be a long time before anyone finds us."

Her heart sank when she realized what he meant and what it meant to her future with Jeff.

"But, you know I'm married."

"Don't worry about it. That is a minor detail for now but will be taken care of very soon."

"What do you mean?"

"One of my associates will be taking care of that husband of yours shortly. Then you'll be all mine to do with as I wish. Of course, I won't be marrying you like I had planned before. After all, you've been with another man, and I can't have that kind of woman as my wife, but you'll make a nice mistress."

Tears welled in her eyes when she thought about losing Jeff. "You can't be serious, Gregory. You'll never get away with killing my husband even if you didn't do it yourself. What if your associate is caught and he tells everyone you were involved? You'll hang for sure."

"I'm perfectly serious, my dear. No one will know I'm involved in your husband's murder anymore than they were aware I was involved in your father's murder. They can't even find out who is running the rustling in the area, much less if there is one more murder to add to the list."

"You killed my father?" she squeaked with a heart-wrenching whisper.

"I didn't kill him, sweetheart, but some of the men working for me did. I really hadn't planned on his death, but it made continuing to pilfer the cattle from the area ranches easier without him involved. I really did admire your father, and I was saddened that he was eliminated, but it was a necessity under the circumstances."

She fell quiet for the remainder of the trip, while the overwhelming grief tore at her heart. Maybe he hadn't done it himself, but he was to blame just the same.

When they rounded the corner and she realized where they were, her heart sank even further. She knew he would be taking her into the cave behind the waterfall. She had been the one who told him about it when they had picnicked near there some months ago. No one knew of the cave except her. Her brothers didn't know, and she knew her husband wasn't aware of it either. They would never find her.

When he had ridden as close as he could with the horse, he stopped, dismounted, and pulled her down with him in such a manner she fell to her knees, scraping them badly in the fall. Gregory jerked her to her feet and dragged her along in the direction of the waterfall.

"Come along, my dear. I've set things up nicely for you even if it is rather primitive."

They climbed across the rocks and boulders to reach the cave. He had let the horse go when they had reached the rocks, but she hadn't gone far. She grazed near the pond, drinking the fresh water after her long trek. Elizabeth hoped and prayed someone would find the horse and wonder what it was doing out here.

Once inside the cave, Gregory took her hand with one of his as he reached for the shackle attached to the wall, looped it around her wrist, and closed it with a clank. She knew it hadn't been there before. He really had planned this out rather well if he was going to keep her chained up like a dog.

"Do you really think it's necessary for you to chain me to the wall? I don't think I'll be going anywhere."

"Well, you see, I don't trust you, so yes, you must be chained at least for now. We shall see in a few days time when you haven't eaten or drank anything, how compliant you really will be."

He started a small fire in the back of the cave in order for the smoke not to be seen and he started making something to eat.

She watched his every move while trying to think of some way to get away from him.

He really is crazy if he thinks I'll come to him after he kills Jeff in cold blood.

Her mouth watered when the smell of cooking food wafted toward her. She hadn't had anything to eat today except a small bite before they had left the Rocking W this morning. She had been so nauseous because of the baby, she hadn't wanted anything, but now, her stomach growled in protest.

He smiled at her as he heard her stomach growl and took pleasure in her misery. After he finished eating, he made a bed near the fire for himself and rolled over to get some sleep.

"You aren't even going to unchain me to allow me to lie down? I thought you were more of a gentleman than that," she said, trying to goad him or make him feel at least a little guilty for leaving her chained to the wall. If she could just him to unchain her, she could probably get away. She knew these hills better than most and much better than he did.

"I'm sorry, but no. You won't be unchained even for sleep. You'll have to make due against the rock there. Good night."

He rolled back over. It wasn't long afterwards, she heard him snoring softly and her anger began to rise to new heights.

That bastard! If Jeff or my brothers don't kill him for this, I will and I'll do it with my bare hands.

As she clenched her fists, her nails dug into the palms of her hands almost to the point of making them bleed.

God please let Jeff be safe. Even if Gregory manages to take me with him, please make sure my husband and child are safe.

Hot tears rolled down her face, and she buried her head against her arm so that the crazy man holding her prisoner couldn't hear.

CHAPTER 24

The next morning found Elizabeth still chained to the wall and she had fallen into an exhausted sleep with her arm hanging above her head in the most uncomfortable position. Gregory almost felt sorry for her, but then he remembered how she had chosen that cowboy over him and he hardened his heart to her again.

She will choose me, once the cowboy was dead or she'll die right alongside him. He got up and moved about the cave.

The sound of movement around her woke Elizabeth.

She jerked, almost pulled her arm out of the socket. "Ouch!"

"Ah! I see you are awake. I was just getting ready to make some breakfast. Would you care for some? Oh that's right." He snapped his fingers. "You can't have any until you've begun to comply with my wishes. I'm sorry, sweetheart."

"You really are a bastard, Gregory. I never realized it before, but you truly are cruel," she growled, rubbing her wrist as best she could under where the shackle rested.

"Actually no, darling, I'm not a bastard. I'm very much the legitimate child of my parents. I am really surprised at your language, Elizabeth. I really thought you were a well-brought-up lady who didn't use that kind of language, especially around a man who desires your affection."

"I really don't care what you think of me or my language. Just for your information, my parents did bring me up to be a lady, but you just bring out the best in me, I guess."

"Yes well, we shall see how well I bring out the best in you. Taming you will be my pleasure," he replied as he skimmed his eyes over where her dress had been torn at the neckline, revealing the upper part of her breast.

"No matter what you do to me, I'll never submit to you willingly. You should know that. I thought you were a gentleman, but obviously, that part of your upbringing must have gone right over your head," she spat in defiance but regretted it as soon as it left her mouth when he stood up, moved toward her and slapped her full force across the face, leaving a huge welt along her jaw line knocking her unconscious again.

"Sorry, my beauty, but we will have to tame that mouth of yours. Maybe a gag would be in order." He ran his fingers along her jaw, down her neck, and cupped her breast and was satisfied when her nipple responded to his touch with a mind of its own.

Smiling to himself at her body's unconscious reaction, he turned on his heel and went to the mouth of the cave to smoke. She always did get his anger to rise rather quickly, and that was something he would have to learn to tame. It would do no good to physically hurt her, nor would it do any good to completely break her spirit. Part of his attraction to her was her spirit, and if he completely broke that, she would no longer be attractive to him.

* * * *

When they heard the horse whinny softly in response to their horses, they walked around the backside of the pond to see where the noise came from. Jeff saw the horse first and walked up to it, took its brindle in his hand, and softly stroked the horse's nose to calm it. The horse clearly belonged to someone because it still held its saddle on and its bridle still in place.

Maybe someone had fallen off and gotten hurt. Or maybe it belongs to the bastard that now held his wife captive.

"Who do you think it belongs to?" Matt asked.

"Not sure. Let me see if I can find a brand," Ray said and walked around the back of the horse.

"There isn't a brand on her, but the saddlery looks like what old man Jefferies has in the livery in town. See—the blanket has his stitching on the underside." He lifted up the corner of the saddle blanket.

"Why would one of the livery horses be out here?" John asked. "Unless our friend Gregory brought it."

"That's my thought, which means he should be around here somewhere close with Elizabeth, but where?" Jeff wondered aloud as he started back toward the pond.

"Let's tie her up to that tree there so she doesn't wander off again, and then we can look around the pond for some more clues," Ray said to Matt.

Matt tied the horse up and then followed his brothers back around to the other side of the pond.

"Let's see. Where would he go from here if they were now on foot? It can't be far." John looked around, trying to decide where they could be hiding. "There are no line shacks in the area that they could have walked to. The nearest one sat two miles away and on foot, which would be difficult especially dragging and uncooperative woman."

Jeff stood near the pond looking at the waterfall when he saw a small puff of smoke come from one of the rocks to the side of where the water cascaded over the rocks.

That's odd.

He tilted his head to one side and squinted against the sunlight, trying to figure out where it had come from when he saw it again.

"Hey," he said in a bit of whisper to Elizabeth's brothers. He didn't want anyone to hear him if there was someone up there. "I just saw smoke coming from that rock up there."

"The rock? Are you sure?" John said.

"Yes, I'm sure. Is there a cove or something back there you think?" Jeff asked.

"I don't think so, but then again, I've never really gone back there," John replied.

"I'm going to have a look." Jeff tried to quietly scramble up the rocks toward where he had seen the smoke.

"Be careful. If they are up there somewhere, he could be armed," Ray warned Jeff as he started up the side of the hill.

* * * *

Gregory stood at the mouth of the cave smoking and when he saw a glint of reflection, he peered through the water cascading over the rocks. After a moment, he saw someone at the bottom near the mouth of the pond. He threw down his cigar, crushed it with his boot, and walked back to the rear of the cave. Taking a bandana from his pack, he walked up to the still-unconscious Elizabeth and bound her mouth with it.

It would do no good if she screamed and someone heard her.

After the gag was secured, he went back to his pack and removed the pistol he had stowed there. Checking to make sure the bullets were in the chamber, he spun the barrel and clicked it in place. He returned to the cave mouth so that he could see what or who was near.

Gregory squinted through the water so he could try to see what was going on. He moved to the left of the mouth, to see a little better, and when he did, he could see Elizabeth's three brothers standing near the pond at the bottom looking up to where he now stood.

"Damn it! How did they figure out where we were?" he wondered aloud, before he turned and went back inside.

Elizabeth began to moan when she started to awaken.

He paced near his pack, mumbling to himself while he tried to figure out a plan to get them out of there without being seen.

I know. I'll use her like a shield. I'll have to leave her behind, but if I shoot her while I get away, they will be too concerned over her to worry about chasing me. It's perfect!

He went to Elizabeth, pulled the gag from her mouth, and took the key from his pocket to unlock her wrist. Not quite arouse, she slumped against him, almost taking them both to the floor.

"Come on, sweetheart. We're leaving." He pulled her up against him, and used a piece of rope he'd had stashed at the cave to bind her wrist behind her back.

"Leaving? Where are you taking me now?"

"We must leave now, my dear. We have unwanted company, and you are going to be my leverage out of here," he said, replacing the gag. It wouldn't be beneficial to him if she screamed, alerting her rescuers before he could get away.

Pulling her up in front of him, he stuck the pistol in her side. "Now, walk toward the mouth of the cave, sweetheart."

When they reached the mouth of the cave, he peered out trying to gage where her brothers were. Seeing that they didn't appear to be aware of his presence, he pushed her out the side of the cave toward a path leading down the back of the hillside away from her brothers. She stumbled, almost fell, as he pushed her along, but he grabbed her arm to steady her, sending some small rocks cascading down the hillside in front of them.

* * * *

Jeff crouched next to the trail when small rocks rolled down.

Working his way up the front of the hillside, he'd seen the path leading down the back and forking off from the path he climbed. Movement at the mouth of the cave, alerted him to the occupants whereabouts before they emerged.

The boulder where he now watching the man force his wife to walk in front of him, kept his presence hidden. Gregory didn't appear to be aware of Jeff's position, and he wanted to keep it that way.

When the pair walked so close to him he could smell the fear emanating from Elizabeth, Jeff grabbed her from Gregory's grasp and pushed her behind the boulder. The rope on her hands had come loose enough, she was able to work her hands free and pull the gag from her mouth. He jumped on Gregory, knocking him to the ground.

The gun lay trapped between them while they rolled on the ledge. A gunshot echoed loudly off the canyon walls and Elizabeth screamed.

"Elizabeth, get back!" Jeff shouted, as they continued to struggle.

Gregory punched him in the face, knocking him back against the rock. The pistol now pointed straight at his chest.

"You bastard!" Gregory yelled. "You've taken everything away from me, and now you'll both pay! I'll kill you both right here, right now."

"Gregory, please," she said, pleadingly to him with her hands outstretched. "I'll go with you if you'll just let him go."

"Elizabeth no! Don't even say that," Jeff yelled, not daring to move.

Ignoring his plea, she continued, "Gregory. I know you want me still. I can see it in your eyes. Let him go, and I'll go with you. We'll be together, just like you want."

"Really Elizabeth? You'll go with me?"

"Of course. You know I've always cared for you. We can be together like we've always planned."

Jeff watched his wife talk to the crazy man, playing along with his mind-set, as if she truly understood how to reach him.

"I knew you loved me and not him." Gregory wiped away the sweat that ran down his face into his eyes. "We'll be together always. We'll travel the world and see all the faraway places that you've read about in those books."

"Yes. We can travel and just be together. Just you and me."

"I need to kill him though. He'll come after us," Gregory said, leveling the gun at him again.

"No!" she shouted. "No, he'll promise to leave us alone, won't you, Jeff?"

"Yes," he replied, choking back what he really wanted to say. He was afraid the man would shoot both of them if he did.

"See? He'll leave us alone. We can go off and never see him again. Please, just give me the gun." She reached for it.

"No! I can't do that, Elizabeth. I have to kill him," Gregory said again, pointing it at him and pulling back the hammer back.

A moment later, the gun exploded.

CHAPTER 25

Ray appeared out of nowhere and jumped Gregory. They struggled over the gun while Elizabeth ran to her husband. Blood streamed from the wound in his shoulder.

"Jeff? Jeff? Oh God! You've been hit!"

She had never cried so much before in her life, but now she was bawling over her husband, and it felt good.

"It will be all right. It's only a flesh wound." He pulled his bandana from around his neck and placed it against the wound.

They both turned to see Ray still struggling with Gregory before the gun went flying. Ray punched Gregory, going after him again as they got closer and closer to the edge of the trail.

Gregory stumbled backward.

Everything seemed to be in slow motion. Gregory began to flail while he tried to right himself and keep from falling. His eyes widened when he lost his balance and fell headlong over the side. He tumbled down the hill coming to a stop near the bottom.

Elizabeth buried her head in Jeff's neck.

"Are you two all right?" John asked.

"I'm fine but Jeff's been shot. We need to get him to the doctor." She held her husband's head in her lap. "He's bleeding pretty badly."

"Can you walk?" Matt asked.

"Just get me to my horse, and I'll make it back to the ranch." Jeff got up from his position against the rock.

"You can't ride," she said as they walked back down the hill.

"I'll be fine. I told you, it's only a flesh wound," he insisted when they reached the bottom and walked to where Gregory lay completely still with his eyes permanently looking at the sky above.

"We need to take him back to town with us. There will be questions, I'm sure."

"I'll go fetch his horse."

John wrestled with Gregory's body to place him over the horse.

"Elizabeth, you can ride with me." Jeff steered her in the direction of his horse. "Jack here can handle both of our weight. John? Why don't you and Matt take the body back to town? Elizabeth and I will head back to the Rocking W so I can get this shoulder looked at. Send the doc out when you get there."

"Sounds good to me."

* * * *

When they reached the front gate of the Rocking W, they all split up. John and Matt took Gregory's body into town, and the other three rode toward the house.

When they rode into the yard, Donna and Ernest came out to greet them. Elizabeth dismounted first, and Donna almost fainted when she saw the blood on Jeff's chest and down the sleeve of his shirt.

"My God, son! What happened? You're bleeding," she said, coming to his side after he slid off the horse with a groan of pain.

"I'll tell you the whole story in a bit. Right now, I need to lie down before I fall down." He stumbled, but Elizabeth caught him under the arm and he leaned on her heavily.

"Has someone gone for the doctor?" Ernest got under his son's other arm to help him into the house.

"Yes. John and Matt went into town to fetch him and deliver the body."

"Body?" Ernest asked while they made their way into the house.

"Just let me lie down and rest for a bit. Then I'll explain. Just a little bit—" His voice trailed off as he finally lost consciousness from the loss of blood.

Ray took her place, while he and Ernest carried an unconscious Jeff into the bedroom and gently placed him on the bed. She worked efficiently to remove his shirt, but almost passed out herself when she saw the hole in his shoulder.

She took a deep breath to steady herself. "Donna? Can you get me some warm water?"

He needs me right now and I will not pass out.

When she had worked the shirt from his upper body, his mother brought the warm water and a clean cloth.

The doctor will need to be able to see it when he gets here.

With gentle strokes, she cleaned the area, and applied pressure to it to stop the bleeding.

The doctor arrived about an hour later only to find a disgruntled Jeff sitting up in the bed arguing with her about whether he could get up.

"You will stay there until the doctor can have a look at that shoulder. You lost a lot of blood, and I won't have you causing it to bleed again now that I've gotten it to stop." Her hands were planted firmly on her hips while she glared.

"I'll be fine. I just need to get up and move around a bit."

"You'll do no such a thing. Stay right there," she ordered and pushed him back down on the bed, but he wrapped his arms around her, taking her down with him.

"Only if you stay in here with me." He chuckled with that sexy half smile of his that could melt her heart.

Her eyes softened as she looked her husband and said, "There will be none of that for a while, sir. You won't be up to that kind of activity for a bit."

"Wanna bet?" he whispered against her lips.

"Now what have you two gotten into? Gunshot?"

"How'd you guess?" Jeff inquired a bit sarcastically.

"Well the shot went clean through so I think you'll heal just fine. You'll need to take it easy for a couple of weeks," the doctor stated after he had examined the hole and applied a couple of stitches to hold the skin together. "And I mean really take it easy, Jeff. If you tear that open again, I'll just have to come back out here and stitch it shut. Besides, your wife needs to take it easy right now too with the baby coming."

"I'm sure we can find something to keep us busy for a few weeks," Jeff said with a devilish grin and a quirk of one eyebrow.

The next day, the sheriff came out to the ranch to question Jeff and get his statement as well as her on what happened with Gregory. After hearing their story pretty much corresponded with what John and Matt had said, he closed the case and wrote out a statement to Gregory's parents about the demise of their son.

Epilogue

The sun rose in the sky and burned away the fog settling over the ranch house. Jeff stepped onto the porch to greet the morning. It had been a long night while Elizabeth struggled with the birth of their son, but now it was over and he was here. The baby was beautiful, and his birth had brought Jeff to tears.

He'd refused to leave her side even when the doctor tried to send him away. The helpless feelings engulfing him tore his heart out while the pains grip her with each contraction. Watching his beautiful Elizabeth struggle with the pain of their son's birth made him even more in awe of her. She was so strong spirited and such a fighter, he was proud to call her his wife.

The last several months had brought them closer together than ever before. Even as she had gotten bigger with every month their child grew inside her, she worked alongside him to make their ranch prosper. She had been his partner, his love, and he had grown to love her more and more each passing day.

When the notice had come about the contract with the government to train horses for the Texas Rangers, he had been ecstatic and she had been by his side the entire time. The Circle W was now theirs to hand down to their children and their grandchildren.

"How are you doing, Papa?" his father asked, coming out onto the porch to stand next to him.

"Tired, but elated. He's beautiful, isn't he?"

"Yes, he is. He looks a lot like you did when you were a child. You should be very proud."

"I am," Jeff replied with tears in his eyes.

"Have you two decided on a name?"

"Yes. We are going to call him John Ernest Walker, after both his granddads," Jeff said with a proud smile and an arm around his father.

"Thanks, son. He'll be a strong man just like you are," his father said.

They both turned to look at the door of the house when they heard a baby cry, and with a big smile, Jeff turned around and headed back into the house to be with his wife.

* * * *

Ernest stood on the porch for a bit looking up at the clear sky above him and said, "John. I'm sure you are up there watching over those two, and you'd be very proud of your daughter. She's given us both a wonderful grandson. Watch over him from God's side, will you?"

A bird whistled from the tree near the house in response to Ernest's plea and he smiled knowing his friend watched over them all from heaven above.

THE END

ABOUT THE AUTHOR

Sandy Sullivan is a romance author, who, when not writing, spends her time with her husband Shaun on their farm in middle Tennessee. She loves to ride her horses, play with their dogs and relax on the porch, enjoying the rolling hills of her home south of Nashville. County music is a passion of hers and she loves to listen to it while she writes.

She is an avid reader of romance novels and enjoys reading Nora Roberts, Jude Deveraux and Susan Wiggs. Finding new authors and delving into something different helps feed the need for literature. A registered nurse by education, she loves to help people and spread the enjoyment of romance to those around her with her novels. She loves cowboys so you'll find many of her novels have sexy men in tight jeans and cowboy boots.

CHAPTER 26